Nick Kent is an award-winning journalist and author. Over the decades he's crossed paths – and swords – with rock musicians as varied as Jerry Lee Lewis and Prince, survived two tours with the Rolling Stones and Led Zeppelin, and even found himself briefly playing guitar in an early iteration of the Sex Pistols. These and other adventures are recorded in his books *The Dark Stuff* and *Apathy for the Devil*. *The Unstable Boys* is his first work of fiction.

THE UNSTABLE BOYS

NICK KENT

CONSTABLE

CONSTABLE

First published in Great Britain in 2021 by Constable

This paperback edition published in Great Britain in 2022 by Constable

1 3 5 7 9 10 8 6 4 2

A CIP catalogue record for this book is available from the British Library.

ISBN: 978-1-47213-291-8

Typeset in Adobe Caslon by Hewer Text UK Ltd, Edinburgh
Printed and bound in Great Britain by Clays Ltd, Elcograf S.p.A.

Papers used by Constable are from well-managed
forests and other responsible sources.

Constable
An imprint of
Little, Brown Book Group
Carmelite House
50 Victoria Embankment
London EC4Y 0DZ

An Hachette UK Company
www.hachette.co.uk

www.littlebrown.co.uk

A selection of press clippings through the ages pertaining to the subject matter, rock combo the Unstable Boys.

'Scoops from the Scoot', *Tigerbeat* (May 1966)

Pop-a-doodle-doo, pussycats and all you smitten kittens. It's Scooter McLain, roving reporter and dude-in-the-know-deejay for Radio KSOQ checking in again to fill you all in on the beat on the street, and there's no shortage of sizzling scoops every night on the swinging Sunset Strip where the stars come out to play.

The hot poop this week? The Stones have been in town recording. Mick, Keith and Charlie broke from their busy schedule to take in a smokin' hot performance by the Ike and Tina Turner Revue at the Whisky a Go Go. Whilst Tina was getting the dudes and dudettes all worked up, I slid into the booth next to Mick and asked him 'Hey man, what's shakin'?' He shot me a hinky look and turned his head away. Goddamn limey fop. Hey get over yourself, Mr Big Shot.

Little Lord Jagger could learn some lessons in good manners from his fellow countrymen, the Yardbirds. That crazy quintet were driving the young set wild at the Whisky after Ike and Tina had finished their run. Between sets I got talking to one of the guys – his name was either Chris or Jim – and over a few drinkiepoos he filled me in on what was really going on back there in old London town and gave me the skinny I was after. Said the hot new act busting out of Blighty right this minute is a quintet of rebellious young roustabouts called – get this – the Unstable Boys.

So I did some digging and – yikes – that bird boy was right. They've got a single 'Dark Waters' that really rings my chimes. And my spies tell me that when they play live the audience pack together so tight you couldn't even swing a cat in the joint – not that I'd ever consider doing such a thing of course. I'm a feline fancier at heart.

The point I'm making – and would have made earlier had the Benzedrine not just started energising my old ever-lovin' noggin – is this. The limeys can't get enough of these moody hunks. And anything the limeys like the yanks are going to adopt. Am I right? Of course I am. Hell I've already signed the adoption papers. I'm so cock-a-hoop for this crew, I'm ready to get rash with my predictions. These Unstable Boys are nothing short of musical game-changers and they've got just the kind of under-nourished look the young cutie pies love to gaze longingly at. How can they fail? Answer: no way, Doris Day.

Mr Jagger, consider yourself forewarned.

'Unstables ousted from package tour drama', *New Musical Express* (3 February 1967)
Current chart successes the Unstable Boys ran into a spot of hot water last week that ended up causing the quintet to be sacked from the ongoing package tour of the British Isles headlined by

middle-of-the-road recent chart-topper Bobby Grit and his back-ing band the Wandering Hands. The bill also featured Australian folk-pop up-and-comers the Gentle People, best known for their recent smash recasting of 'The White Cliffs of Dover'. Cliff Dogsberry, their bassist, harmony singer and unofficial leader, took immediate exception to the Unstable Boys' backstage behaviour. 'They swore like pommy troopers. We've got a sheila in our combo – young Nathalie – and I had to go and remonstrate with them. I told them – "Listen, mates, there's a lady present. No call to adopt the language of the gutter snipe." And one of them – the singer – responded by spewing up a stream of four-letter-strewn insults which he concluded with what I can only call a noisy eruption of rectal gas. I was left speechless.'

Nathalie Peters, the Gentle People's auburn-haired singer, went even further in defaming her former tour mates.

'Every venue we played they left the backstage toilet in an unspeakable state of disrepair. They criticise us Aussies for being coarse and ill-mannered but I've seen nothing in the outback to match the kind of grubby tomfoolery those fellows routinely get up to. As a good Christian woman, I was appalled. Vulgarians – that's the only word that fits their kind. And vulgarians have no place in today's entertainment industry.'

The group was pulled from the tour after the Aussie hit-makers and other participants complained to the promoter. Contacted by the NME, the Unstable Boys' manager brushed the expulsion off by saying that his group had been 'going over far better than any of the other acts' and had been axed 'out of envy'. He also pointed out that the group's third single was still in the Top 10 despite the controversy and that their debut album had just charted over in the States.

The group's unpredictable singer was later sighted in London nightclub the Bag O'Nails. Asked about the tour sacking, he launched into an unprintable stream of insults directed at all who'd shared the bill and organised the jaunt. Then he retired to a dimly lit corner of the venue to throw up over a large potted plant.

The Unstable Boys meanwhile are set to begin their first tour of America a month from now.

'Unstable Boys prove true to their name' by Stu Ginsberg, *Rolling Stone* (October 1969)

There's something about touring America that has the effect of ripping to shreds certain bands who fly over from the UK to ply their trade up and down our highways. The latest casualties would appear to be the Unstable Boys. Only last year the quintet were a name on every music-biz-insider's lips. Some even dared to call them the new Rolling Stones, others England's answer to the Doors. Their albums and singles have all garnered healthy chart placings throughout Europe and here in the States.

But the group has also weathered its share of tragedy and controversy. Their lead guitarist Mick Winthrop was recently killed in a road accident while several drummers have passed through their ranks, some disappearing altogether soon after their departures.

'I don't know what it's all about,' sighed lead singer 'the Boy' when we spoke briefly in a San Francisco bar. 'People talk about us being cursed. Someone asked me the other day – do you think you suffer from bad karma? I said "I wouldn't know, man. I don't eat Indian food."'

Guitarist Ral Coombes is more circumspect about the group's recent trials and tribulations. Interviewed in a candlelit hotel room, he admits that Winthrop's death is 'something we're still working through' and that the 'many changes on the drum stool' have had a draining impact on their potential. Currently the group's three original members are touring the States with two new players. 'Mick died two weeks before this tour was set to start. We tried postponing the dates but the management here wouldn't hear of it. They found these two guys we're playing with now and stuck them in the line-up as a kind of fait accompli. They're doing the best they can but obviously it's not the same. I've played twelve shows with the new guitarist but I've yet to have a significant conversation with the guy. I only found out the other day he might be half-Mexican.'

The fifty-two-date tour which began last month in Sacramento has so far been 'a bit of a topsy-turvy type of experience' according to 'the Boy'. Coombes elaborates: 'The venues this time around aren't always suited to what we're trying to achieve live. One night we played on a bill with Albert King and his band. That was challenging. But the next night we had to go on after a juggler and a ventriloquist act. That sort of thing can really do your head in.'

According to their third original member, bassist Mark McCabe, the group's two principals have been 'fighting like cats and dogs' for some time now. The guitarist readily confesses that he and 'the Boy' are 'not kindred spirits . . . our sensibilities and musical agendas are very different. For a while those different sensibilities have flourished when fertilised by a strong musical chemistry. But that chemistry may well be over. In which case there would be nothing to tie us together. We can go our separate ways. I'd be lying if I said it wasn't something I was looking forward to doing.'

The singer's outrageous behaviour both on stage and off has fuelled much of the current antagonism. His recent arrest for allegedly defecating on the forecourt of a used-car dealership in Oakland made the local news there. 'I was looking for a new motor,' claims 'the Boy' who had to pony up a 250-dollar fine in a subsequent court hearing. 'And the geezer kept asking me to leave a deposit. So I dropped my slacks right there on the lot and obliged the man.'

Some may find this hilarious. But the Unstable Boys guitar player and bassist are not so easily amused. For them it's the last in a long list of last straws. The guitarist talks longingly about returning to his home in London and recording a solo album – 'something more serene'. The bassist claims to be 'thoroughly fed up with the music industry' and is thinking of going into some unspecified sort of 'retail business' with his brother.

This leaves the singer to carry on the group's name, a task he claims to be pondering the wisdom of pursuing. His views on his co-workers are bluntly expressed. 'Wankers' he calls them repeatedly. Apparently it's limey-speak for guys who masturbate a lot. No love lost there then. And no big deal in the larger scheme of things. Just another hot little combo biting the dust while the world still turns.

'Unstable Boys', *The Encyclopaedia of Rock* (2017)
One of many noteworthy UK beat group ensembles that formed in the mid-1960s, the Unstable Boys are now rightly being feted as one of the better second division acts from an extremely fertile era for pop and rock. Initially influenced in equal measure by the songcraft of Lennon and McCartney, the intricate folk guitar stylings of Bert Jansch and Davy Graham and the less

sophisticated groove-based rhythm and blues of the Rolling Stones and the Pretty Things, the group scored a Top 5 hit with their second single 'Dark Waters', a minor chord-dominated lament to a drowned paramour. Critics and record buyers alike found the song haunting in an out-of-the-ordinary way further highlighted by the vocalist who, known simply as 'the Boy', managed to convey the lyrics by adopting a tone that was both chilling and mellifluous. The single even scraped into the US Top 50.

Between 1966 and mid-1969 – three tumultuous years – the group recorded and toured incessantly. In 1967 they released four singles and two albums to great acclaim. The psychedelic era was in full bloom and their recordings during this year reflected this state of affairs with phasing, flanging and backwards guitars liberally garnishing the tracks they made. One album in particular, Capture the Rapture, was hailed as one of the year's most radical releases and rose to no. 8 in the UK hit parade and an encouraging no. 22 in US Billboard charts that year. A live album – released posthumously but recorded at Los Angeles' Whisky a Go Go during the fabled summer of love – demonstrates the band could be a fiery-sounding live act spicing up the well-constructed melodic thrust of their self-composed songs with an anarchic jolt of menace that came from the unpredictable singer who increasingly seemed to be operating from a different perspective to his fellow group members.

By 1968, though, the divisions in the line-up were starting to make themselves increasingly manifest. Guitarist and main songwriter Ral Coombes wanted to further develop the eclectic experimental approach already hinted at in previous group waxings, but 'the Boy' was gung-ho to strip the music down to a simpler, rhythm-centric essence. The bass player apparently *wanted the other members to transform themselves into a country and western band like the Byrds and the lead guitarist caused even more inner-group dissent by dying in an automobile accident just as the ensemble were finding their bearings in a Connecticut recording studio, there to record a projected double album.*

A number of tracks were completed despite the grim reaper's inconvenient cameo but the record company, spooked by the death and weary of the group's in-fighting, chose to just release a single album, which they then systematically under-promoted. The result was a flop, their first record not to graze the Top 100 on either side of the Atlantic (a second album from the sessions was released posthumously).

The group broke up almost immediately afterwards. Songwriter Coombes was the first to jump ship. He released a solo album in 1971 that sold dismally at the time but has since become something of a cult 'cause célèbre'; a second solo album was also rumoured to have been recorded but the tracks – if they exist – have never officially been made available. Bassist McCabe went on to play briefly with a number of bands, most notably the Gladstones, the Irish vocal quartet who enjoyed chart success throughout Europe during the 1970s. Various drummers came and went during the group's duration. According to a reliable source, most of them are probably dead now.

'The Boy' meanwhile continues to live on, though oftentimes in reduced circumstances to those he enjoyed in his heyday. After the Unstable Boys he formed his own blues band. It lasted all of three gigs. In the early 1970s he tried out as the lead vocalist for several reputable hard rock acts (both Jeff Beck and Deep Purple gave him auditions) but to no avail. Yet he persisted in trying to re-establish

himself in the forefront of public scrutiny even if it meant jettison-ing his dignity in the process. An ill-starred attempt at leap-frog-ging onto the glam-rock bandwagon is best consigned to the waste basket of history. On his 1978 'punk' cash-in, he's featured on the sleeve waving a machete, his face smeared in a brown substance that he claimed in interviews to be the contents of his rectum. Neither time nor shame would appear to have withered his resolve to continue as a force in music though of late he's been uncharacter-istically elusive.

This is a genuine mystery because his old group have recently enjoyed a renaissance via three old tracks resurfacing as soundtracks for high-profile ad campaigns. As a consequence, were they to reunite and tour again while this second wave of mainstream acceptance is still cresting, the group's members would be virtually guaranteed sold out crowds throughout the British Isles. They'd also get prestigious bookings at various summer festi-vals in Europe and America.

'1960s cult act brought back from obscurity by high-profile ad blitz' by Duncan Pertwee, *Financial Times* (23 February 2015)

Ancient 'freak-beat' quintet the Unstable Boys are the latest unlikely candidates for a new millennium makeover. It has come in the form of Technokratix's latest multi-million ad campaign which features the group's music as its soundtrack and even name-checks the long-defunct band in its slogan – 'If you're feeling unstable, we will enable you.'

With most vintage pop and rock acts from previous decades reuniting these days, it would make sense that the Unstable Boys' three surviving members would do likewise in order to further capitalise on this unexpected up-turn of good fortune. But – according to bassist Mark 'Clint' McCabe, the only ex-member available for comment – that is extremely unlikely. 'Too much water has passed under the bridge. We're all different people these days. We've grown so far apart that I can't imagine us having anything in common – not even the music. People like to imagine young rock bands as gangs – four or five guys bonded around the same sensibility. But it's never as simple as that. There were always conflicts: you get caught up in an endeavour with a bunch of egomaniacs and head cases and it's like walking around with a sack of wild cats on your shoulder. It does bad things to the central nervous system.'

Asked if he'd learned anything from his four-year stay in the often trouble-prone combo, McCabe replied without hesitation: 'Yeah, not to do it again under any circumstances. Not a tour anyway. I've just had an operation that I'd rather not go into detail about. I'm not about to run the risk of haemorrhaging internally in front of a paying audience.'

His two former bandmates – singer Dale 'the Boy' Royston and guitarist/main composer Redmond 'Ral' Coombes – meanwhile have yet to express themselves publicly on the subject of their old group's sudden phoenix-like rise from the boondocks of cult-within-a-cult obscurity to the high streets of mainstream visibility. Their former manager Brian Hartnell claims to be unsurprised by the turn of events. 'The Unstables were a funny bunch. Not funny ha ha – funny, as in fuck me, a couple of these lads are in urgent need of heavy sedation or a spot of institutionalisation. Shepherding them around was no piece of cake, I can tell you that. But even when I wanted to throttle them – which was often the case, let's be frank – I was still won over by the *talent those boys could pull out of the hat. I knew they'd get their second day in the sun. Those songs of theirs – and that Ral had mad skills in that area – they've got legs.'*

Hartnell, like McCabe, is doubtful the ad campaign windfall will prompt a re-formation of any sort. 'But then why do they need to? The Unstable Boys were an enigma. They came, they cast a long fleeting shadow over the late 1960s rock landscape. Then they left. Like thieves in the night. Men of mystery. That's what this industry was once based on. Creative ground-breakers who knew when to say their thing and then knew when to shut the fuck up, lie low and watch their legend expand.

'If they did attempt some form of reunification – it would probably end in a bloodbath. Paramedics lurking at the side of the stage every night in case one of them keeled over. Cruel snipes in the press, I can see the headline now: "From Unstable Boys to incontinent old men".'

CHAPTER 1

It was well past the midnight hour when Trevor Bourne relented and let his fingers do the walk of shame. He'd intended to watch a YouTube documentary on the political upheavals felt throughout Great Britain during the 1980s – call it a spot of background research for a future journalistic endeavour – but finally couldn't stomach the idea of seeing Margaret Thatcher strutting around in the starring role and had opted on a whim to ogle more erotic female flesh instead. It hadn't taken more than three mouse clicks to find Pornhub. Bollocks to the Iron Lady. More shapely bodies were the order of the hour.

He'd sat there glaring at the screen. Porn clips came and went. Nothing to truly engage the libido though. He was waiting for that tingle in the loins but couldn't locate it. Too much wine in the belly probably. Trevor knew the syndrome all too well: the drunker you get, the randier your thoughts become, the softer your dick gets.

But that's what sites like Pornhub were good for. Why go through the humiliation and expense of chasing down potential sex partners that you'd almost certainly disappoint when you can simply sit back alone at home and watch others performing sex acts you don't have the stamina to enact yourself?

And it wasn't just about craving an orgasm. Watching porn could have cultural implications. You could learn a lot about different countries from simply studying their pornographic output, Trevor had lately come to believe. Take the French and the Italians, for example. Their porn films were too pretentious. They liked to weave in actual plot lines. The men and women being filmed often attempted to display themselves as credible actors and not just fuck puppets. By contrast, the Germans cut to the chase. Why waste time on superficial dialogue when a close up of an erect penis penetrating an orifice is what the customer is really paying to see? And why waste money on glamorous-looking sex performers when you could simply get a couple of local debauchees drunk and then film the consequences?

He sat there staring intently at the screen, watching people engage in various hardcore sex acts. But the images stirred nothing within him below the waist.

It was at that moment his train of thought entered a tunnel of self-reflection, the one marked 'shame'. What he'd just witnessed left him struggling to justify what he'd sat through unblinkingly. The thing had been sick and sordid to behold. And those poor women! How much were they getting paid to be treated so brutally? Whatever it was, it wasn't enough.

A deeper question was forming a frown on his still relatively youthful brow. Why was he exposing his brain cells to this filth? What did it say about his current lot in life that he was reduced to finding some kind of sick solace from the sight of people behaving like human toilets?

Trevor suddenly felt unclean, his senses soiled by toxic smut. And that's when the self-disgust started to seep in. Why was he – a grown man, a thinker, an aesthete – reduced to this pitiful predicament where he felt compelled to stare zombie-like at other human beings behaving like beasts of the darkest jungle? Yes, the writer/journalist – and he was both – was something of a voyeur by the very nature of his and her chosen profession but like everything else, voyeurism had its limits.

The answer came to him at once like a piercing scream: Jessica. Once the love of his life, now the humongous thorn impaled inside his haunted heart. Less than six months ago, she'd spoken the unspeakable. Something about 'a trial separation' and 'maybe seeing other people'. So now he was alone in a flat – their old love nest – that he could no longer afford to pay the rent on while she was living the high life in the luxurious apartment of her new boyfriend, a thirty-something merchant banker with perfect teeth and all the depth of a speck of drizzle rolling down the surface of a windowpane.

Don't mention his name. Don't even go there. Because – as Trevor reluctantly concluded – his current loveless existence was inextricably bound up in his recent problems in securing any kind of lucrative work. In his mind, Jessica had fallen out of love not with the man himself but with his circumstances. Love's raw flame could still be rekindled but it would not be easy to find the matches. Doing so would have to involve radically changing his ways, which leaned mostly towards sloth.

The night before, he'd been on YouTube smirking at the late comedian Peter Cook impersonating a gruff-voiced northern football manager. Cook had been in tip-top comedic fettle as his character solemnly shared the secrets of his soccer coaching skills with a balding talk-show host. 'In this world, it's all about the three Ms: [pause] Motivation, [longer pause] Motivation, [even longer pause] and Motivation!' That's what Trevor needed at this harrowing juncture of his life: motivation – in triplicate jumbo-sized, steroid-like doses. The advent of a stout-hearted stoicism. The compulsion to claim bold accomplishments. To be reborn as a phoenix arising from the ashes of heartache.

But then his old sour mood would boomerang back on him. *Who am I kidding here?* he'd think and the sudden gust of doubt would derail his lofty pipedreams about standing tall.

The bigger picture was this: Trevor was trapped in a world that currently held no significant context for him and his kind. His backstory was not untypical of the generation who'd spent their formative teenage years grappling under Thatcher's boot heel through the 1980s. There was a broken home, the deeply eccentric mother and the rich but rarely present daddy. By the time puberty beckoned, he'd spent his short life in a state of bookish timidity. Music began casting a spell over him at age twelve; he tried to learn to play a Smiths song on a guitar a friend owned but the fretboard was too big for his hands and the chords too complicated for his fingers.

But then just as his genitalia were becoming framed by an anarchic moustache of pubic hair and his voice had suddenly descended a full octave, the acid house rave scene broke loose. Trevor spent his late teens necking back Es and inhaling reefer at many such soirees held during the decade's final gurning days. The immediate upshot of this – beyond the lost brain cells – was that his A level results were nothing to write home about. No matter: his B in English would be enough to land him a place in a college specialising in 'Media Studies', which is what he wanted to do in the first place.

When 'Media Studies' were first taught at places of higher education, the role of the journalist or social commentator could still be called a potentially lucrative career option. But the affordable home computer arrived on the scene and the realm of the print media was duly hit with diminishing sales figures and advertising revenues as a direct consequence.

By the time Trevor had graduated and was actively seeking work, the internet storm was gathering but the old print order were still top dogs in terms of feeding information out to the masses, and no one in their network could foresee what lay ahead. This being so, work was still plentiful and Trevor was fortunate enough to be 'interned' by a music editor at the *Independent* who felt his initial reviews showed 'pluck'. He spent several seasons in a state of steady employment there, covering the on-going late 1990s pop/rock landscape with what he intended to be wry wit-drenched detachment but which often took on a tone that was more flippant and hectoring.

By the turn of the decade, he'd had enough of trying to drum up another glib glob of text focusing on the sociological significance of Noel Gallagher's monobrow or why Coldplay were such a dreary bunch of fellows. Jessica was in his life now – sweet Jess, oh God those green eyes so wide and so wanton. When did the love dust fade from those heavenly orbs?

God, the pointlessness of it all – alone, half-drunk and staring at a computer screen with only a half-empty bottle of red wine for companionship. 'Cheap but cheerful,' the man behind the counter at the offie had called this particular cut-price bouquet for the taste buds.

But trying to eke pleasure from frugal circumstances was never Trevor's particular forte. He'd been born to a man of considerable wealth and had always been secure in the knowledge that whenever the rent was overdue, the credit cards all 'maxed' out and no payment from the print media forthcoming, he could always make another awkward pleading phone call to the old man who would then chew him out for ten minutes saying hurtful stuff about how he was a 'bloody terrible disappointment as a son' before begrudgingly agreeing to pay off his latest overdraft.

Father and son had never seen eye-to-eye on career choices and general lifestyle issues. His father was a boundlessly ambitious, go-for-the-jugular business tycoon who'd made his reputation as the closest thing Wolverhampton had ever come to having a captain of industry. In that region – and others – he was known as the takeover king.

Their relationship could best be summed up in the remark his father had made in front of him, Jessica and his interfering, loathsome stepmother. 'The doctor told me today, "Jack, you're a fucking miracle – you're still as bloody robust as a strapping twenty-five-year-old bricklayer." I said back to him, "That may be, doc, but I'm still suffering from the rich man's worst disease." "What's that then?" he asked. "Bloody useless, money-grabbing offspring," I replied.' The stepmother – a coarse, pushy Australian woman called Yvonne with skin like sun-baked Naugahyde – had tossed her head back and gracelessly cackled while Trevor felt like every atom of his being was in the process of reducing itself down to a puddle on the floor. Jessica's eyes had suddenly turned from limpid pools to frosty slits. Oh Jess – I wasn't worthy of you.

Bugger all this. Time to smoke some wacky instead. The wine had made him maudlin. Pot by contrast promoted a sense of (mostly) pleasant befuddlement that he needed right now. A joint was swiftly fashioned – rolling spliffs fast was one of his few real skills – while his mind wandered through the details of his most recent attempt at summoning career initiative.

One evening recently he'd found himself at a social gathering idly conversing with a middle-aged woman, a slightly dotty self-proclaimed interior designer who specialised in the feng shui approach to redecoration – soothing colours, banish all the clutter and bric-a-brac, leave wide-open spaces for the mind to meditate in. That sort of thing. In a mildly inebriated condition, Trevor had nonetheless listened to the woman's words intently – particularly the part where she boasted she was making lots of money from her practice – and then been struck by an enterprising idea of his own.

If well-to-do people were so anxious to give strangers money and carte blanche to reorganise their living space, then surely those same pampered beings would welcome someone into their house – a bona fide music expert en plus – and pay him handsomely to 'reorganise' their record collections. In the circles Trevor generally frequented, one was often judged by the contents of one's record collection and he felt he possessed exactly the right sensibility to help others attain the ideal musical selection for all moods and occasions.

He placed an advert in one of the London evening papers but got no takers. Then a cousin of his connected him with a couple living somewhere in Berkshire who seemed interested. He ended up taking a taxi out to their place. By the time he arrived at the destination, he was already over £100 out of pocket. The man was possibly called Dennis. His wife was definitely called Beryl. Trevor remembered her name. There weren't many Beryls left in the world. They were a dying species. No food was offered – no alcohol. Trevor sensed he was in the presence of teetotallers. The offer of a cup of coffee was eventually made and he accepted. But the absence of biscuits – that rankled him.

He duly studied the contents of their record collection while doing his level best to tamp down on the disdain he felt at what he saw displayed before him. From his perspective, it looked like these two were a lost cause straight off the bat, and duly proceeded to lecture them on their lack of good taste in a manner that immediately created a chill in the room.

Why two Kenny G CDs and nothing by John Coltrane? Why several Pink Floyd recordings from the latter Dave

Gilmour-helmed years and not a sign of anything involving Syd Barrett? And what on earth were all those Chris Rea albums doing there when both Leonard Cohen and Tom Waits were conspicuously absent from the couple's playlist? Trevor then committed his most significant faux pas. He pointed to a Supertramp album and said something about it being 'music for plebs'.

The Dennis fellow went ballistic. 'That's my all-time favourite album,' he protested. 'Well, none of us is perfect,' Trevor had responded without thinking beforehand.

The encounter ended shortly after that exchange. Dennis called him 'a snooty cunt' and told him to vacate the premises at the earliest opportunity. Trevor responded by marching to the front door while suggesting the homeowners 'stick your Kenny G CDs up your bums'.

Once outside the house, he had the devil's own job to find a taxi back to his London mancave. He'd spent around £250, money he'd never see again. And what had been achieved? Apart from a frank exchange of views with two people saddled with limited conversational skills, excruciating bad taste and even worse manners who couldn't even muster up a plate of biscuits – nothing. In fact, a new low had been plumbed and rank desperation was battering at the door in the immediate aftermath of the above-described incident.

Two factors spared him from a total meltdown. One was a bag of skunk that someone – he wasn't sure who – had left by mistake during a recent social evening at his apartment. Four or five tokes and he'd been sent reeling into another stratosphere. It was pure escapism of course – not any sort of solution – but when times grow hard, it's important to cultivate your own private comfort zone and self-medicate your way through adversity.

But the second factor offered more than just a reassuring sense of woozy languor. It represented the only tangible ray of hope he'd been privy to in recent weeks. Just one month earlier, he'd received an email from someone he'd never corresponded with or previously encountered. But he knew the name of the sender – everybody in the United Kingdom did.

Michael Martindale was a very rich and successful man who'd somehow managed to make millions as a writer of crime fiction for the past twenty years. He was generally considered a consistent rather than an outstanding literary talent but he had an undeniable knack for creating characters that the public in the United Kingdom – and elsewhere – fell head over heels in love with. Back in the 1990s, Trevor had read one of Martindale's books – skimmed through it, more like – and while he managed to actually get to the end, he'd been left somewhat underwhelmed by its contents. Nowadays he felt more a sense of peevish indignation towards the man's uncanny and – to his way of thinking – unwarranted run of success. His books sold in their millions, were translated into every foreign language imaginable and spawned big budget films and TV series. Meanwhile Trevor and his media cronies were subsisting on starvation wages and coming to realise that readers of thought-provoking literature were probably doomed for wholesale extinction.

Of course, all that envy vanished from his mind the instant he saw the correspondent's name on his computer screen. It was replaced in a flash by a brand new agenda, one harnessed to a sudden yearning to exploit the man and his circumstances. It turned out that Martindale was contacting him because of an article Trevor had written for *Mojo* magazine some months earlier.

It concerned the Unstable Boys, a late 1960s rock combo who'd enjoyed three bountiful years of hit records and sundry misadventures before breaking up and becoming yet another vaguely recalled footnote in the annals of rock history. Then in 2014 a leading technology firm ran a series of high-profile ads for their latest mobile phone featuring one of the Unstable Boys' songs (not even one of their hits) as the soundtrack and for a while there you couldn't escape it – it was everywhere. A swiftly released remix of the original recording brusquely elbowed its way to the top of the charts and the tech firm then followed things up by sanctioning two more ad campaigns featuring Unstable Boys material. Both songs managed to dent the charts as well and the media started to focus on this lost band of bickering boys whom blind fate had chosen to bless with a second wind.

Martindale had been an Unstable Boys fanatic as a teenager and his eyes would still glaze over – Trevor noticed – like those of a love-struck girl whenever their name was mentioned in interview. This shouldn't have surprised him. As a side-bar to Trevor's *Mojo* piece, Martindale had contributed a short, gooey testimonial to the group. He'd proposed in his introductory email that the two should get together, that there was a project he wanted to discuss involving the Unstable Boys. Two days later the pair were furtively scoping each other out in a pub in World's End.

From where Trevor sat, Martindale, despite his bumper paydays and shed-loads of popular acclaim, didn't appear to be a man to be envied. He looked more like a man on the threshold of poor health – shapeless, audibly wheezing, slow in his gestures. The brain was still agile but his animus was sorely depleted. 'I suppose you know about my recent predicament,' he'd mentioned, partly as a way to explain his lack of personal dynamism. In fact, Trevor hadn't known at the time – though he'd nodded to Martindale – that the author had been 'outed' in an extramarital dalliance by a tabloid and was currently living alone, away from his wife and two sons.

It all started making sense then. The cavalier manner in which Martindale would throw alcohol down his throat the way you'd toss a beaker of water over a budding conflagration. The veiled references to writer's block. Above all, the sense of utter desolation pouring out of the man. It felt quite enjoyable to Trevor to see a rich man suffering, to have solid proof before him that mega-success was not a guarantee of lasting contentment.

Martindale's pitch was this. Although he'd never engaged in anything of that kind before, he wanted to make a documentary about the Unstable Boys, their rise and fall, their wilderness years, their second wind and their current existences. A rockumentary by any other name.

Martindale then mentioned that everyone – his agent and sundry nosey colleagues – had tried to dissuade him from pursuing the idea and urging him to stay with what he knew best: crime. He'd signed a deal a year before to pen a new volume featuring his two best-loved detectives and had pocketed a £2 million advance as a result. But he had yet to write even one word of the hotly anticipated text, he'd muttered to Trevor in that conspiratorial way of the intoxicated sharing bar space with people they scarcely know. The drink was starting to light a fire in his brain. His voice grew louder and its tone turned bellicose, an unsettling turn of events because the man was clearly acting way out of character.

He sat and seethed for a while. He cursed his business associates, he cursed the publishing world, he cursed the media – few were spared during this disturbing tirade. He even began to invoke his family into the verbal fray – 'And even my own beloved wife and two ingrate sons ...', he'd barked out before suddenly realising he'd overstepped a line and promptly fallen silent. Trevor was just thankful the verbal tempest had abated. Martindale had got so carried away during it that he'd failed to notice that he was moistening the journalist's face with tiny flecks of spittle.

He then told Trevor what their meeting was really all about, that he was about to get a production company interested in the Unstable Boys project and that he wanted to employ him as both journalist and 'creative consultant' (whatever that meant). No sums of money were discussed during their initial tête-á-tête. But the man was obviously loaded and Trevor wasn't about to look a gift horse – or indeed any semblance of gainful employment – in the mouth. This could be a genuine money-spinner, he'd instantaneously calculated – at least six months of all-expenses-paid guaranteed income with the possibility of more to follow.

There were caveats, mind you. When Trevor had researched his article on the Unstable Boys, he'd managed to secure interviews with a former manager, a roadie and the group's

A & R man back in their golden era. But actual former group members were harder to coax out of obscurity to query in person about those long-gone crazy days. In the end, Trevor had managed to snag the bassist Mark McCabe – a talkative chap – and two drummers who'd put in time flailing the skins for the group – salt-of-the-earth types the pair of them, but mentally fogbound and incapable of recalling salient details about their younger years.

The supporting players had their share of spicy anecdotes to recount but the two main protagonists of the saga – the singer and the guitarist – had been impossible to pin down. They were still alive but nobody knew where they were currently holed up. The singer apparently floated around the globe, settling briefly in various parts of the world and then, having quickly outstayed his welcome, departing in haste. He had sometimes retreated to Switzerland where he lived rent-free in a mansion owned by a rich woman rumoured to have been some kind of practising witch. He owned no mobile phone, generally refused to pick up landlines and – although he'd coerced someone to create an email address for him – apparently lacked the skills to operate it so was in effect completely unreachable.

Martindale, however, wanted Trevor to focus on tracking down the singer's similarly unreachable guitar-playing former amigo. Generally considered the most talented member of the ensemble, Ral Coombes had basically written and arranged all their original material alone, even though the composer credits often featured other names alongside his. A genuinely gifted musician who lacked the temperament and sense of his own specialness to attain anything more than fleeting success, he'd embarked on an ill-starred solo career after leaving the Unstable Boys. A long stint as a reclusive drug addict had taken him completely off the rock radar throughout the 1980s but somewhere in the 1990s he'd cured himself and reports surfaced of new songs being demoed. Nothing got released, however, and no public sightings were forthcoming.

Trevor had spoken to a 'business associate' of the former group who'd been rehired to negotiate the windfall advertising revenue that had started pouring in. He was one of the only people alive who could still manage to contact Coombes and the singer through some channel or other, possibly carrier pigeon. He told Trevor that Coombes in particular would not be tempted to talk about the past or about anything. His teenage son had been hit and killed by a lorry while riding his skateboard. 'There's been too much tragedy in his life,' the business associate concluded. 'It's not something you'd want to shine your flashlight on.'

He spoke with tenderness about Coombes but was less charitable when summoning together his thoughts on the singer whom he referred to as 'a bit of a mad lad'. In early photographs of the Unstable Boys their vocalist looks brazen, insolent and scarily self-assured. If the group's odyssey through the late 1960s had been made into a film, then a young Oliver Reed would have been ideal as the actor playing the singer's role. They shared a number of traits: cruel eyes, a rugged physicality, unpredictable mood swings, menacing manners and a fondness for hellraising to which women were often helplessly drawn despite their better instincts.

Trevor had asked the intermediary the inevitable question – was any kind of reunion possible now their commercial clout had been exhumed from the grave? 'Not a chance,' came the reply. 'They detest each other still.' These words were replayed in Trevor's mind when Martindale – unprompted – had stated that the programme they'd be working on would – all being well – act as a trigger to reunite them. The narrative would then magically morph from a conventional rockumentary into a heart-warming human interest story about ageing men regrouping to take care of unfinished business and settle old scores.

That's when Trevor's eyebrows had arched and, for perhaps one whole second, he'd stared at Martindale as if he was beholding an irredeemably stupid man. He'd snapped out of it quickly enough and retreated back behind his mask of meek civility but a distinct impression had been left – he was dealing with an idiot.

First of all, how was he going to reunite the Unstable Boys when its two principals apparently loathed each other to the degree where they literally couldn't live in the same country, never mind occupy the same stage? Did he really think one could put back together a cranky bunch of deeply eccentric and dysfunctional musicians in the way your average handyman could superglue a broken teapot back into active service?

Trevor studied Martindale and saw little to be impressed by. He'd toyed with the idea of being candid with the man but quickly concluded that it wouldn't be in his best interest. He needed employment, he needed money, and this was the closest thing to a cash cow that he'd encountered in many a moon. He'd play the duty-bound hired hand. Whatever Martindale wanted, he'd attempt to comply. The trick was to disengage from the creative process and just follow orders. That way, when things began to unravel – as he suspected they would – he could avoid getting drawn into the gathering storm while still receiving a fat pay cheque for services rendered.

Trevor was not a deep-thinking man but he had developed his own instincts about human nature as he'd stumbled into adulthood and felt he could 'read' the inner characters of those he interacted with fairly adroitly. Martindale was an open book and a sorry saga it was too. He should have been out living the life of Riley – whoever this Riley was – with all the money, exposure and acclaim he'd accrued but instead he was just wilting away.

His family had essentially exiled him from his own home and hearth, he was holed up alone in an apartment his agent had quickly found him but was having difficulty operating many of its utensils. He was approaching a crucial deadline for a new crime novel but hadn't typed one word. Instead he seemed hellbent on focusing his depleted energies on reanimating a long-dead rock group from his long-gone youth. What sort of melancholy madness was this?

Trevor had long recognised the lure of nostalgia that held sway over all generations but perhaps most notably the 1960s baby-boomer fraternity. Folks twenty-odd years his senior were always lecturing him about the 'true golden age of rock' in ways that implied that while they'd been privileged to attend a full-scale banquet, folk of Trevor's young stripe had only crumbs left to nibble on.

Trevor couldn't stomach most of these people. They reminded him far too much of his disapproving dad. And he didn't much rate 1960s rock anyway, despite the lip service he'd dutifully displayed towards the era's best-loved icons in his columns. His musical tastes had begun with the likes of Joy Division and the Smiths and he tended to look at late twentieth-century popular music as a prelude to or aftermath of those two acts. Most 1960s music sounded dated, quaint and corny, and the Unstable Boys' output was no exception.

But he wasn't going to tell his new employer that, just as he hadn't mentioned his antipathy to the *Mojo* editor when he'd offered him the assignment that had set this whole ball rolling in the first place. He wasn't passionate about the project yet sensed that it was still the correct career path to take. Nostalgia was selling like hot cakes and, after all, he was brainstorming with a real literary high roller despite initial appearances to the contrary.

If only Jess could have seen the two of them together deep in conversation at that swanky restaurant. Would she have reconsidered and come to her senses? Just thinking about her set off an incendiary sensation in his chest, a kind of existential heartburn.

When it grew more intense, he cast his eyes downwards to where the pain was seated. The joint he'd been smoking had fallen from his hand and was burning a hole in his T-shirt. He'd just set himself on fire. Having patted down the gathering conflagration, he stared for a while at the hole it had left in his clothing. That T-shirt was a write-off for a start. And for one split second he asked himself the question – is this a portent, an omen of things to come? The answer came quickly. No, it's just what happens when you get too cabbaged. With this conclusion safe in his cerebellum, he staggered off to pass out fully clothed on his lonely bed.

CHAPTER 2

A few months before he hired Trevor Bourne, the esteemed author squinted stonily at the images staring back at him from his computer. Aubrey, his agent's assistant, had just emailed him a series of new photographs – portrait shots of the novelist that were intended for publicity purposes. Dougie Ogilvy had taken the photos – he was A-list all the way – and only a curmudgeon would dare even imply that he'd hadn't done a splendid job of giving a somewhat bland and inexpressive face a much needed shade of gravitas and intensity.

It was all down to the lighting: dark shards framed each portrait with the subject's face lit cautiously in the middle, turned slightly away from the camera so that a hint of cheekbone could be captured. At least three shots from the session were ideal for the back of his next book jacket because they captured his role as a writer succinctly: as the narrator of his crime novels, he was constantly peering in and out of dark places.

The photographs were also flattering. The sympathetic lighting gave his weak chin a sharper curve, the wrinkles, crow's feet and fleshy bags around his eyes had all been rendered invisible and his ever-receding hairline artfully concealed under the camouflage of darkness. A man with confidence in his own physical appearance might even have had one of the images blown up and framed to decorate the wall of his private abode.

But Michael Martindale was not such a man. For most of his life he'd often found himself plunged into a state of abject gloom about the skin he'd been born into. He hated his body – it was so shapeless. And his facial features appalled him. As a teenager he'd dreamed of having roguish good looks and a lean, long physique, but it was not to be. By age sixteen he'd achieved his full height – five foot seven inches – and had inherited a physique best described as dough-like or, if one was being charitable, cuddly. He wasn't fat or even particularly rotund – just a spud-like creature on two bandy legs.

His physical shortcomings were even more torturous because he became a teenager in the 1960s, just at that moment when young people discovered the joys (and perils) of rampant narcissism. Suddenly you had to be part of some preening tribe but Michael was too misshapen to ever pass for a mod, too inherently sweet-natured to be accepted as a rocker and too reassuringly bourgeois-looking to make it as a hippie. He remembered once being at home with his parents. His hair was just starting to protrude beyond his shirt collar and he was wearing a pair of sandals with no socks. His mother called him 'ugly' right to his face.

But he'd somehow prevailed through those blighted years. As time had marched on, so his capacity grew for resigning himself to any predicament and shaping his life accordingly.

Women were never going to swoon when he entered a room. Good looks and rakish personal magnetism were not his to exploit. And so he found himself ambling down a life path that was fashioned more by his inherent timidity than by youthful ambition. He may have secretly yearned to be a rebel and a bit of a social outcast but knew instinctively that he didn't possess the kind of barmy self-confidence one needed to go out there and kick up some dust along culture's slippery ledge.

So he did well in school. Which led to university and an eventual PhD in twentieth-century literature. It also led to Jane, his first and only love, then a fellow student. Both were without brothers or sisters, both had been raised by strict, attentive parents in small uneventful English towns, and both were bedroom hermits wary of actual physical contact.

They first bonded over a Joni Mitchell record Jane was playing in her dorm room. He was a fan too and – as her door was slightly open – he mustered up the courage and stepped forward to congratulate her on her good taste. It was something of a brazen gesture on his part: at that stage of his life, women still generally terrified him. He was expecting the usual reaction from females of his generation – the underwhelming stare, the look that screamed 'unsuitable future boyfriend material'. But Jane was different. There was kindness in her eyes from the first second she surveyed him. That kindness penetrated him like a beam of light – not just a sparkle, a steady searching ray of empathy pouring into his lonely soul.

They fell into an animated conversation focused on the merits of La Mitchell's songwriting that lasted for several hours and numerous cups of tea. From that evening onward, they became inseparable. They liked many of the same books, films and musicians. They liked taking long walks together. After three weeks of non-stop courtship and collusion, they took the giant step of actually deflowering each other. It was a tender event; they fitted together well. From that point on, they were so interconnected they'd routinely finish each other's sentences.

In 1973 both graduated from university and chose to waltz down the aisle together shortly afterwards. Nothing was going to part these two lovebirds – or so everyone including the lovebirds themselves felt at the time. In the process, Michael put aside his dreams of becoming a journalist and opted instead for the same vocation Jane was set on pursuing – English teacher. For the rest of the 1970s and most of the 1980s that is what they did – introduce largely disinterested teenagers to the contemplative joy to be gained from reading quality (if sometimes outmoded) literature.

Aside from having to confront the occasional psychotic pupil with authority issues, it was steady, undramatic work, fleetingly rewarding but mostly a matter of adhering doggedly to a set routine. Still, he learned something that would serve him well in his next vocation: the attention span of the average human being – be they young or not so young – is so minuscule that in order to hold their attention, you have to hook them right from the very get-go and then stealthily reel them in until what you have to say has been digested.

By the mid-1980s Michael had much to feel good about: a secure job with excellent holiday options, two strapping young sons, a nice house with the mortgage almost fully paid up. And the still unshakeable love and devotion of a good woman.

And yet something was missing in his life, something he couldn't quite name. A challenge. A new liberating outlet. Some form of self-expression. He'd always sensed that – given time and the right stimuli – he could one day blossom as a writer of credible modern literature. But timidity still lurked within him. As a youngster, he'd read a biography of an author he admired who'd been quoted as saying 'real writers are born that way. It's in their blood.' The words had unsettled him. Sometimes he'd lie awake at night listening to his blood pumping through his veins, searching for some sign that poetry might be flowing alongside the red ooze.

Fortunately, his adult years coincided with the more mature realisation that writing – great or otherwise – issues not from the blood but the brain and that the budding scribbler was best served cultivating his or her mental faculties to maximum effect.

Still, it was Jane who first set the ball rolling. After the birth of their second son, Theo, she'd found herself unable to juggle the roles of teacher and mother, and had opted instead to stay at home and concentrate on her maternal duties.

Then clear out of the blue a former colleague had called her. In certain tight academic circles, Jane was an acknowledged expert on the 'noir' crime fiction of Raymond Chandler and Dashiell Hammett, and the colleague – recently employed at a most reputable publishing house – was overseeing the imminent publication of a one-volume compendium of Chandler's short stories for which she was adamant Jane should supply a lengthy preface. Delighted by the offer,

Jane diligently complied and the resulting text – which ran to over 8000 words – was singled out in reviews as one of the most insightful and cogent essays on Chandler and his oeuvre ever committed to print.

Seeing his beloved wife so feted and so aglow with the lustre of accomplishment at first overjoyed Michael. But that joy became increasingly more confined. The inner conflict it ignited within was at first hard for him to fathom. He was palpably proud of his wife and yet he felt suddenly competitive towards her. It was a difficult situation to adjust to, because he couldn't talk about it to Jane without potentially igniting a conflict between them. He tried brooding for a while but that only made his predicament more vexing.

What really ate at him was that Jane was a better teacher than he was and also a better literary critic – and now it had been made official. He was adept at making language sound quite interesting and could talk with impressive gusto about the skills and shortcomings of numerous pen pushers but he lacked Jane's analytical edge, her scrupulous, detail-dense extrapolations, her eloquence and nimble-wittedness.

To counteract his feelings of inadequacy, he placed himself in front of an old ribbon typewriter one rainy day in May 1985 and proceeded to will himself into hesitantly tapping out what started out being a short work of fiction. A prostitute had gone missing somewhere in the Yorkshire Dales. He commenced his tale with just this sliver of information to further spark his imagination. A strange hippie commune led by an intense and volatile leader with piercing eyes and habit of speaking in sinister riddles was then quickly conjured up into the gathering theatre of conflict in order to start establishing some kind of plot line.

Having written ten pages, he realised that he needed to catapult the forces of law and order into his narrative. So partly as a spoof on the popular TV cop-buddy dramas of the 1970s and 1980s, he invented two police officers: Adrian Cheeseman (youngish, left-leaning, popular with the ladies, a reasonable man in most circumstances but who, when sufficiently angered, was not to be trifled with) and Reginald 'Chalky' White (close to retirement, rabid right-winger, big drinker, sufferer of a plethora of health issues, possessor of a prickly, curmudgeonly exterior that in truth masked a heart of pure gold), thrown together against each other's express desires in order to solve crime and placate their long-suffering superintendent.

Michael often had them stuck together in a car as it sped along the Dales. They'd start out bickering on any number of topical subjects – the miners' strike, Maggie Thatcher, the rising price of tobacco – but when the subject turned to actual crime solving, they'd find themselves suddenly on the same page – the one bookmarked 'rogue action first – consequences later'.

Initially the budding author had envisaged his endeavour lasting little more than twenty pages but when he noticed that he'd just finished page seventy-eight, he recognised two things. The first was that for the duration of this writing exercise he'd been utterly spellbound. Time had stood still. The real world had receded into a misty backdrop. Creating fictional characters and situations using only words and then shaping their urges and destinies – it was like playing God. An intoxicating role.

The second thought was that he needed to tie up the loose plot threads smartly, solve the mystery and conclude his story at full speed. He made the murderer the prostitute's former pimp – an appropriately seedy individual the author had referred to only sparingly in the text, exiling him to the outskirts of the plot until the dramatic climax where both White and Cheeseman watched him fall to his death from the roof of a high-rise block without offering assistance. White also got to bust the commune for drug dealing and plant a bone-crushing haymaker on the face of the bogus guru. Justice had been served and the Dales were once more safe for law-abiding ramblers. End of story.

He gathered together the 111 pages that represented its totality and – after some nervous editing – presented it to Jane. Her opinion mattered to him in that moment above all else. And her reaction was sublime. After she'd put the pages down and taken off her reading glasses, she looked at him with such warmth and such pride that he felt he might actually faint. 'You have a real gift,' she told him. 'You have skills.' And the joy of it was – she was being sincere.

At first she felt that the overall plot line needed at least one more twist in its tail but Jane was more drawn to character development than tricky plot twists, and her husband had just presented her with a text rich with memorable, entertaining folk. She particularly liked the friction-filled rapport he'd cultivated between the two cops, whom he'd nicknamed Chalk and Cheese. She'd immediately told him that *Chalk and Cheese* should be the work's official title, not *Dark Doings on the Dales* (his initial idea).

She also pointed out that the narrative lacked any kind of strong female presence. The dead prostitute was little more than a convenient corpse and the girls in the hippie commune could have been replaced by sheep, so passive were their portrayals. She suggested that he introduce a female police officer into the tale, a self-confident yet vulnerable beacon of womanly intuition who could talk reason to both Chalk and Cheese when their personal animosities were threatening to turn ballistic, and could rein them back together as an unstoppable crime-busting duo.

Michael acted on this immediately. He also heeded her advice about expanding the dead prostitute's role in the text. He wrote tender paragraphs about her short life and wrong career choices. And – at Jane's insistence – he inserted an episode early in the text where the doomed girl actually conversed with her future assassin.

Finally, it ran to 249 pages. And then – wonder of wonders – the text was deemed so 'sprightly' by Jane's pal, the commissioning editor, that she pushed to have the thing published by her company.

The advance and royalty rate he ended up with – he had no agent at the time – were a mere pittance but Michael was still ecstatic. The effect of being published for the first time – in book form moreover – can often be akin to injecting a syringe full of pure adrenalin-like self-confidence into a neck vein: a dizzying, self-empowering rush ensues and the writer is never quite the same again.

Then the reviews came and though no one went out on a limb to talk him up as the new Raymond Chandler, the majority of critics applauded his debut work as a first-rate page turner. The book's key virtue – all concurred – was high-lighted in the terse, antagonistic and yet often darkly droll dialogue between Chalk and Cheese that held the whole narrative together like a spine.

The book sold modestly at first but then a TV production company stepped forward and bought the rights to *Chalk and Cheese* with the firm intention of turning it into a six-episode series. Michael was suddenly the recipient of serious money but still managed to fret furtively over the fact that another script-writer was being employed to do a rewrite and that his charac-ters had effectively been taken out of his hands. Suddenly he felt like a child whose most prized possession had been stolen.

The way things turned out, he needn't have worried. *Chalk and Cheese* was transmitted at midweek peak-time viewing and millions throughout the UK were transfixed. They became strangely attached to the two cops and much of the credit for the series' populist appeal had to go to the 'other scriptwriter' who significantly amped up the comedy factor peeking through the two main characters' often tense exchanges. Also – as luck would have it – the powers-that-were had snagged two of the UK's best-loved 'thesps du jour': fifty-two-year-old Ralph Blakley, then hailed as the West Midlands' answer to Anthony Hopkins, and twenty-eight-year-old (thirty-three really – but who was counting?) Gavin Maloney, renowned for his youthful good looks and impres-sive grasp of a host of regional accents and dialects. They became Chalk and Cheese to the degree where the viewing public perceived them as being umbilically connected one to the other – a single combative-but-unstoppable-when-a-good-fight-was-called-for entity.

The series' success changed many aspects of Michael and Jane's lives. First and foremost, the sudden downpour of money into his account meant that he could take a long sabbatical from teaching and pursue his lucrative new passion with a single-minded fervour. So much money was flooding in that they bought themselves a holiday home, a cottage by the beach. Nothing ostentatious, just a snug little retreat.

At the same time, everything was starting to accelerate. The BBC craved more *Chalk and Cheese*. The production company and the publishing house were equally ravenous. No problem. Michael simply churned out two stories featuring the pair and they were eagerly filtered through to the general public. Royalty rates were dramatically increased in the author's favour and the two books that resulted were reviewed sympathetically, though one or two mean spirits made disparaging remarks about Chalk and Cheese's relationship becoming 'somewhat formula-driven'. The two resultant TV series at first drew strong viewing figures, but by the end of the final episodes the critics were saying that the magic chemistry had run its course and that the two crime fighters ought to be put out to pasture.

To his credit, Michael was not massively upset at seeing his once loved creations getting the brush-off from the cognoscenti and viewers alike. Secretly he agreed with the naysayers. Chalk and Cheese had spent too long clumping around in his imagination and needed to be evicted at full speed. Exiled. Excommunicated even. Whatever it took. Of this he was adamant.

One afternoon he was seated at his typewriter staring into space when he began conjuring up a fresh fiction. An

American special ops expert gets a hit placed on him by an all-powerful consortium of gangsters and has to change his identity and home base at the earliest opportunity. He chooses to relocate in the sleepy low-profile town of Shropshire in Devon where he ends up working as a night-time DJ on local radio. It's a midnight-to-six slot that allows him to play his favourite music – old-school country and 1970s southern rock – and indulge in lengthy bouts of whimsical philosophising in between the song selections.

One of his few listeners is an insomniac female detective on the regional task force, who shares his love of Willie Nelson and who finds his radio voice deeply soothing. Fate brings them together one evening and they quickly become drawn to one another platonically, although a palpable frisson of mutual carnal lust lurks just below the surface.

They begin sharing secrets. The lady detective divulges details of ongoing investigations to the DJ who duly comes clean to her about his special-ops training and the reasons for his new identity. They decide to become an unconventional crime-fighting duo. The DJ goes under the radar and employs his own special skills to aid the female cop in her cases. He then feeds her the clues that he's uncovered via his radio show by means of coded messages only the two of them can comprehend. 'The Race is On', 'Ring of Fire' and other ever-greens are suddenly transformed into ominous messages that some dastardly deed is about to kick off in the immediate vicinity. Sometimes the lady cop steps into the inevitable danger-filled house of looming death alone with only his clues to guide her, but most of the time he manages craftily to pre-record his radio show before sneaking out to join her for some good old one-on-one, knee-to-groin crime fighters.

The signature tune bookending his broadcasts is J.J. Cale's 'Call Me the Breeze' and he adopts the nickname himself. He becomes 'The Breeze' or just 'Breeze'. All references to his real name, place of birth and early life are to be left shrouded in mystery for the time being.

Michael named the female Eleanor after a song by the Turtles that he'd been fond of as a youngster. Eleanor and 'The Breeze'. He'd found his next two fictional protagonists just like that – to quote Tommy Cooper, another of his childhood fascinations. The plot line of course needed actual criminal activity to set everything else in motion, and so Michael created his first serial killer, a psychopathic mastermind whose evil ways were credibly concealed behind the role he'd affected as a harmless simple-minded local yokel generally well regarded by the community.

His publishers were exultant after reading the first draft of *They Call Me the Breeze*. The writing was crisp and bristled with tension-packed scenarios that set the blood racing with gory detail followed by even gorier detail. Eleanor and the Breeze were a pair destined to win the hearts of that oh-so-lucrative mainstream demographic who'd once been so fond of Chalk and Cheese. The book became his first no. 1 bestseller in the UK, topping the fiction charts there for nine sweet weeks in the autumn of 1993.

After that, it was full speed ahead. The book was immediately turned into an award-winning series that attracted record viewing figures. The actor playing the Breeze won the 'world's sexiest man' accolade in the Brit tabloids, while a female scribe at the *Guardian* dubbed him 'the thinking woman's crumpet'. The woman playing Eleanor was glowingly likened to a younger Helen Mirren. And the writer who'd set it all into motion was starting to feel the tantalising glow of the spotlight inching his way.

Conventional wisdom states that when someone becomes very successful but only for one brief interlude, that person is lucky – but little else. If, on the other hand, that person is able to duplicate or even further amplify that success with their later work, then they are indisputably 'damn good' at what they do. This was an intoxicating thing for Michael to experience. Just thinking about it – his new status, his new bank balance packed with more zeroes than you could shake a stick at, his new admirers – made him lightheaded.

Fortunately a fierce work ethic kept him mostly grounded. Between the mid-1990s and 2010 he completed five more books featuring Eleanor and the Breeze, hot on the trail of a veritable rogues' gallery of modern-day wrongdoers. The formula worked like a charm throughout most of those years. More TV series followed. A film was made with Jason Statham filling the Breeze's cowboy boots and breaking out a plausible Marlboro man-sized Yank accent; one of the *Game of Thrones* actresses played Eleanor.

Walking the red carpet at the film's London premiere was a moment he'd often find himself reliving. Crowds screaming frenziedly, flash bulbs popping away, mobile phones held aloft. But most of all, that look he'd long ago concluded that he would never be the recipient of. The look of a crowd of people saying 'We find you desirable' with their eyes. The look of love. Part of him found this predicament preposterous but another part was captivated by this newfound power to elicit even a soupçon of awe from the masses. It gave his spine a hot jolt that spread throughout his bones and stayed there incubating daily.

His life started to take a somewhat precarious turn from this point on. Thus far everything had been peaches and cream. The 1990s had witnessed him become a successful writer, his books sold spectacularly well and spawned equally lucrative films and TV series in their wake, his marriage had remained strong and mutually supportive, his two sons were both doing well in different but equally prestigious colleges. He'd even won an award from a bunch of fellow scribes situated somewhere in Scandinavia. Its compact form and curious metal shape made it an ideal paperweight for his writing desk. And every week new offers poured in.

At a certain point it just went to his head.

He started getting requests to appear on BBC panel shows. Back in the 1990s he would have flatly refused such offers because he understood implicitly that, though he could sometimes come up with genuinely humorous dialogue for his fictional characters, he lacked the quick-wittedness to be able verbally to joust with people who did that sort of thing for a living and who could be quite merciless to those with whom they tangled.

But in 2003 he'd become a hot property. Everybody in the media seemed to be seeking him out for comments and soundbites and his business associates were always aggressively prodding him to get on the telly more. But it was vanity finally that prompted him to take the plunge. Vanity and a lack of self-awareness that was alarming to behold in someone who'd formerly been so cautious in his general comportment.

He became a regular on *The News is Dead – Long Live the News*, a satirical half-hour show, but did not blossom in these exacting new circumstances. The comedians were invariably more mercurially witted than he, nailing their punchlines like champion darts players while he looked on silently, still struggling to come up with one vaguely droll zinger.

And the political experts – well, the problem there was that they were actual experts on the subjects they addressed and he wasn't. Oh, he'd read a newspaper and make a point of watching the news on the telly at least once a day, but the information he gleaned from these daily routines wasn't really sufficient to enter into meaningful discussion with those whose job it was to regulate such issues.

So he was outgunned from the start, and reviews of his appearances on the show were quick to point it out. But a form of blindness prevented him from reading the writing on the wall. Instead of phasing out his TV appearances and taking the J. D. Salinger route to media invisibility, he became ever more visible on the box. He'd got the bug and appeared determined to master the art of self-projection through cathode ray with the same positive results he'd achieved from making his mark on modern crime fiction.

But it wasn't going to pan out that way. The public may have loved what he dreamed up in his head but when faced with the man himself they preferred to change channels. A backlash formed – as it always does, particularly in England where the populace habitually turn on those they feel have become too successful.

It was around this time that things started to come unglued between him and Jane. Through all their preceding years the bond between them had stayed strong and mutually support-ive. Jane had persevered with her own writing though her efforts – all critical theses on her favourite nineteenth- and twentieth-century novelists – were destined to appeal to only a fraction of the mighty mainstream demographic her husband had managed to tap.

Not that the disparity in literary success caused the couple any significant inner conflicts. Jane was happy with her life during the 1990s. All through the decade she'd been an attentive mother to her two sons. Her status as a literary critic during this time had brought her numerous well-phrased plaudits from fellow pundits and regular work reviewing the latest books in the *Observer*'s culture pages. And she'd been ecstatic about her husband's new career path for many years.

But then somewhere in the noughties that thrill curdled into something that felt more like a muted form of disap-proval. Old friends would see them out together in public – an increasingly rare occurrence as Jane chose to accompany her husband less and less on his nocturnal sorties – and later note that the tension between them was as palpable as the frosty look on Jane's downcast features.

And the worst of it was Michael didn't seem remotely aware of his wife's unease; he was too busy holding court with his new cronies. And what a shower they were: self-absorbed actors, ruthlessly ambitious social commentators, preening media networkers, all of them drunk on a cocktail of alcohol and self-importance.

Jane observed them and shuddered inwardly. They reminded her of comic-book characters out of the *Beano*: Lord Snooty and his pals. And the way her husband soaked up their odious company made her recoil from him. Weeks would go by and they'd barely speak to each other even though they shared the same home.

Then the scandal blew up and Jane was placed in an intolerable position. The tabloids and some of the upmarket dailies duly portrayed her as the injured little wife, the victim of a fool's outed infidelity. The role infuriated her beyond belief, maybe even more than the betrayal itself. Suddenly these parasites were at the front door baying for quotes and filming empty rooms from the outside of the house. A private woman, she reacted by expelling the perpetrator of the nightmare scenario – her husband – from the premises and terminating all contact with him for the foreseeable future. Their two sons – now in their thirties – quickly followed suit.

So he was all alone in the world and feeling generally sorry for himself. Actually the first part of that last sentence wasn't entirely true, he reminded himself. His agent was still in his corner. He'd found Michael this more than acceptable maisonette in Mayfair to rent and rest his weary bones within. But the blighter was always on at him to finish his next literary opus. The first deadline had been and gone, the advance long banked away and still not one finished word existed. And you know what? He didn't give a monkey's bum.

He was drinking a lot these days. People could probably smell it on him. He didn't care. Give a man a break. His wife and kids had just abandoned him. And the muse hadn't been making any house calls of late either. What else was there to do but to pour yourself a good stiff drink and neck it back while listening to some stimulating music?

He headed first for the cupboard where the hard spirits were kept. The vodka bottle was empty. Brandy it would have to be. Filthy-tasting but reliably obliterating. Then he moved over to the CD player. What to play? A touch of the classics perchance? Nah, too cerebrally demanding. Some modal jazz à la Bill Evans? Another time. His mood demanded old-school rock by any other name.

He didn't have to dither about. The choice was pretty much made for him. He opened up the CD case of *Capture the Rapture*, the Unstable Boys' second album, placed its contents on the system and pressed play.

The music started up fast and feisty. The guitar riff driving the song along so relentlessly sounded a lot like the Johnny Burnette Trio, had Johnny and his brother Dorsey dosed themselves on LSD instead of moonshine and ampheta-mines. Then the vocalising began – a feral howl devoid of conscience.

> There are bad men
> And there are worse men
> Then there are cursed men
> I'm all of those
> You can see it in my face, dear
> You can smell it on my clothes
> The places I frequent
> And the company I keep
> Always up for mischief
> Got no time for sleep

Me and the devil rolling side by side
Working that whip on a midnight ride
Looking to prey on all who call this loveless sphere their
    home
Me and the devil – that's where we like to roam

There are strong men
Right-and-wrong men
'Life goes on' men
I'm not their kind
There is nothing
Strictly nothing
But self-interest
On my mind

This word 'morality'
Don't mean a thing to me
I take what I want
I break what I want
I'm a real go-getter
A people upsetter
Me and the devil coming over the rise
With our minds full of mayhem and our empty eyes
The night is young but the pickings are ripe
I'd cut that girl but she's not my type
God is dead but we are very much alive
Me and the devil – we were born to thrive

Don't have to call him cos he's right here next to me
Don't have to call him cos he's right here by my side

'Me and the Devil' (not to be confused with the Robert Johnson song of the same name) was never released as a single for good reason – its lyrics would have got it banned from global radio airplay – but it remains the Unstable Boys' supreme moment as a group, the one recording of theirs that merits being placed in some kind of time capsule and preserved for the ages.

Their other recorded output was worthy and inventive and featured some wonderful examples of late 1960s-era songcraft, but this one track caught them briefly operating on an altogether higher plateau. Like the Rolling Stones' 'Gimme Shelter', the song chills as it thrills. The listener becomes so focused on the song's mesmerising beat and rapid-fire chord changes that the lyrics sometimes get downplayed.

Michael had been listening to the track – often obsessively – on and off for decades but rarely delved too deeply into what the song was saying. Had he read the lyrics, he might have recognised it as a treatise on the banality of evil. But all he knew was what he heard. The words often appeared garbled and hard to decipher. But the overall sound was unmistakable. It was the sound of freedom. The song played on and the years fell away. He was a teenager once again dancing alone in his bedroom. The brandy was making him wobbly but he was still game for a shimmy around the room. Who cared if the drapes were open? Let them stare. He put the track on rotation. You can't have enough of a good thing when times are bad.

His life had taken an unexpected and treacherous turn. What more was there to lose? The future was uncertain and

the present a catastrophe. Suicide – the coward's way out –
was not in his nature. That left only the past to scurry back to
in search of sanctuary. The lure of nostalgia was on him like
a robber's dog. It gave him that peaceful easy feeling he
desperately lacked in any other aspect of his life.

Well, that and the brandy. So keep that music playing. Let
it cast its spell. The universe it was giving expression to was
where he wanted to emigrate to full time. Be careful what
you wish for, a wiser head than his had once advised him. But
he'd forgotten the remark and the encounter that prompted
it.

CHAPTER 3

Motherhood can do strange and complicated things to female morale. Nine long months of carrying an ever-expanding alien form in your belly that culminates in an extremely painful expulsion of said form into the world at large is a big enough burden to endure. But then the form gets brought home to begin a daily routine of raucous screaming at inopportune moments, coupled with defecating at least once every four hours. The mother – still recovering from her agonising ritual in the hospital – has to suddenly put her own life on hold and concentrate instead on feeding, protecting and constantly coddling her newborn.

Some women soon start to buckle under the strain. The frazzled young mother stares at the tiny bundle howling in the cot and sees only the dead corpse of her once-carefree youth. Resentments begin festering; the seeds of rejection are sown.

Happily this was not the case for Hilda Royston née Grantley when in 1948 she conceived for the first and only time. It was a baby boy with eyes like sparkling sapphires and a significant head of hair who made gurgling sounds from his tiny mouth. The first time the nurse let her hold him she felt like a little girl again, a little girl who'd just been given her very own living breathing doll. The explosion of love that swept through her when she looked at her son that first time never left her for the rest of her life.

Love and disapproval – those are the two cardinal rules of parenthood. You ladle out the affection but whenever your child transgresses – as children always do – you have to rein in the love, act stern and call their behaviour into question in ways that can humiliate and spark resentments.

Hilda never felt the compulsion to implement both of these parental tools. She showered her son with such a relentless downpouring of affection and attention that her love for him veered sharply towards the 'suffocating'. Everything he said or did within her presence caused her to garland the infant with gushing praise. His first scribbled words and pictures were hailed by Hilda as works of a future genius. Nothing was too good for her boy.

Hilda wasn't the self-analytical type, so she rarely if ever considered the possibility that her ever-mounting adoration of her son seemed to coincide with her ever-lowering opinion of her husband. Donald 'Tiger' Royston had been quite the catch once upon a time, or at least back when they'd married in 1946. A fighter pilot during the Second World War, he'd dispatched several boatloads of 'gerries' to their watery graves and even had medals to prove it. The war years had brought out the best in him. He'd exhibited real courage and skill as well as a capacity for staying wide awake during forty-eight-hour-long missions that made him much admired by his fellow airmen.

But that all ended in 1945. Suddenly he no longer had any reason to daredevil his way across the skies of Europe and the change of pace left him deflated and a bit gloomy. Always a robust consumer of alcohol, his intake increased significantly during the months following the war's cessation.

Some say he proposed to Hilda in a drunken fit one night and then forgot the next day what he'd done. Hilda hadn't, though, and was determined to be his bride. She was taken by his rakish air and was physically attracted to him because he bore an uncanny resemblance to a caddish comedy actor then in vogue for whom she had a bit of a thing. Donald was at a loose end, casting around to find new prospects for himself in peacetime Britain and she – in the role of devoted wife – would be his shepherdess gently guiding him through this uncertain new world to arrive at their personal pasture of plenty.

The long and short of it: Donald never found a job he managed to stay afloat in for more than two months before being asked to leave. His consumption of hard liquor kept teetering upwards. He rarely acknowledged his newborn son. He became increasingly belligerent around the house and once threw a glass at Hilda's head (it missed) while their child looked on from his playpen.

Finally, Hilda was told by a neighbour that Donald was 'involved' with a woman named Mary Bryce who ran a bed and breakfast establishment less than one mile from the Royston homestead. This knowledge, coupled with the glass incident, had hardened Hilda's heart sufficiently to the point where she saw no option other than to rid herself of this man's presence for good and all.

This she managed to accomplish by creeping up on him one night and beating his horizontal and inert body into wakefulness with the aid of a large wooden walking cane that had once belonged to an uncle who'd suffered from gout. Neighbours who overheard the incident taking place later agreed privately that, though the act itself was probably warranted, it was also carried out with an uncommon degree of savagery.

Donald Royston was in the hospital for three weeks with broken ribs, a broken pelvis and a massive dent in his once breezy hale-and-hearty demeanour. His central nervous system had evidently taken quite a pummelling too. Five years back he'd been out every night zapping around those treacherous clouds staring death full in the face. But now he couldn't face a mere woman, albeit one with a blunt weapon and a long list of grievances. All the fight had gone out of him. He didn't report the assault, recognising correctly that bringing the incident to trial would shine a fiercely unflattering light on his own recent extramarital activities and only make his current predicament worse.

Grasping at straws, he somehow convinced his paramour Mary Bryce – a portly red-headed woman with a throaty laugh who was the antithesis of the bird-like Hilda – to sell her bed and breakfast and elope with him to a beach resort located somewhere in the Outer Hebrides.

After that, Donald's personal odyssey becomes increasingly disjointed and difficult to detail. He and Bryce remained an item for nine or ten years but seem to have spent most of that time traversing the British Isles aimlessly. Six months in Cornwall, fifteen months working on a farm in Wiltshire – bobbing around Britain like a boat without a rudder.

By the time they'd worn each other out and were set on going their separate ways, the 1960s had begun and their freewheeling chaotic lifestyle would suddenly become not merely acceptable but actively desirable to the youth of the age. But by then it was too late for Donald Royston.

At the end, it was the drink, always the drink. The alcohol would drip-drip-drip into his bloodstream and send signals to his brain. Sometimes in the early stages of his daily consumption the signals would stimulate benign inner feelings. But then as his intake increased, the signals would stimulate raucousness and something distinctly nasty. He'd find himself overtaken by feelings he had no control over, negative emotions and vile thoughts. He regularly hallucinated that the people caught in his path of destruction – boatloads of dead Germans, an abandoned child, a wronged wife and scores of others he'd duped and discarded – were standing only a few feet away staring in silent judgement over him.

The liquor was poisoning both his brain and his liver. Cirrhosis was cited as the main cause of his death. Hilda was sent the autopsy report – it was the first piece of correspondence involving Donald that she'd received in over ten years. She read the report and then calmly put it back in its envelope.

Death often prompts conciliatory emotions from those who've endured conflicted relationships with the dear departed, but Hilda was having none of that. Donald Royston had been a dishonourable man and the gaping void was welcome to him. She scrunched up the envelope and tossed it vigorously into the flames leaping up in the grate of the living-room fireplace.

She never mentioned his name again. She didn't even report the death to friends and neighbours. And she never informed her own son that his father had passed away (it transpired when he was twelve years old). In fact, the boy would only learn about his father's death and sundry life details years later, when he read an article on his group in one of the more upmarket periodicals written by a journalist who had some grounding in investigative reportage. His reaction to the exposé was interesting. He hated its snarky tone. The piece had called him a 'small, feral force of nature' at one point and, though he didn't quite comprehend what the phrase meant, being referred to in print as 'small' was enough to send him apoplectic with anger. The revelations about his dad by contrast passed over him like water off a heron's hindquarters.

On one level, this was understandable. Donald Royston had been an infrequent and erratic presence during the first two years his son had been alive. Then he'd disappeared, never to be heard from again. How was the child supposed to forge any kind of emotional bond with a rank stranger, a fogbound inebriated ghost from some charmless corner of his infant past?

Armchair psychiatrists would find no difficulty in explaining away an individual's lack of interest in exploring any connection with a man whose sperm had been a vital factor in their actual creation but who had contributed little else to their upbringing. But those same often-pitiless judges of human behaviour would be hard pressed to have mounted a cogent defence for the boy's frankly odious treatment of his own mother. It was almost always played out behind closed doors but the locals caught glimpses and would sometimes discuss the disturbing details.

As an infant, the boy had seemed . . . well, 'withdrawn' was one word that was bandied about. Except it didn't truly apply because 'withdrawn' is a word that's often used to define the overly sensitive and the boy seemed devoid of sensitivity altogether. There was a film doing the rounds in the early 1960s – a science-fiction fantasy in spooky black and white called *Village of the Damned*. The plot centred on a brood of alien children with soulless expressions who had been programmed to take over a small English village and then the world at large. When the film was shown locally, several pointed out that Hilda Royston's lad had the same emotionless quality as those diabolical kids.

Though never to Hilda's face, of course. Nobody could say a bad word about her son to Hilda Grantley (she sometimes reverted back to her maiden name) without her responding verbally with a venom that instantly reminded those in the firing line that this woman had almost beaten a man to death.

On the one hand, Hilda could be a genuinely kind person, someone who only truly came alive when engaged in acts of selflessness. So it was little short of tragic that the person she chose to lavish most of that kindness on – her only child – turned out to be someone genetically and temperamentally incapable of cherishing and reflecting back that rushing river of adoration. His mother would always be smothering him with hugs and big sloppy kisses, and he'd generally squirm and slither away like some two-legged snake. By the age of nine he routinely regarded her with a look of unalloyed disdain.

And yet the evident disinterest he felt for his protector failed to make any impression on her whatsoever. Even if he never said anything sweet and was generally sarcastic and belittling during those brief spells when he felt compelled to directly address her at all, he still needed her and Hilda understood and responded to neediness far better than she ever understood the ways of love. For her, love truly was blindness. She'd been blind to the fact that her husband was a lush and a scoundrel and she was blind to the fact that her son was becoming a monster.

Then the boy turned into a teenager. At the age of thirteen he became interested in music – rock 'n' roll they called it. Hilda bought him a piano. Since Donald's departure, her well-to-do parents had been helping out financially but Hilda had also taken on a number of part-time jobs, albeit ones that allowed her to remain in close proximity to her cherished offspring. The boy fitfully clanked away at the keyboard for something like nine days and then never touched it again. After that, she bought him a guitar, a model he'd shown enthusiasm for when they'd passed a local music store. For three weeks he half-heartedly endeavoured to shape an E major chord on its wooden fretboard before declaring that the strings hurt his fingertips too much and abandoning the instrument altogether.

It was during these same years that the boy developed a lively reputation for being 'a bit of a tearaway' in the community. He'd often been sighted committing some senseless act of petty vandalism; he seemed to take a delight in scaring both dogs and cats and was sometimes known to be excessively violent towards others in his age group.

One time Hilda was summoned to her son's school, only to be confronted by a very common woman with an impenetrable northern accent who claimed her own son had just been kicked down a flight of stairs by Hilda's boy and was now lying in the infirmary awaiting stitches to the forehead. 'He's a wrong 'un, your kid,' she'd said through gritted, stained teeth. The woman's tone and grating voice convinced Hilda instantly that the story was an utter fabrication. Why would her offspring have anything to do with such low-class people?

Obviously the reverse was true. Her son was the victim, not the aggressor. But the headmaster – who'd witnessed the assault – was adamant. The boy was banned from attending all classes for a month – which is partly why he'd committed the assault in the first place, knowing full well that the act would pre-empt his expulsion from the stultifying confines of academia, at least for a while. His mother should have been crestfallen but she secretly cherished the possibility that her son would be home more as a result, a hope that was soon dashed when he elected to spend 95 per cent of his waking hours outside, looking to create mischief and mayhem wherever he lurked.

At this precise juncture of his young life, he got his first taste of (relatively) big time notoriety. At the dawn of the 1960s, trad jazz was extremely popular among the young and not-so-young. The form itself was a tame retooling of old New Orleans rhythms played by middle-aged men in waistcoats, bow ties and bowler hats. The boy – like others of his generation – outwardly despised its lack of sonic swagger, tepid links with conformity and corny melodies. Everything about it in short.

Sometime in June 1962 the Acker Bilk Big Band was scheduled to play a concert at the local town hall. Back then Bilk was trad's reigning potentate: a dreamy clarinet-guided instrumental he'd recorded for a TV series entitled *Stranger on the Shore* had sold through the roof. Even Hilda had bought a copy. She'd also considered attending the concert but something else had come up and she'd had to beg off going. This was just as well. For had she been present she would have witnessed Bilk and his ensemble being urinated on at one point during the set, followed by the spectacle of two policemen roughly manhandling a youth, who looked exactly like her perfect son, towards one of the exits and then out of the building.

The events of that night were told and retold so many times by its perpetrator that inevitably the truth was often side-tracked in his desire to iron a new crease into an old tale. He often claimed that he was lurking in the rafters of the town hall for the express purpose of registering a public protest against trad jazz. As Acker Bilk and his henchmen began their set below him, he'd taken the opportunity to relieve himself on to the stage, a significant quantity of his bladder's contents splashing onto Bilk's signature bowler hat as the clarinettist played on, oblivious to the downpour. Ten minutes later, the police stormed in and he was carted off to jail.

Much of the above-stated is based in truth. The youth was indeed lurking in the rafters, he did indeed pass water from that location on to the stage itself while Acker Bilk's combo were in session and he was – briefly – jailed for the offence. But he was not alone in those rafters as he'd later pretend.

Another boy – one Gerald Holstroad – had accompanied him to the spot. Both were inebriated, he more so than Gerald. Holstroad later remembered that – contrary to his claims of staging a protest against trad – the boy had seemed to be thoroughly enjoying the event. But he was also very, very drunk and it was lack of bladder control more than any other consideration that caused him to do what he did. Holstroad also contradicted him on the subject of soiling Acker Bilk's bowler hat. He recalled the arc of the urine landing well short of Bilk himself (though he allows that some splashback may have lightly flecked the back of his shiny waistcoat). He quickly added that the rhythm section weren't so lucky and that the drummer's cymbals and big tom were drenched, and two musicians' suits in need of an emergency dry clean. 'People like to make out he had some vendetta going against Acker Bilk but that's all tosh. He was just bladdered and had to relieve himself. Mind you, if it had been Elvis Presley performing below he'd have at least turned around and pissed against the wall instead.'

Holstroad wasn't detained by the local constabulary that night, partly because he had done nothing wrong, but mostly because he'd quickly vacated the scene of the crime and was on his way out of the building when the police had arrived, thus narrowly avoiding what the boy was about to experience. The latter had remained up in the rafters hooting like an owl at those below. Two uniformed constables had to restrain him; he wasn't being particularly obstreperous, more limp and legless, which made him difficult to manoeuvre down the several flights of winding stairs, then across a crowded room and finally through the exit door out into the chilly night air and the stationary kerbside paddy wagon.

The youngster sobered up in a small grey cell that night. He'd stopped hooting like an owl and had fallen into a deep slumber. Sergeant Terence 'Ferret' Ferris who ran the constabulary was an avid Acker fan and felt personally aggrieved by the youth's loutish gesture towards a beloved entertainer whose trim goatee and haunting woodwind skills were the very stuff that he'd often maintained still made Britain great. He'd heard about this young monkey already – apparently he'd been witnessed tossing lit fireworks at a terrified kitten – and was determined to press charges. But then Hilda arrived and he was duly forced into reneging on his original intentions.

As soon as she'd stormed into the building, she'd fixed Ferris with a look that he instantly recognised was her own customised version of the old 'evil eye' – the gypsy's curse. Then she spoke. How dare you incarcerate my son! How dare you take a mere child and treat him like a common criminal! On and on. They say hell hath no fury like a woman scorned, Ferris remembered thinking midway through Hilda's escalating tirade. But they're way wrong. Hell hath no fury like Hilda Royston when her precious son gets incarcerated.

Finally, after an hour of being verbally pilloried and threatened with lawsuits, he let the bugger go. One of the team had spoken to Acker about the incident and he wasn't interested in pressing charges – which only goes to show you what a class act the man was. Acker Bilk was a forgiving soul but that forgiveness was wasted on his assailant. If charges had been filed and he'd been sentenced to a short stretch at Her

Majesty's pleasure, he might have learned something important, namely that actions have consequences, particularly rash, thoughtless actions.

But this whole incident had demonstrated that the opposite was also true. You could lose all self-control, behave shockingly in a public place and still get away scot free. Best of all, you've suddenly got yourself a reputation. Older guys – serious hard cases – stop you in the street and say, 'You're that mad lad who pissed on Acker Bilk.' You look back at them like Billy the fucking Kid and say, 'What's it to you, pal?' And you can see the respect flashing in their eyes. Girls – and some actual women – grew more flirtatious towards him. This infamy lark was a real win–win lifestyle option from his point of view. You just behaved in a moody and generally unpredictable fashion and the seeds were already planted. Then you just sat back and watched your legend grow.

It was at this time he christened himself 'the Boy'. Capital letter, of course. He liked the sound of it. Not 'a Boy'. Nothing wishy washy. The Boy. The one and only. The seventh son. The Peter Pan man. A handle for the ages and a way of warding off age and responsibility. From there on he wouldn't respond to any other name.

One night in the early spring of 1963 the Boy accepted a lift from some local lads who were driving to a town close by where 'mucky stuff' was on the menu. They pulled up outside a club called the Black Cat and entered the premises one by one, having been frisked at the door.

At first, the Boy was distinctly underwhelmed by what amounted to his first brush with adult erotica. A young woman was coyly gyrating onstage to the accompaniment of a trio – pianist, double bass and small drum kit – who played dopey supper-club jazz instrumentals as she disrobed. Nothing about the spectacle caused him to sprout an erection. The woman was too homely looking. She should have been working in a biscuit factory, not wiggling her breasts at the losers lurking in the shadows and smoke of this pitiful excuse for a house of sin. The same held true for the ladies who followed Miss Pixie (the homely girl's *nom de scène*) onto the cramped stage. The Boy turned his gaze towards them only fitfully as he nuzzled a bottle of gassy stout close to his mouth. The women were ugly and graceless, and ugly graceless women trying to behave like sexual temptresses – well, it was borderline indecent. It wasn't alluring, it was desperate and the Boy knew instinctively that there was nothing less exotic than plain old desperation.

He'd just come back from the toilet – where he'd overheard a heated verbal exchange in an adjacent cubicle between a male customer and the venue's hat-check girl about money and 'services rendered' – when he walked into what felt like a completely different room. The lights pouring onto the stage seemed to sparkle more vividly. The clientele seemed to have woken up. The scent of expectation was in the air – or it would have been if the place wasn't already stiff with the slightly sickening odour of cheap aftershave and underarm deodorant. A bald man bounded onstage to introduce 'our star attraction – we know you can't get enough of her – so hold on to your hats, gents, and whatever else comes to hand. Miss Linda Lu is on the prowl tonight and she's looking for fresh prey. So without further ado . . .'

A tape of Gene Vincent singing 'Woman Love' began playing over the PA though the three musicians from before remained onstage doing nothing. Then a woman in a tight black satin dress strode out into the spotlight, moving like a panther through a mist. In a flash, the Boy was all aquiver. Vincent's voice had a uniquely breathless quality to it; the sound of a young man barely forestalling a premature ejaculation. And Linda Lu was a bona fide top-shelf looker, big boned but startlingly fit. Yet it was the way she toyed with her audience that set her apart. She had them salivating. When their eyes met hers, they melted down to greasy puddles. It was part animal grace and part inspired stagecraft. She dominated both the stage and the clientele with sudden unpredictable gestures. She'd muss up one punter's hair and then turn her back on him with an air of catty disinterest. The trio had recommenced straight after the Gene Vincent track had run its course, and as they played 'Fever' at a suitably torrid tempo, she would suddenly stop moving in the middle of an athletic interlude and stand there like a statue.

At one point she slapped the pianist full in the face – you could actually hear the blow from the stage. It was hard to tell if it was a spontaneous act or choreographed, but those in attendance let forth a collective gasp when it happened. The pianist didn't appear to take offence. On the contrary, the assault seemed to bring him to life and make his playing more alert and engaged. The bassist meanwhile was getting quite physical with his cumbersome double bass, strumming big fat chords and even attempting the odd flamboyant run up and down the fretboard to further prod the rhythm into interesting new places. And the drummer was in rimshot heaven. Every time Linda Lu made one of her special pelvic thrusts – which she did often – he'd respond with an enthusiastic and on-cue cymbal splash.

Her final gesture was to let her ample but well-toned physique slowly shimmy in just a bra, panties, stockings and high heels while her arms were outstretched and her fingers fluttered like leaves on two tree branches in a stiff wind. She then removed the bra and wiggled her pendulous breasts but her lower extremities remained covered. There was no glimpse of vagina. Nobody in the room protested at this oversight. They were all too smitten and slack-jawed by Linda Lu's smooth moves and raw sexual magnetism. In a world full of pinched-faced clueless English roses who smelled of too much hair lacquer and bargain-bin perfume, the Boy could see she was the real thing. A goddess.

Later in life he would tell the story that once her performance had ended, the Boy approached her while she was standing at the bar. After the usual introductory chit-chat he'd suggested they both repair to a more intimate location and she'd said 'all right then' – and acquiesced to his every desire. The claim that he lost his virginity to this sultry temptress was described in details that changed with each retelling.

The truth was he didn't lose his virginity that night. (That took place a month later with a neighbourhood lass called Eileen, who then claimed to have gotten pregnant by him in an attempt to snag herself a husband, only to have her dreams dashed by her prospective bridegroom's mother turning up at her parents' house and throwing an epic fit.) He'd thought of approaching Linda Lu – real name Catherine McKinney, Glaswegian by birth, blessed with a Betty Page level of sexual magnetism that could set the heather on fire – but hesitated when he saw her deep in conversation with a well-muscled man sporting a handlebar moustache and a short-sleeved shirt. The man had what looked like prison tattoos on both arms and one of those arms was coiled around Linda's lower torso, the hand resting firmly on her left buttock. It turned out he was also her fiancé and a professional wrestler of local renown who worked under the sobriquet the Merchant of Venom. Together they made a striking, intimidating-looking couple and clearly shared an emotional complicity that even the deeply self-deluded Boy thought twice about trying to infiltrate. He wasn't even able to summon up the nerve to look her in the eye and strike up a tepid conversation.

He left the Black Cat with his fellow revellers in the wee hours of that Sunday morning, seriously liquored up and still uninitiated in the art of love.

But he came away with something more precious. In Linda Lu's insolent, ruinously sexy act he'd received his own 'eureka' moment. A blueprint for a career all his own. Like her, he would become a performer, a people enchanter, a wayward sprite, a hypnotising shapeshifter. Puck to her Aphrodite. He'd do it not by stripping, of course. He'd achieve his ends by becoming a singer in a group and then incorporating Linda Lu's tempestuous body language into his live performances. It was in that moment of realisation that it all began to come alive.

CHAPTER 4

Fast forward four months. The Boy has been actively culti-vating an acquaintanceship (the word 'friendship' would be pushing things; the Boy didn't have friends as such) with a local youth who'd managed to cultivate a reputation in the area that was even more corrosive than his.

Michael 'Madman' Mulvaney was a piece of work that could have turned up darkening the side streets of any of the sleepy shires dotted around early 1960s Britain. He terror-ised sheep for fun and routinely managed to insert the word 'fuck' at least three times into every sentence he ever uttered. He enjoyed a caveman-like relationship with his parents, both of whom were far too partial to alcohol. Excessive drinking was the only trait the three had in common. There was the farm work too – the old fellow owned a broken-down house, a couple of barns and half an acre of wheat fields – but the family's astonishing indolence had meant that their farm had dwindled to a derelict shadow of its former self. Nobody could be bothered to do a stroke of work on the place.

While his parents slept for up to sixteen hours a day, every day, Madman opted to further develop his work-in-progress skills as a young criminal and all-purpose menace to decent society. He was an insatiable kleptomaniac, starting out like a magpie drawn to pilfering small shiny objects that looked expensive, though he'd often later discover they were mere cheap copies of the real thing. In due course he became more ambitious and started robbing houses, using his dad's Land Rover to haul the booty back to his lair. On one such occasion, he came across a drum kit set up in someone's cellar, promptly dismantled it and spirited it back to one of the empty barns in his folks' dysfunctional farmstead.

Though such terms weren't bandied around much back in the early 1960s, Madman was a chronic sufferer of – among other things – attention deficit hyperactivity disorder, but this shortcoming didn't deter him from spending hours in that barn, aided only by bottles of cider and some diet pills he'd stolen from his auntie's medicine cabinet, just thrashing and crashing away, splashing the cymbals, hammering the big tom like a blacksmith shoeing the Devil's own racehorse – bish, bash, boom, bang! When he'd start warming up behind the kit, all the animals in the immediate vicinity would scurry away as far as possible from the source of that infernal racket.

Madman was not by any measure of the imagination skilled as a conventional time-keeping, groove-setting drummer. He was more of a law unto himself. The kit he'd stolen had been a big one and he liked to employ all its possibilities all the time, which meant that ballads and mid-tempo tunes were off the musical menu. He was in his element only when playing frenziedly and even then he had a tendency to slow down and quicken the pace several times during a single number. But the Boy was drawn to the sense of loony abandon that Madman brought to the task at hand. The brazen lack of discipline, the deafening volume, the ostentatious way he lay his kit to waste – all these factors were more impressive to him than the skills of someone more adept at executing a deft paradiddle.

Other recruits were enlisted in the pair's quest to bring their version of musical anarchy to the surrounding villages and shires. The school the Boy had finally been expelled from at age fifteen provided two likely candidates. Mark McCabe had played the double bass in the school orchestra and knew an older lad with an electric bass guitar he wanted to offload. So he was in, even though his personality was too inherently pragmatic and reserved to blend in well with his loose cannon co-conspirators.

Something of a timorous soul, Mark wasn't one for small talk. The same could be said about Ral Coombes who was also inward-looking and hard to read. A complicated young man. His parents were Quakers. But Coombes brought something to the fledgling endeavour that no one else in the outfit knew about. He understood songcraft. He was a proficient guitarist – good rhythm chops, knew a lot of chords, even some tricky jazz shapes, held the instrument properly as though it was an extra limb and not just a piece of amplified wood strapped around his neck – and could strum out the skeleton chords of practically any old rock or R & B number you'd care to call to his attention. This skill extended to composing his own tunes. He'd even written some lyrics for them but turned all coy whenever he was asked to present them at practice sessions.

Their rehearsals took place at the barn where Madman's drums were stored bookended by bales of hay. The guitar and bass were amplified by a single AC30 amp the drummer had stolen during one of his ever more frequent robbing sprees. There was no public address system so the Boy's bids at vocalising were generally drowned out by the other instruments, particularly the drums. A Bo Diddley song was attempted and then brusquely rejected once it was ascertained that the drummer was having insurmountable difficulties holding the rudimentary rhythmic pulse in check. A Buddy Holly cover was also swiftly jettisoned once it became clear the Boy couldn't remember any of the lyrics. Everyone was scratching their heads and frantically searching for the elusive thread that could weave together four disparate youngsters still deep in the formative stage of their musical development. Ral struck up a two-chord rhythm on his unaccompanied guitar based on the changes propping up the opening verse of George Gershwin's 'Summertime' and the bassist started to noodle along. The Boy stopped vocalising in the whiny, insolent tone that came most naturally to him and introduced a sound from out of his lips that was higher in range and borderline mellifluous. Of course, the Madman soon ruined the ambience with some inappropriate skin-beating but the prior two minutes in that barn sired a sound with a future.

After they completed their first attempt at actually playing together, they repaired to the local coffee bar in order to brag about their new endeavour and hopefully impress some girls in the process. Spirits were high at first but soon became deflated by the absence of fellow caffeine-seeking post-adolescents to awe. Only two other customers were there to share their adventures with and neither looked like they were in a sharing mood.

One of them was rather well known in the region. Every little village in the British Isles during the 1960s had its token bohemian, usually someone of the male sex who believed he was touched with a unique creative vision even though no actual proof existed. 'Perce the Poet' was such a creature. His real name was Percy Dalgleish and he was a terrible old con act. Contrary to his boastful assertions, he was not a published poet. No slender volume of verse bore his name in gilded letters on its cover and no poetry magazines had printed any of his many attempted contributions to their pages. He was now in his early twenties and reduced to haunting the same dismal locales he'd been frequenting since before he'd reached puberty. A portion of him was brash and boastful but another part was utterly paralysed by inertia, or by the fear of chancing his arm in some bigger goldfish bowl and getting eaten alive.

Perce's way of sidelining his personal woes was to adopt the high-handed persona of the young artist as wilfully misunderstood maverick. Many saw through it instantaneously, but a certain breed of middle-class small-town girl nonetheless found his haughty manner oddly enchanting and failed to spot the lecherous agenda it inevitably concealed.

One such female in a PVC raincoat was seated beside him and staring up at his face as he spoke in the voice of a seasoned thespian about his 'gift'. He called it 'word-juggling', though his verse had more to do with simply slinging words on to a page without concern for rhyme or meaning. He likened this approach to the way abstract painters defiled their canvases with random blotches and splashes, or modern jazzers abandoned chord structure and melody in favour of unrestrained cacophony.

It was then that the girl asked Perce about his 'poetic process' and he went into oratorical overdrive.

'It's more than a process, my dear. It's a purging, a cleansing – a vomiting forth. Only the poet is vomiting forth ideas and half-digested crumbs of wisdom while the peasant' – and here he cast a disparaging glance at the Boy and his hopelessly juvenile-looking amigos – 'is on his knees in his outhouse vomiting up only . . . yesterday's carrots!'

'Yesterday's carrots!' the Madman shouted while stirring a swastika symbol into the froth of his cappuccino with his index finger. 'That'd be a cracking name for our combo.' He was serious too. No one chose to disagree at that particular moment so that's who they became. But only for a week or two. First, the 'yesterday's' was dropped: it sounded retro. Then they played their first gig at a local pub and the owner had introduced them by bellowing, 'They call themselves the Carrots, folks. Guess which one is the donkey?' The Boy had almost brained the man with his microphone.

A name change was urgently required. Finding the right one was a crucial concern as it needed instantly to signal the band's DNA to the general public. Many bad ones were considered and then discarded until the afternoon the group were supposedly rehearsing but were listening to a transistor radio and generally larking about. *Round the Horne* was being broadcast and its cavalcade of mirth and high-spiritedness was having an infectious impact on the young men. 'Welcome to Jollity Form,' Kenneth Horne, the show's avuncular host, beamed forth over the airwaves. 'We've got something for the stable boys. And something for the unstable boys too.'

The Unstable Boys. Genius. And so utterly appropriate.

Their early gigs were invariably shambolic affairs. The Boy and his drumming compadre were both massive fans of the Pretty Things, a London-based quintet of loutish beatnik types then performing dog-eared renditions of American rhythm and blues records. The Boy was grooming his hair daringly long like the Pretty Things' singer Phil May – practically down to his shoulders – and also aping his sneery guttersnipe vocal approach while the Madman's favourite drummer and all-purpose role model was the Pretties' human firework Viv Prince. But the contributions from a decent rhythm guitarist and nimble-fingered bass player couldn't quite steady the ship, which was doomed to crash onto the jagged rocks of cacophony as soon as Madman decided to turn the group's evening repertoire into one long deranged drum solo.

Even the Boy was losing patience with his daft ways. But no one had the nerve to sack him. He was a big lad with deep-seated issues and could've easily put the other three into the intensive care unit at the hospital a half-mile down the road if spoken to the wrong way.

Fortunately no one had to give him his marching orders. The local constabulary took care of that detail. The Madman's criminal activities had become too numerous to ignore and their perpetrator less cautious. They caught him in the town centre one starless night blind drunk with a television set clutched to his chest like it was his first-born child. He'd just removed it from the broken window of a shop he'd been lurking in front of. They then drummed up a warrant to search his home while he was sleeping off his stupor in a cell.

In the family's house, stables and barns, the forces of law were shocked to discover the sheer range and quantity of stolen goods being stored within their walls. From that moment on, the Madman's goose was cooked. Two years hard labour at Her Majesty's pleasure. All in all, it was for the best. Jail time afforded Madman ample opportunity to further hone his one true calling in life as a career criminal and it freed the Unstable Boys to cast their net for a drummer who knew how to play a kit in sync with other players.

This all took place in early 1965 – February through March. But by Easter the ensemble not only had a new drummer, but had also located a fifth member to further swell their ranks.

The latter was a real find, an art-school dropout called Mick Winthrop, then biding his time at his parents' house in the neighbouring village. Ral had seen him in a pub playing some seriously intimidating lead guitar solos that put all the other pickers in the area to shame. His band had been a bunch of two-chord deadbeats and so Coombes had felt no remorse when he approached him during the intermission to suggest he throw in his lot with the Unstable Boys instead.

Likewise, he and the bassist made sure they had the last word when it came to picking the new drummer. They, after all, were the ones who actually had to play with the lucky recruit. And one loose cannon in any band is enough. Their singer had that role already well mapped out. After being pummelled mercilessly by the Madman's wayward rhythms for too many months, they were looking for a drummer who was spry, energetic, with great hand and feet coordination, but was most of all steady. A steady beat and a steadying influence. Both would be a welcome change. And for a while Alan Dyson, a twenty-year-old son of a vicar and veteran of numerous local popular music combos, was able to supply those skills to most of the group members' satisfaction.

But the Boy was not happy. From the outset he'd perceived the group as his personal little army. He was the singer and frontman, the one bathed in the big spotlight every time they performed, the one channelling the energy and setting the agenda, the one all the boys and girls were staring goggle-eyed at. To his way of thinking, it was as plain as day: the Unstable Boys were his invention and plaything, he was their leader and their destiny was reliant on the others acknowledging his pre-eminence at all times.

But it wasn't working out that way. That sneaky Ral Coombes was asserting himself far too much, bringing another guitarist into the fold without properly consulting the boss first. Granted – the guy could work the fretboard like a magician and had moreover brought some much-needed fire and finesse to the overall sound. His inclusion was a no-brainer. But the way he'd been sneaked aboard by Coombes – that was cheeky.

The Boy also had his misgivings about the new drummer. A part of him genuinely yearned for Madman to still be raising merry hell behind the drum kit. He knew it wouldn't have gained them much in the way of live work; he just had

a soft spot in his otherwise cold, cold heart for mayhem
magnets, no matter how problematic they inevitably turned
out to be. So he was undecided about Alan Dyson. On the
one hand, the group now had a bona fide timekeeper behind
the drum kit, someone who could stay in the pocket while
further goosing the groove along with skilful tom-tom fills
and cymbal splashes. On the other, he wasn't an exhibitionist
and his approach to percussion – like his general demeanour
– was a touch too reserved for the Boy's taste.

Still, he'd caved. What else could he have done? He hadn't
been able to rustle up a suitable replacement for the drum
stool himself in the weeks following the Madman's incar-
ceration. In letting others call the shots for him in his own
organisation, however, he now faced the unsettling realisation that the group's inner dynamic was shifting more in
favour of the actual musicians and away from the singer, the
man with the plan, the true mesmeriser of the masses.

Things were happening far too fast for him to seize back full
control of the enterprise. Because the group were now way more
musically proficient as a quintet, they found themselves more in
demand as a live attraction. This led to concerts in some of
merrie olde England's bigger cities. Promoters were putting the
word out: 'The Unstable Boys – book 'em. They're on the up-and-
up.' Then came the night in Ipswich (when they supported the
Huddled Masses, a local beat group whose gimmick was dressing like monks in long brown habits and partly shaven heads)
and the A & R man from Fontana came round and made his
pitch: sign with me and I will guarantee your (almost) instant
stardom. Intoxicating words to young men each in their own
way obsessed with career self-advancement and the fever dream

of being an object of adulation. The Beatles were out conquering the world. The Rolling Stones were redefining the very concept of rebel clout. Heady days were looming. And if you had the right look and made the right kind of brave-new-world foretelling racket, it was harvest time for you and your merry tribe.

And so it came to pass. Contracts were signed. A pitiful royalty rate was agreed upon. The group had no manager to work their corner. It was highway robbery. But who seriously thinks about future royalty statements when the enticement of sudden fame is being dangled before them?

A manager was quickly chosen to guide them through the tricky machinations of the mid-1960s UK music industry. He wasn't that bright and lacked real business acumen but he was flush with his newly deceased daddy's money and at a loose end so a deal was done. The group moved down to a cold-water three-room flat in Hemel Hempstead.

They then recorded their first single, something of a career misstep. The Boy wanted to do a cover of a particularly raucous-sounding R & B single he owned, a song called 'Justine' by Don and Dewey. It was a full-tilt screamathon with two black singers barking the lyrics out at each other like pistol-strapping robbers taking down a 7-Eleven. The Righteous Brothers also covered it just prior to hooking up with Phil Spector.

As a piece of music it was untamed, brutish and, given the right backbeat, joltingly danceable. But it was also fundamentally a duet – you needed two singers with loud, lusty, beseeching voices to nail its mercurial essence. The Boy failed to recognise this and set about recklessly vocalising the piece with only his single-tracked callow wail to carry the day. The band gave it their best shot but the backing track they ended up with sounded tepid compared to the song's testosterone-drenched original. Still, in early 1966 it got the green light from Fontana who pressed it up and generally hawked it around hoping for a freak first-time hit. Someone working for the label tried to buy it into the charts – he knew the addresses of the record stores that furnished the hit parade with their sales stats – but it only rose to no. 27 and then sank into the sunset.

They continued to be increasingly in demand as a live act because they'd actually become good at what they did. The music gelled, it had a flint-hard backbone, a standout lead guitarist and a grasp of dynamics in the way it was arranged that few other groups of the hour could marshal together for their own repertoires. And there was something about that singer that guaranteed you couldn't keep your eyes off him when he was onstage.

The second single, the record company impressed on the Unstable Boys collective, was make-or-break. This is where Ral Coombes stepped into the breach with one of the songs he'd composed himself. The Boy had nothing to offer and so was press-ganged into going along with the decision even though the song itself didn't exactly correspond with what he felt his group should be playing. There was too much melody for starters. And too many chords. The arrangement was bonkers and required he actually sing the words as opposed to just slurring syllables in a malevolent monotone. He sulked a lot whenever they'd rehearse the number and was still in a strop when the day came to wax it for posterity.

Coombes had foreseen such problems arising and instinctively stepped up to take the reins. It was his song after all and he'd arranged it – with minor contributions from the other players – so he was already hearing in his head what he intended the finished product to sound like. But he also knew that to achieve his ends he needed to be as diplomatic as he possibly could. The producer of the session – an old-school hack – was proving to be something of a hindrance: he'd voiced the opinion that the song needed a harpsichord playing somewhere in the mix. It was his only suggestion throughout the entire session. The Boy had told him exactly what he could do with his harpsichord and the middle-aged gent had promptly exited the premises in a pipe-smoking huff.

This left the engineer and Coombes to commandeer the session which – as it turned out – was a blessing for all concerned. The engineer David Barnes had young ears and an adventuresome approach to capturing sound on magnetic tape. He was able to record the group in a way that maximised their potential and, after fifteen takes, a suitable backing track was minted.

Then the real drama began. The Boy was already playing up. He was in the early stages of inebriation thanks to the several cans of ale that had been clanking around in the lumpy pockets of his duffel coat and was in no mood to be told what to do – by anyone. Ral let him act out at first. He'd dealt with him long enough to recognise the routine by now. Let him blow off smoke until he'd exhausted his desire to be infantile and contrary, and then quietly coax him into providing what the rest of the group needed from him – a credible vocal performance. His first attempt had been painful to listen back to – he'd bellowed the words out like a hard-of-hearing rogue solicitor reading out a court summons. Coombes steeled himself for what was to come – the inevitable confrontation. And he knew in advance that there might be dire consequences. But there was no other solution. Their make-or-break moment could not be scuppered by egocentric tomfoolery and knee-jerk unprofessionalism.

So he got right in the Boy's face, removed the headphones from around his ears and began reading him the riot act. He didn't try to placate or indulge him, he simply but firmly impressed upon him what was about to happen. He – the Boy – was going to sing the song exactly the way it had been conceived – as an expressive pop lament, not as some drunken braggart's petulant rant. He was going to have to employ that light tenor voice he'd once or twice slipped into during rehearsals instead. It might just do the trick.

The Boy's reaction was as expected. 'And what if I don't?' he fired back. 'Well, if you don't,' Ral replied, 'this session will have been a waste of time, our second single will go unreleased and our career will peter out like a damp squib. You'll go back to living with your mother and the rest of us will splinter apart to embrace other pursuits and projects. But this will be over, finished, done. Full stop.'

He kept staring deep into the Boy's face, willing him to lock eyes, to grasp the severity of the situation. It was hard to tell how his words were registering so he had to go that extra mile and further stoke the brewing drama.

'Oh and another thing,' he added. His voice remained neutral but the half-whispered tone sounded more

threatening than a full-throated shout. 'If you continue fucking up tonight, you and I will most likely end up squaring off
in the car park outside and trying to beat seven shades of shit
out of each other. That's not an idle threat, by the way. It's a
guaranteed reality. Now, you may think you can take me in a
fight – and that may indeed be so – but be warned. I've been
studying you and you're not nearly as hard as you perceive
yourself to be. Disruptive? Yes. Troublesome? Guilty as
charged. But when it comes time to face the music, ball your
hands into actual fists and wade into the conflict you've
invariably instigated, then you tend to suddenly make yourself very scarce indeed. That mêlée you started in Birmingham,
which ended up with the barman scarring that punter's face
with a broken glass – where were you exactly? Under a table?
Or did you lock yourself away in the men's toilets?

'The point is – if you continue behaving the way you've
been behaving tonight, you're going to lose big time so focus
on that. Let it soak in. But don't take too long reaching a
conclusion. Time is money, after all. We're in a recording
studio, for Christ's sake.

'It's your choice. You can be a legend in your own lifetime.
Or a legend in your local off-licence. Which is it to be?'

The Boy stood there thunderstruck, staring daggers at Ral
Coombes but unable to summon up one pertinent comeback. His guitar player had established his superior standing
in the line-up and the Boy was left with no other option than
to do what he should have done all along – sing the bastard
as required. It took thirty-five takes and seventeen cups of
black coffee but when it had reached completion, everyone
knew they had a winner on their hands. Everyone, that is, but

the Boy. He sat in sullen silence during the playback watching his bandmates' goonish displays of giddy enthusiasm without ever joining in. He didn't like the song and thought his vocal was too much Matt Monro, not enough Mick Jagger. He thought about having to perform it – and sometimes mime it when the telly shows would start booking them – night after night and groaned inwardly. But the die had been cast.

Most of all, he couldn't get his head around the way he'd been spoken to earlier. No one had ever dared confront him like that before and the more he obsessed about it, the more intolerable it felt. He'd buckled too. He'd shown weakness. Ral fucking Coombes was going to have to be taught a lesson or two in respecting his betters. The gauntlet had been thrown down.

He'd started out distrusting the guy – he was too bloody clever by half, knew too many big fruity words, looked at you as though he was constantly sizing you up, judging, scheming. Now he hated him. Unreservedly. Nothing would have given the Boy greater pleasure than to push him under a passing train. But he needed him too – that was the real thorn in his side. The Boy may have despised the song they'd just recorded but even he could tell that it would more than likely be a hit. Like the rash on his penis he'd come away with after they'd played in Bradford, it was infectious.

And so it came to pass. The song 'Dark Waters' was perfectly in sync with its time (mid-1966 to be precise) – a fusion of olde English folk song and new-fangled drone rock. The minor chords that shaped its melody lent the song a plaintive air but the groove was also perfect to dance to. The lyrics concerned a lovesick young man anxiously awaiting his 'one true love's' return from a mysterious sea journey on a ship with black sails. Would she reappear to calm his beating heart or had she drowned, lost to the briny deep? The Boy had managed to tap into the song's mysterious subject matter by summoning from his larynx a voice that conveyed presence and power but also – as is often the case with men singing in a close to falsetto range – a distinct vulnerability. The public loved it. Its rise in the UK charts was slow to begin with until the pirate radio stations started playing it more and more frequently and the momentum built from there and just kept expanding. At the end of its run, it had peaked at no. 2 in the UK charts.

Suddenly they were the toast of the town, the new breed, the ones the scene makers suddenly wanted to be seen with. Cathy McGowan on *Ready Steady Go!* called them 'a really lovely bunch of fellows' and had batted her fake eyelashes flirtatiously at the Boy when the group had guested on the show. All the London nightclubs let them in for free, their smoky interiors rife with a worldly set only too eager to make the acquaintance of the latest pieces of young flesh being thrown into the Tin Pan Alley shark tank.

There was a photo that Hilda Royston kept on her bedside table from that golden era back when her son and his playmates were rising young stars. It was a black and white snap taken at an awards ceremony sometime in late 1967 or early 1968. The winners are all lined up together waving their trophies and grinning triumphantly. Lulu is on the far left in a satin micro-dress, one of the Bee Gees is next to her, a fellow with mutton-chop sideburns who might be John

Lennon or else one of Manfred Mann stands alongside him – and there in the middle, her darling Boy with a big wide uninhibited grin on his face. That was why she loved the picture so much: it was the only one she owned where her son was smiling.

These days when she surveyed the photo, her attention would sometimes shift to the man standing on her son's left with the outrageous dyed blond hair and the fat cigar protruding like a phallus from his lips. It was hard to mistake Jimmy Savile. Hilda had heard the stories about Savile that came out after his death. And she didn't believe one of them. The man had dedicated his life to entertaining decent working people and tirelessly promoting charitable causes – and this was his reward? Balderdash! Furthermore her son – who'd known Jimmy Savile personally, lest we forget – had once told her that 'Jimmy's a bit odd but a diamond geezer through and through.' So it was written in stone as far as she was concerned. It wasn't the Jimmy Saviles of this world who needed to be put under scrutiny, but the mischief makers in the media who were always meddling in other people's private lives and fabricating lies in order to sell their tawdry journals.

Her son had suffered at the hands of these press jackals, too. From the very beginning he'd been targeted. One of the scandal sheets had referred to him as a 'degenerate'. Incidents of an unsavoury nature involving her son would get reported now and then. She didn't believe a word they printed but it made life disruptive. Why, one time in the local supermarket a young lass had run up to her and shouted: 'Your son is a dirty beggar.' Just a slip of a girl too. She'd run off before

Hilda could react. If she hadn't, Hilda would have boxed both her ears, dragged her to the nearest sink and washed her mouth out with soap and water.

They didn't understand how complicated and all consuming it was, being an international celebrity. The media built them up only to chop them down mercilessly and tarnish their reputations. The venomous stuff they'd written about her son over the years – all of it spiteful, salacious and plain wrong.

Why didn't they praise his accomplishments instead? Only last year he played top of the bill to 150,000 satisfied customers somewhere in Serbia. He told her that himself. Said the show was 'a blinder', whatever that means. Why didn't they write about his wealth also? He'd told her the last time he visited that he was worth millions. He had it securely placed in several offshore accounts, he said. Then he'd added that his accountants were busy transferring his wealth into new less taxable locations and that as his money was 'all tied up' for the moment, he needed to borrow 'a modest sum' from his old mum to tide him over for a few weeks.

Of course she gave it to him. She only had twelve grand in her savings account but immediately withdrew 80 per cent of the sum and handed it over to him. She didn't give it a second thought. Her son the multi-millionaire. He'd pay her back. One day he'd maybe even pony up for a nice care home in a well-heeled part of some sleepy English hamlet. But that wasn't what she really wanted. What she wanted desperately was for her son to need her. Everything else was superfluous.

Right now she was all alone. Not a word – no midnight phone call – in months. He's gone to ground, she reckoned.

The poor lamb. Maybe he's brainstorming up a new act. Or monitoring his millions. No matter. He'll be back. And when he walks through that door, first thing he'll head straight for the kitchen, open the fridge and reach for the jelly. He always loved Hilda's jellies.

INTERLUDE: RAL COOMBES'S LAST INTERVIEW

First published in 1976 in the fanzine *Wipe-out* and reprinted in 2015 in *Mojo*. The interviewer is credited as Sandy Harvester.

SH : It's been a while since we've heard from you, Ral.

RC: Well, exactly. That's why I can't quite comprehend why this interview is taking place. I haven't released anything in five years. I have no band, no record label, no manager, no agent. Surely your readers would be more interested in reading about someone younger who has actual career prospects.

SH: But then again you must be aware that several of the new punk acts who've sprouted up in 1976 cite you and the Unstable Boys as an influence?

RC: Really? I think they're probably more influenced by my old singer's barmy stunts onstage and off than by the music itself. Still, it's nice to be saluted by a younger generation, I suppose.

SH: What's your evaluation of punk then?

RC: It's . . . interesting. I saw the Sex Pistols on a friend's TV a couple of weeks back. They certainly held my attention. All the ingredients are there. The big fuck-you power chords. The hooligan swagger. The singer reminded me of the Boy but with an actual brain between his ears.

SH: Does this music excite you?

RC: Not really. I'm old school, I'm afraid. Ask me about the sixties instead. I'll be more inclined to marshal some enthusiasm and provide you with detailed answers.

SH : OK then. First of all, why don't you talk a little about your origins?

RC: I was born in 1947 – a Pisces, not that it matters. It was two years after the Second World War and my parents had both been robbed of their youthful vitality during that six-year ordeal. They'd been bombed and shot at. Every evening they'd return to their lodgings never knowing whether the building was even still standing.

So when the war came to an end they were hellbent on leading as quiet and non-confrontational a life as they possibly could. The war itself was never mentioned. For a while everything felt calm. Then my mother found religion. A friend introduced her to a local Quaker church and she got hooked on their doctrines. She became well-known throughout the community for her endless acts of kindness. My father didn't really share his wife's new-found Quaker zeal but nonetheless went through the motions of being a believer simply to placate her.

Then rock 'n' roll happened and I became a lost cause almost overnight. Something about the sound of young men wailing to jungle rhythms made them think that it was ungodly music, and anyone who listened to it was dancing to the devil's drumbeat. I'm surprised they didn't try to have me exorcised.

SH: They weren't supportive of your musical ambitions then?

RC: In a word, no. God love them. They tried so hard to wean me off the stuff but it was already too late. When I was twelve an uncle gave me an old hollow-bodied guitar that he'd picked up somewhere in France during the war – that was all it took. It was actually a decent instrument. Later I got a pick-up attached to it and played it through an amp with the first Unstables line-up.

SH: How was the first line-up actually formed?

RC: I knew the Boy from school, when he was just Dale Royston. 'Roy the Boy' was his first nickname. Then he dropped the 'Roy'.

I was a bit leery of him at first. He had a reputation even then. There was something about his demeanour that made you feel like he'd be the ideal figure to stand behind were a major ruck ever to break out in the playground.

Then one day he sidled up to me and asked if I played and owned a guitar. I said I did and he invited me to bring it to a rehearsal taking place in a barn that weekend. He mentioned that a lad from his class was playing bass and that he'd found a drummer too.

SH: And how did it go?

RC: Oh, it was a shambles generally. Godawful. But we had nothing better to do so we persevered. Shortly after that the drummer was forced to leave, which was a shot in the arm for us musically. We got better drummers to fill his shoes. And then a genuinely spectacular lead guitarist came along to round out the sound.

SH: And the Boy, how did he react to it all?

RC: Not well. Always complaining. Shiftless too. Always expected everything to be done for him.

The worst of it was that he was utterly clueless about what his real skills were. He could have been a decent singer but ended up as a cut-rate vocalist. He could have been an outstanding live performer but chose more often than not to play the exhibitionist card, doing or saying something specifically designed to pinball an audience into a state of unrestrained thuggishness.

Now, the rest of the band were not violent people. So to have to withstand these stage assaults night after night became increasingly difficult for us. That and our frontman's frequent assertions that we were just his backing group.

SH: When in fact you were writing all the songs?

RC: Well, that only caused more conflict between us. Because we had different agendas. I wanted our music to develop and take full advantage of all the styles and techniques of the day. The Boy just wanted it as a rowdy backdrop to his cavortings, a vehicle for him to smother the spotlight.

That's why Mick Winthrop was so important. He was one of those happy-go-lucky young guys unburdened by neuroses: a natural jester. When it got close to daggers being drawn between the Boy and me, he'd know just when to step in and defuse the situation with some daft quip. He could talk to the Boy, make subtle suggestions and get him to at least listen. When I tried, usually he'd just turn on his heel and exit the building.

Mick became the glue that actually held the Unstable Boys together. The moment he was pronounced dead from that car crash, I knew the group was finished. Don't forget, he was becoming a rising guitar hero at the time. Half our live audience were teenage girls and boys who'd come to see the Boy run wild, but the other half were musos there to marvel at Mick's playing.

SH: What effect did Mick's death have on you?

RC: When you're in your early twenties and someone of your age who you've cared deeply about passes away, it's literally too much to take in. I remember feeling a stabbing sadness followed by complete and utter numbness. No tears. I got high instead. Then there were all the questions: Would the upcoming US tour be cancelled? What would be the fate of the new album we'd just started recording? After a while I told myself why worry? We had a nice run. But then the stars above simply turned against us. It was all over.

Only it wasn't, of course. The tour went on. Over fifty dates. Replacements were found. Rehearsals took place at the sound-checks prior to the show. Everyone was looped on different chemicals. All in all, an episode best forgotten.

At the same time I was trying to complete the record which – in a fit of youthful hubris – I'd decided should be a double album. I had the songs but suddenly had no bandmates to record them with. Session players were called in and the work slowly got done. The Boy never turned up to the sessions so I laid down the guide vocals myself. When he finally showed up at the studio and heard my hesitant voice on the tracks he went ballistic. After yet another heated exchange in the car park, we parted company, never to speak to or work with each other again. That must have been December 1969. By then it really was over. The record company wouldn't pay for our airfare back to England. The managers changed their phone number literally overnight.

SH: And what was the fallout like?

RC: Well, part of me was elated not to be in a state of constant conflict with at least one of my bandmates. It felt liberating at first. Being essentially a one-man act and calling your own shots. I'd already had an offer to record a solo album as soon as we went public with the break-up. But I was also plagued with doubts about whether I could flourish on my own. As a result the tracks on my solo album featured a lot of other instruments to the point where the arrangements overwhelmed everything with their invasive clutter.

I can't listen to it these days. I should have worked with just a rhythm section and a pianist, but I was too self-conscious about my singing voice and a spare, intimate backing would have forced it too much into the foreground. I've always been looking to capture a sound from my lips that I can instantly identify as my true voice. But I never have, not so far anyway. I know it's inside me somewhere but I can't for the life of me find the way to channel it through my larynx.

SH: Did you play any concerts to promote your album?

RC: Five or six. Then I had to jack it in. They were solo shows – just me and an acoustic guitar. I'd performed once or twice at a local folk club in my teens, but that was the only experience I'd had standing alone performing before an audience. I thought I could anaesthetise my pre-show nerves with enough drugs but nothing I took did the trick. Remember, in the past I'd stood onstage as part of a gang with big amps and a PA system that could instantly drown out any hecklers and stun the rest into respectful silence. Now I was a distinctly vulnerable-looking troubadour trying to pour my heart out in intimate numbers to the unruly masses. Every night I heard the booing. I was the support act and they just wanted the main attraction. You can't blame them, really. I brassed it out for the first five shows and then quit the tour. And the music business, effectively.

Several sessions for a second album were subsequently taped but those tapes were destroyed when the studio caught fire and burned down. And my reputation as an unreliable druggie kept growing. The phone calls from high rollers in the biz stopped coming. And then I gradually accepted my new status as a twenty-five-year-old has-been.

SH: And what was that like?

RC: Difficult. Money was always a problem. My wife was an out-of-work dancer and I was a failed musician – what other prospects were there for two people without skills, training or diplomas?

She ended up getting a job at a clothes shop three days a week and I do gardening work in the area. Hedge-clipping and lawn-mowing. There's something very peaceful about mowing a lawn. You survey what you've accomplished at the end of the job and the parallel lines of shaven grass you've painstakingly sculpted – 'perfect' is the only word that comes to mind. It can be almost as gratifying as writing a good song. Almost, but not quite.

SH: Over the past six years, have you ever crossed paths again with the Boy?

RC: Funnily enough, a couple of years ago we found ourselves in the same room. It was in that nightclub the Speakeasy. I was with an entourage at one table and he suddenly materialised with a crowd of his own who noisily commandeered a table not far from ours. He looked the same, a bit more weathered in the face perhaps. When he saw that I was there too, our eyes locked together for what seemed like an eternity. Like snakes. It was like each of us was willing the other to come over and ... what? Pat each other on the back? Spit at each other? Attempt some kind of small talk? Not a chance. Everything we had to say to each other had been said already years before.

SH: So I take it there's no reunion on the horizon?

RC: That's never going to happen. Get used to it. I have.

SH: In conclusion, any last words on the subject of the Unstable Boys ?

RC: Too young, too overworked and too underpaid but on a good night we gave it our best shot. Our tombstone should read 'They were green but they were keen.' Green but keen: there, I've just given you the headline for your piece.

CHAPTER 5

His body supine and curled horizontally under a beige duvet, Ral Coombes rested his head on the pillow and waited for the cares of the day to dissolve from his thoughts and free his subconscious mind to journey across the threshold into dreamland.

Five minutes later he'd made the transition. He was in another land, one very different from his current earthly location. It was like magically merging with an old black and white movie from the 1940s about carefree natives making merry around a fire on some dark exotic beach. He was no longer the careworn old man he'd lately become, but a smooth-skinned youth once more, one of several impulsive young hombres parading around on the moonlit sand.

The focus of their attention was turned towards a group of young women who sat on the shoreline singing from time to time. These were rare beauties with heavenly voices that when blended together in song forged a sensuous sirens' chorus as spooky as it was bewitching.

In order to court their attention, the young men were plunging one by one into the dark foaming surf and then resurfacing minutes later with their hands clenched in fists. They'd been diving for pearls on the ocean bed to give to the singing girls. Still glistening with saltwater wetness, these lusty athletic creatures would then prostrate themselves before the females and place their newly discovered bounty before them. One pearl warranted singing. Two or more secured some kind of physical contact with at least one of them.

And so he'd heedlessly dived into the foam himself in order to retrieve some ocean-bed booty. He'd traversed the watery depths until he touched its floor and began casting around for something shiny to grasp. He saw small gleaming objects and lunged for them. When he'd made it back to the beach, his hands clasped what he took to be precious stones. The women would be ecstatic, he sensed. He threw himself down on the sand before them dramatically and then opened his fists to let his treasure be visible to all.

Their reaction tore him apart. Their eyes weren't aglow with gratitude and desire, they were more like slits through which contempt spat out at him like poison darts. He looked down at his stones strewn across the sand and suddenly realised that they weren't pearls or precious jewels – they were glassy trinkets. He'd risked life and limb and all his youthful pride on procuring a fistful of rhinestones.

In shame and sorrow he gathered them up and – amidst the jeering laughter of the women and their tightly muscled male suitors – retreated alone, deep into a jungle forest where he found shelter in a cave. There he fashioned a guitar out of wood, shredded vines for strings, and committed himself to learning to sing and play the music he'd heard those accursed girls performing that humiliating night. Then he sewed the rhinestones on to his only clothes – a pair of jeans and a white shirt. An unloved exile in this primitive dreamscape, he would seek vindication of his own self-worth by first honing and then pedalling his formative musical skills far away in some neon-strafed city of sin.

The dream abruptly changed locations at this juncture, the ways dreams do. In a flash he was standing on a stage in a noisy, smoky nightclub. He was all decked out in his rhine-stone-encrusted outfit and had his homemade guitar slung low around his shoulder. A man in a cowboy hat with shaky hands made a brusque introduction before an audience of maybe one hundred people. Two female go-go dancers bookended him and stood there chewing gum noisily as he tuned up.

He felt the expectation in the room. He knew this was his big shot, his make-or-break moment. He said a silent prayer and struck a hesitant chord. But eight bars into the first song, things began to go seriously awry. The guitar strings refused to stay in tune. He had to retune the thing during a song and, even then, it was never right. He tried to project his voice further out in order to camouflage his instrumental problems but the toxic mix of nerves and smoke in the room was drying out his throat and causing his larynx to clutch up whenever he strayed beyond a restrictive single octave range.

And as he struggled and sweated up there under that piti-less spotlight, he saw the faces of the clientele, at first intrigued, one by one morphing into dismissive sneers. It was just a big-city repeat of what had transpired on the island. And then – to further compound the misery – the rhinestones had started tumbling from his clothes onto the stage around him. He stopped playing and gathered them up. The audience had left anyway. The gum-chewing dancers too. He was all alone on an empty stage. Just him and a fistful of rhinestones.

It was then that the banging began. It made an oppressively insistent impact on some dim corner of his brain. This unsettling dream needed to resolve itself somehow but something more powerful was shutting it down and erasing it from his mind. Reality was intruding again. He woke up.

Ral would have spent a few seconds pondering the symbolic significance of those damn rhinestones had he not been rudely yanked from slumber by the loud banging noise coming from his front door. Scraping the sleep from his eyes and wrapping the duvet clumsily around his lower frame, he pulled back the latch and opened the wooden door tentatively.

Before him stood a sight that had become all too familiar to him in the past week: an old woman in a floral dressing gown with a look of stark terror in her eyes babbling away in Dutch, beckoning him frantically to enter her apartment. The woman was his neighbour – he was currently living alone in a four-room residence only a few streets away from Amsterdam's red-light district – and she was going insane. Ral couldn't understand one word she ever said but he recognised mental illness when he saw it. The old woman lived alone too, talked to herself incessantly and was up all hours obsessively (and very noisily) cleaning her apartment.

She was a royal pain for all who lived in the building. But Ral still followed her unquestioningly into the flat which, though spotless, was nonetheless tainted with a stale, musty odour he'd always associated with looming death as a child, the same smell that he'd encountered the last time he'd seen his Auntie Geraldine before she died of cancer. The old woman gestured fearfully at the wardrobe in her bedroom and uttered a number of sounds that he couldn't make head or tail of.

This was not the first time he'd been in this situation. A week earlier the same routine had occurred. From what he could tell, the old woman was hallucinating that strangers had taken over her wardrobe and were plotting to murder her in her bed. Ral Coombes reacted the same way then as he did now. He calmly walked to the wardrobe, opened its doors and drawers and painstakingly demonstrated to the woman that no human beings – or extraterrestrials – were living there and that what she'd mistaken for homicidal predators were in fact items of her own clothing.

It took about twenty minutes of very patient miming to convince her but after that, she suddenly snapped out of her panic attack and calmed down long enough for him to brew a pot of relaxing herbal tea. The pair then sat sipping their beverages in silence. Before she'd emptied her cup, she fell asleep, affording Ral the opportunity to – once fully dressed – descend to the ground floor and inform the concierge of his neighbour's fragile condition. The concierge then contacted one of the woman's relatives by phone who arrived an hour later and took control of the situation.

Ral returned to his apartment unfazed by what he'd just witnessed. Nothing surprised him any more. His own wife – the love of his life – was currently in a home for Alzheimer's sufferers back in England. He'd fought to keep her at home but the doctors were adamant that she needed 'full time treatment'. He'd visited every week but most times she was unable to recognise him.

The last time he'd seen her, it was two days before he'd decamped to Amsterdam. He'd gone to the home to cover the finances for his wife's immediate future. Then he'd gone in search of her – to say goodbye. He found her in the company of three other residents. They seemed to be carrying on a conversation only the four of them could understand. His wife was seated next to a late middle-aged man named Alfred, and she stared at him when he spoke with a tenderness and empathy that were nowhere to be found when she turned her gaze on Ral. She simply didn't acknowledge his presence there. She'd looked through him like he was a plate of glass. This was the way their world ended.

Most men in the same situation would have come apart, but Ral Coombes had managed to stay stoic and walked away without tears forming in his eyes. He was past the point of heartbreak because his heart had already been broken ten years earlier, when their son had been taken from them at just eighteen years of age. He'd always been a wild kid – good hearted but reckless – and, after starting to watch the TV show *Jackass*, he'd become besotted by its presenters' daredevil tomfoolery and determined to enact similar feats in his own neighbourhood. This resulted in him skateboarding off a viaduct wall, mistiming the leap and flying instead into the grill of an oncoming haulage truck under whose wheels he perished before the stunned lorry driver could step on the brakes.

When Ral had been given the news by the authorities, he'd identified the corpse and then walked for miles until he'd arrived at the top of an isolated hillock. Dusk was descending all around him and he had stared up at the gathering darkness and screamed at God, calling him the vilest of names, taunting him to appear from out of the gathering gloom and explain this act of wanton sadistic barbarism. His beautiful son had never stood a chance, a chance to grow, a chance to ascend into adulthood, to fall in love, to avail himself of the full force of youthful self-empowerment. He screamed until his voice grew so hoarse it hurt as though a blood vessel were about to burst inside his throat. Then he just stood there – spent, like a scarecrow – and listened to the silence. No stars lit up the sky.

Several hours later, he managed to navigate his way back home. But from that night onwards, he was a changed man. He shut down. He socialised rarely. At the same time his wife started behaving in ways best described as slightly unhinged: strange lapses of memory, blank stares, the sense of someone gradually losing control over their own identity. Over the course of the following years, he started getting the deeply unsettling sensation that his wife's personality was being invaded by some alien entity, like in the old black and white movie *Invasion of the Body Snatchers*. At first he thought it was grief for their dead son that was causing her to experience a breakdown in her nervous system, which was in turn triggering some form of mental disarray. But he slowly became aware that whatever ailed her was turning the love of his life into someone else entirely; a stranger both to him and herself.

It happened in stages. First came the vagueness – the long sorrowful stares out of the window, the losing battle to retain simple information and act on it, the terrible sense of neediness that she projected onto her husband. But then stage two commenced where the neediness began to bleed into resentment on her part. She became abusive when agitated and said a number of wounding things to Ral.

He dealt with it all as best he could. It was exhausting, stressful and saddening but having someone to protect gave him something to do – a calling in life – and a reason not to sink into the catatonic black hole of grief that had opened up before him since the day his son passed.

Stage three, however, proved to be the bridge too far. She started falling over around the house. One nasty tumble down the main flight of stairs almost left her with a broken back. That's when the doctors stepped in and convinced Ral to put her in care. The look of sudden abandonment she'd given him the day she'd been moved into her new accommodation had chilled him to his very core. Ten minutes earlier, she hadn't even known who he was.

Walking away from the facility, he remembered being a teenager performing the traditional song 'A Man of Constant Sorrow' in a local folk club to muted applause. It had been a shallow spectacle – the sound of a sheltered post-adolescent trying to express emotions only a fully fledged adult could begin to grasp. But now he knew exactly what that song was saying because he was living it right down to the bone.

It was then that he'd started entertaining the concept of 'easeful death' – not a full-blown act of suicide but more a vanishing act into the ether. But how to achieve such a feat? First and foremost, just give up caring. Shut down your inner factory of emotions. Just float down the river of life until it's time to sink.

'Acceptance' seemed to be the key to it all. Just accept what each day brings you. Try to stay active during your waking hours. Don't let the grief bog you down. But be very aware that death will continue to circle your wagon until your last breath is drawn. Are you ready to die? Ral Coombes thought long and hard about that question in the months following his wife's 'departure' before concluding, 'Yes, I am.'

But he also felt no great compulsion to hasten his end or purposefully set it in motion. Back in the day – many years before – he, like so many of his generation, had fallen into drug addiction. The fall had been steep, long and costly. His career and promise as a musician had been derailed by the lifestyle shift and he'd been left sorely diminished as a functioning human being. But he'd got lucky and managed to kick the habit not long before his son was born.

The two occurrences were interconnected. Parenthood furthered his resolve to stay straight and cultivate self-discipline. At first, it was a bizarre sensation being the only sober person in rooms full of drinkers and druggies. But he'd persevered and in due course the pay-off had sprung forth in the form of the unfettered joy he started feeling just being around his infant child and guiding him along as his tiny body grew daily and his personality blossomed within him. Those years were his beautiful reward for all the bad stuff that had transpired prior to this calm-after-the-storm era. But then things started to change.

Still, when tragedy struck not once but twice, Ral wasn't seized with the urge to self-medicate his way back into potential bad habits. In terms of simple practicality, he didn't know any drug dealers anyway. But more than that, he'd outgrown the syndrome of taking spurious concoctions to relieve pain only to have the substance turn around and hoodwink you into believing you couldn't live without it. It just wasn't an option any more.

So what was he doing in Amsterdam of all places, living a mere stone's throw from the city's most notorious thoroughfare of sin? Good question. Around the time his personal tragedies began, Ral had found himself simultaneously being goosed by lady luck. Out of the blue, one of his old songs had been picked to soundtrack an advert and the resulting exposure – plus the use of two more of his songs in follow-up campaigns – had transformed him from living virtually hand to mouth in a council house in Middlesex with a perpetual overdraft to pay off, to someone with almost half a million pounds collecting interest in his bank account. At first, he'd been befuddled by this burst of good fortune and hadn't changed his frugal ways in any significant fashion.

Then – after his wife's departure – he started getting visits from a figure he'd known well in his distant past. Brian Hartnell had been one of the Unstable Boys' many managers during their career duration and had amply demonstrated to Ral that he was that rarity among Tin Pan Alley straphangers – a competent and basically trustworthy business associate. They'd been out of contact for aeons but then the ad-campaign windfalls had brought them back into one another's orbit. Hartnell became the only character from his old days with whom Ral still occasionally socialised. The latter became particularly concerned by Ral's state of mind in the weeks after he began living alone. There are too many ghosts in this house, he'd told him. You need to pack a bag, go outside and investigate some new horizons. Because the old horizons aren't working for you any more.

It was then that he'd suggested Ral get clued into some home exchange network on the internet and had offered to set the process rolling himself. Two weeks later, he'd phoned to say that a Dutch couple with a young child were prepared to occupy Ral's house for between six to twelve months (the husband had sudden work commitments in London) and allow him in turn to live in their four-room Amsterdam flat.

Ral had agreed without even a hint of hesitation. The part of his brain that would normally have been feverishly weighing up the pros and cons of such a life-altering decision simply wasn't functioning at that moment. Fate had revealed itself as a force he was woefully unable to shape. He could only meekly follow where it beckoned. If it pointed towards relocation in a foreign city where the people spoke an incomprehensible language and wore wooden slippers, so be it. He had no special love for the place, though he'd often had an interesting time there when performing as a musician back in the days when a visiting rock group would often play to a completely horizontal audience; everyone flat on their backs, pot smoke billowing like mushroom clouds over their prone corpses.

His arrival in Amsterdam occurred in the late spring of 2016, just as his native isle was grappling cluelessly with Brexit bedlam. Even he – a mostly apolitical animal – was aghast when the vote came through. He was just glad to be temporarily out of the eye of that particular hurricane.

Compared to the rest of Europe – France, Germany, Belgium and even Norway were all ankle deep in the innocent blood spilled during recent terrorist attacks – Amsterdam felt like a sleepy safe haven, a good place to lie low in. The city itself seemed to have changed little in the five decades since he'd visited it more regularly. Not like London, which to Ral had lately become like a long-estranged ex-girlfriend who'd had her face restructured so extensively through plastic surgery she'd become practically unrecognisable.

But Amsterdam somehow still felt the same; the bridges and canals, the plethora of urine-stained side streets, the weaving footsteps of the stoned pedestrians, the prostitutes all warpainted up and cooing sweet nothings to their potential quarry. Sometimes he'd get accosted on the street by some persistent scoundrel trying to sell him what they claimed was cocaine but he'd already perfected the routine – a gentle shake of the head and minimal eye contact – and nothing further would transpire. No knives would be pulled out. No threats would be hurled or shakedowns attempted. He pondered this turn of events before concluding that he'd craved invisibility and now he'd basically attained it. He'd been living with the ghosts of his son and wife for so long now he'd become one himself.

Mostly he walked alone. Miles and miles every day often following a canal along its winding liquid trajectory. After an hour of non-stop promenading, he'd start to feel a pleasant rush rise up his spine and neck muscles and activate a glowing sensation in what felt like the base of his brain. Ah, those precious endorphins! His only real respite from gloom came when he was marching along at full pelt and the buggers suddenly started kicking in and he'd feel an inner jolt, a pleasant cerebral buzz, a sense of air in his lungs and light reflected in his eyes. It wasn't anything truly joyful though. Ral had experienced those back when his family was still intact – those all-too-fleeting moments of pure rapture. But now he knew better. God was asleep on the job or had simply gone AWOL. And all was definitely not all right with the world – his and everyone else's, if the daily news was any indicator.

A light-headed endorphin rush couldn't ultimately compete with spirit-crushing issues like that. Still, it helped soften Ral's mood and gave him some form of routine. He'd arrived in the city with little in the way of baggage. A suitcase of clothes, twelve dog-eared books, some family photo albums, some scraps of distant memorabilia from his rockstar youth. No guitar or any other musical instrument. The flat was part-furnished with some of the previous tenants' belongings – there was a big television, a CD player, a well-stocked kitchen and a number of lava lamps placed strategically to create a more intimate ambience when the overhead lights were switched off. It was ideal for Ral whose homemaking skills were meagre at best. He was required only to buy – and cook – his own provisions from the supermarket handily located just at the end of the street in order to survive in his new surroundings.

At first, the nights spent there were hard to endure. The days he could handle, but when darkness fell he'd feel despair lurking just a heartbeat away. Nothing on the telly could begin to hold his attention. The well-thumbed books in which he'd so often sought solace failed to stimulate him. He kept wanting to reach out to the photo albums and stare at images of the ones he still desperately loved, but he knew no good would come of it. There'd be no catharsis: just more emptiness. And he was all scraped out.

This sense of desolation became so oppressive that he began spending his evenings outside, covering the water-front. He'd walk until the endorphins were crackling inside his head and then return via the red-light district. Someone had placed an old sofa next to the canal in a spot looking directly towards the prostitutes who stood in windows bantering away to those passing below them in strange languages. Ral would sit there alone and watch these women.

He was aware that what he was doing could easily be misconstrued as 'suspicious behaviour', an old pervert's nocturnal stalk of lust. But he didn't much care. Because he knew in his heart of hearts that he harboured neither lustful feelings nor moral judgements towards these creatures of the night, that he posed no threat to them whatsoever. He simply liked staring at them. They were like an old Fellini film come to life. But more than that, their racoon eyes, multicoloured hair extensions, 'come-hither' couture and ostentatious body language triggered a sweet nostalgic flashback that he could luxuriate within for some precious moments. Watching the women reminded him of the first time he'd performed in

America. The venue – the Whisky a Go Go on Hollywood's Sunset Strip – was a nightclub that featured scantily clad girls in elevated, caged glass booths either side of the stage, and they would dance to the live music all night long.

They played a week-long residency at the venue and each night Ral, barely out of his teens, would stare longingly at the sirens in their cages, soaking up the glitz, shaking their pristine bodies, shape-shifting their arms and legs and skinny forms to the beat of the music. The image had always stayed with him: his first encounter with unbridled ecstasy.

He'd been happy then. He'd made it over to America, the land of dreams. He'd thrown off the stultifying boredom and sense of meek containment that had been his lot as a teenager in post-war England. He had catapulted himself to a bigger, brasher, more mind-boggling country, where palm trees routinely grew on the sidewalks – in LA they did, anyway – and surreal shark-finned automobiles held dominion over the countless highways. He had many memories to cherish from that time, but the image he always returned to was the one of those women.

He'd had a premonition even then that it would end badly for them. They were in cages after all, being ogled at. Their vocation was only three short steps away from being a stripper, many would have argued. Their futures looked both shaky and potentially shady. Prostitution, porn shoots, drug addiction, bad marriages and child-support battles were all out there waiting to glom on to their tender bods just as soon as the honeymoon phase of their Hollywood dream had ceased to cast its magic glow. Work dries up, the phone stops ringing. Then it gets disconnected.

But that somehow didn't matter to Ral. Not then and not now. To him those caged girls weren't victims or slaves, they were warrior princesses. They'd dance for ten hours at a time, always on the beat, and the look on their faces never changed – some might call it 'vacant', the less-judgemental would refer to it as 'lost in concentration'. That was the real source of his fascination with them. They had this miraculous capacity to concentrate on the moment and exploit its potential for unfettered abandon right to the end of the line. The erotic charge they inevitably ignited in the club's male patrons was always an inescapable factor but it wasn't what made them memorable to Ral. It was their power, their nonchalant audacity. Playing loud guitar music alongside their thrashing forms was like being part of some unconquerable army back in olden times. If the stage had been on wheels, the world would have been theirs to plunder.

How seductive the right kind of nostalgia can be when times turn hard. It just moves right in and sets up a sanctuary, an undemanding halfway house to discorporate from the gloomy present and temporarily find solace in golden visions of the past. That's where Ral had been trying to escape to over the past months. But mostly he'd been unsuccessful. He was old but he could still distinguish the clear truth from the ripples of distortion.

He missed his wife tremendously but recognised also that their relationship had become increasingly dysfunctional in the years leading up to her illness. He desperately yearned to re-experience the bonding sensation they'd shared as a family when his son was alive, but then remembered that their closeness had really only occurred when he was still a child. As soon as he'd become a teenager, he'd gone his own way. So what was there to miss? Some people remain constant, others change. In the weeks prior to the fatal accident, his son – still living under the same roof – had managed to say no more than ten words to his father. He was always in a hurry – no time for conversation or affection. It was like he couldn't wait to jump into a pair of shoes that were still far too big for his feet. How can one hope to guide a spirit like that when – as Ral well knew himself – it is so easy to disentangle yourself from family ties when you're a teenager desperate for independence?

The night outside was alive with the sounds of modernity. Mobile phones ringing, computers humming, sirens polluting the sound waves – all the sonic clutter that now soundtracked this strange new world.

These days he preferred silence. It relaxed him, gave him a blank canvas to spread his thoughts across. He was lucky he'd never developed tinnitus like many other rock guitarists of his era. When he heard silence, he was listening to the real thing without interference. Sometimes it would get so quiet that he might as well have been completely deaf.

Ral Coombes didn't actively seek music out any more. He didn't listen to records and he'd stopped playing instruments. This was odd. Music had brought him great happiness in the past and he had a genuine talent for making it. Playing the guitar for hours on end had once been his way of meditating, of ascending to a state of sweet serenity as his fingers took on lives of their own and embroidered melodies he'd never heard before.

It wasn't like his love of music was dead. It was more like it was sick. Poorly – that's what his mother used to call being under the weather. When he overheard a piece of music these days, something about it – the tempo, the chords, the vocal timbre – would not sit well with him and invariably start to cloud his mood. When he actually gave the music his full attention, it failed to engage him.

But every now and then, it would sidewind him in the street, wafting out from a bar jukebox or a radio. Something about the sound and the song would pull him in again, reawaken his responsiveness to the invisible art.

He'd been idling away his time in a local bistro just the other day when the music being piped over the PA system changed from Céline Dion to Frank Sinatra singing 'Willow Weep for Me'. And Sinatra's world-weary croon and the spellbinding arrangement had suddenly pierced his heart, causing him to weep openly. Another time he'd been watching a film – nothing worth mentioning by name – when all of a sudden its soundtrack was taken over by a rendition of the opening strains of Ralph Vaughan Williams's *Lark Ascending*, which swept through him like a forest fire.

Classical music, jazz of the non-cacophonic variety and ruby-voiced crooners could still stir his soul, but rock music – his old stock in trade – was more problematic. He'd hear it in the streets when he was out walking and wince. The new stuff was overproduced and under-inspired. It was like food cooked in a microwave instead of an oven. The temperature's perfect but the nutritional value is nada. As for the old stuff, well, he tended to shun all that. Classic rock, they called it now. He shouldn't complain – after all, its continued commercial appeal had meant he'd just netted a lifesaving windfall of money from work he'd done fifty years ago. But something was wrong about a culture that was forever looking back. The world of rock he'd inhabited had been a forward-thinking place.

But now things had turned all topsy-turvy. There was no brave new world for the young and not-so-young to inherit. The future was no longer toothpaste-advert bright: it was dark, fearful and inhospitable. Gadgetry and technology had trumped any kind of radical new youth sensibility. Most musicians were struggling because record companies were struggling. No one was buying records any more. The new music seemed uncertain about how to offer solutions. Young musicians sprinkled the latest range of sonic fairy dust over the same tired set of chord changes and breakbeats and wondered why their music wasn't setting the world on fire. The root of their dilemma was as old as time itself. For just how long can you keep making new soup out of old bones?

Only one old-school rock track had left a lingering thumb-print on his imagination of late. He'd been seated in the red-light zone one balmy night. There wasn't much activity among the prostitutes, so his attention had drifted towards a group of young people about five yards to his left who were smoking pot while listening to some music-playing contraption that was hidden from view. They looked like they were having fun and Ral had felt a twinge of envy at the carefree way they'd carried themselves. One of the girls had jumped fully clothed into the canal at one point. And all the while their high-spiritedness was being further orchestrated by a taped compilation of classic rock evergreens. AC/DC and Guns N' Roses' hooligan laments were further amplified by a strange echoing that seemed to occur as the music bounced off the canal water. The effect itself was rather pleasant to listen to even though Coombes was a fan of neither band.

But then came a song he was more in sync with – Led Zeppelin's rendition of the old blues traditional 'In My Time of Dying'. He sat there and let the strange acoustic of the canal rearrange the track adding a dub-like reverb to the instrumental frequencies. Robert Plant's voice seemed to rise up from the water with a force and pitch that engorged all the oxygen around it. He was beseeching Jesus to meet him 'in the middle of the air'. 'Meet me, Jesus. Meet me,' the voice beseeched. 'Meet me in the middle of the air.'

The middle of the air. Eureka, thought Ral Coombes. Why, that was exactly where he was currently. Floundering between earthly existence and the ether, his will to live waxing and waning tentatively within him like the flame of a melting candle. And no sign of Jesus of course. Why would he bother? The man clearly had more pressing engagements. Why would he want to be slumming around Amsterdam with a bunch of prostitutes, stoners and a deadbeat like him? Surely there were more deserving souls to save.

A spotlight flashed briefly across the canal's waterway but that was the only illumination Ral Coombes experienced that evening. When the stoners' beatbox serenade grew too punky for his tastes, he stood up and walked back to his lodgings.

He'd just pulled the keys out of his pocket when the concierge collared him. Something about a phone call. She spoke pidgin English in such a garbled way it was hard for him to make much sense of her rantings. He thought he heard the words 'journalist' and 'interview' but he wasn't paying close enough attention. His response to this was instantaneous. Whoever was trying to reach out to him – well, if they succeeded it would be kismet but if they failed it would be preferable. He didn't need – or want – publicity. He still craved invisibility.

The concierge asked if he had a message for the caller were he to phone again. 'Tell him to meet me in the middle of the air,' he remarked before mounting the stairwell and vanishing up to his flat.

CHAPTER 6

According to the coroner, Hilda Royston passed away on 4 May 2016 at the ripe old age of ninety-two. 'Ripe' was also a word that those who found her corpse would use to describe the aroma in the living room, where she'd sat when death had made its house call sometime in the late afternoon while she was quietly sipping tea and listening to a programme on the radio. Five days and nights had tiptoed by without anyone in the immediate vicinity noticing anything untoward. Finally, the milkman mentioned something to the neighbours, who knocked on the door but received no reply. After that the police were called in, the back door practically taken off its hinges and the subsequent discovery made.

It looked like her exit from earth had been made painlessly. There was no fear in her face, no visible sign of inner torment or physical discomfort stricken across her features. On the contrary, she looked strangely serene; her mouth was even shaped into a half-smile. All who gazed on her corpse while holding their noses away from the gathering stench of decomposing flesh could see that she had been ready to go.

Her death-mask face betrayed no glimmer of surprise what-soever: more a look of blithe acceptance.

In the final years of her life, she had become increasingly eccentric. Her eyesight was slowly failing her but she refused to invest in new glasses. Several neighbours found her walking the local streets at eventide in a dazed condition. When they attempted to guide her back to her own residence, they were met with a stream of verbal abuse. The locals learned to be wary around her, although she rarely socialised any more. The Hendersons from five doors along had been the last to speak to her. Three days before her death, they'd thrown a garden party for their young children and assorted school chums and Hilda had arrived in a state of some frenzy, brandishing a tray loaded with bowls of raspberry jelly. 'I've been making jelly for six days now,' she explained to Donna Henderson. 'I've made so much my fridge is full to the rafters with it. So I brought some over here for the youngsters because, as we all know, no child can resist jelly.

'Take my son, for example. Dale's an entertainment legend, but he still hankers for my jellies just like he did when he was back in short trousers. That's why I've got to keep making them. I'll have to buy another fridge, I suppose. But I know one day he'll be back and it'll be, "Mum, got any jelly lurking about?" and I'll say, "Go to the fridge, Dale my son, and feast your eyes."'

She'd then placed the tray on a table close by and walked – with some difficulty – out of the ongoing festivities and back to her house. The last words to come out of her mouth had been about her son. Right to the end she'd called his name like a lovesick parrot.

Somehow the news reached him – he was in transit somewhere in Eastern Europe at the time – but his reaction was as expected. He wasted no words on mourning the passing of the one person in his life who'd conceived, fed and indulged him into wayward adulthood and acted as an all-purpose safety net during his later wilderness years. Instead, he focused his mind on more practical matters. What had she left him in her will? As per usual, the Boy's finances were in potentially perilous circumstances. A nice fat injection of inheritance cash would be just what the doctor ordered.

Imagine his ire then when the will was read out and it was revealed that Hilda had died in rented accommodation with only £640 in her savings account to bequeath to her darling son. He'd always thought the old biddy had some secret slush fund hidden away and was doubly gobsmacked to learn that she hadn't owned her own property. He chose to ignore the fact that her financial problems had been exacerbated by his consistent borrowing of funds over the years, tidy sums that he never thought to actually pay back.

So there he was, down on his luck again. Up slack alley with bedlam beckoning. He had debtors he needed at all costs to avoid – proper bad lads. All his old allies had died or grown tired of his poncing ways. And now his old mum in her last dying breath had let him down too. He'd been counting on her death netting him at least £100,000 after tax. What could a man in such circumstances do, apart from feeling supremely sorry for himself and cursing all who had engineered this latest lousy twist of fate into play. From time to time he'd posed himself the question: a mother's love, exactly how much is it really worth? Now he had his answer:

640 measly pounds. All the other stuff – the cuddles, the shelter, the bailouts – didn't count.

There was only one possible solution to his current woes, one final port in the gathering storm. The hour had arisen to get on the blower and summon forth his former personal valet-cum-court jester Johnny Two Livers.

The relationship between Johnny Two Livers and the Boy went way back to early 1966. After a 'difficult' performance at a club in Basildon, during which the singer had kicked a male heckler full in the face, the venue's car park became the location for the inevitable retaliation. The Boy was surrounded by the victim and two strapping cousins out to exact vengeance. The jig looked to be up until three strangers arrived and entered the fray. 'Bog off, young 'uns,' the biggest one had barked at the Boy's trio of would-be leg-breakers. 'You're out of your depth here. It's past your bedtimes. Go on now, shoo!' And the men had scattered like geese. The Boy's chief defender apologised – 'This sort of thing doesn't normally happen in my manor' – and introduced himself as John Eric Luman.

Right off the bat, the Boy liked the cut of his jib. Luman had 'presence'– he was a strapping six foot two inches with muscles all over the shop and a mean look on his face. If an intimidating-looking hombre like Luman was always by his side, the Boy could raise merry hell to his heart's content.

For the rest of the Unstable Boys' career, Luman was paid a modest retainer to be the Boy's personal roadie, minder and enabler. He earned his nickname partly because of the cavalier way he consumed alcohol, but also as a nod to the professional wrestler who called himself Ronnie Two Rivers. Like

Two Rivers, Luman was a man with secrets. The wrestler pretended to be a scalp-hunting half-breed but in reality hailed from Wigan. And Johnny Two Livers' cold, hard stare masked an inner sensibility strangely at odds with both his physical exterior and the situations he got himself into.

It had not always been this way. During the first eighteen months of his tenure as the Boy's all-purpose protector, Johnny Two Livers had regularly doled out beatings without a second thought or a twinge of conscience. The leapers he was always necking back helped, of course. He'd lost count of all the times he'd beaten up complete strangers at the Boy's behest. 'Make it so the bastard never walks straight again,' his young prince would hiss at him and that was all the incentive he needed. He knew his role. And he knew his place. Right there by his master's side.

But then in 1969 he only went and got himself dosed up. Some hippie joker spiked his rum and Coke one night when he and the group were in a Los Angeles nightclub. One hour later he was witnessing the face of God talking to him from a billboard. Twenty-two hours after that, he was still pie-eyed and fading in and out of the real world. His entourage tried to talk him down with little success. 'The body is weary,' he kept repeating during the latter stages of his 'episode'. 'But the mind is fitter than a fiddle. Fitter than a fiddle.'

Eventually he came back to earth, but it had been a bumpy ride and Luman was never quite the same again. In this respect, he was no different from countless others from that era who were transformed inwardly after consuming halluci-nogenic chemicals. But the lifestyle dilemma it confronted Luman with was harder to reconcile. He'd always been a man to whom violence had come as second nature. He'd even managed to make a living out of it. But all of a sudden – post-acid – he found the whole business of throwing punches and breaking bones vaguely repugnant. He was drained of bloodlust.

One night in Reno, Nevada, things started kicking off. The Boy was playing up again, taunting a bunch of Mormons in big Stetson hats about their lifestyle choices and general appearance. Fists were getting bunched, tempers were frayed and ever escalating, the first punch was one heartbeat away from being thrown. The Boy had looked over at his Two-Livered henchman, fully expecting him to intercede on his behalf. But John Luman had just stood there like a fucking statue, motionless. 'What are you donkeying around for?' the Boy had yelled at him. 'You need to show these Yanks what the old bulldog breed spirit stands for.' Luman's reply stunned his employer. 'Why?' he'd muttered. 'Why bother?' In that instant it became clear as day to the Boy: Johnny Two Livers had lost his bottle.

He was all set to give Luman the heave-ho when the Unstable Boys broke up and the pair were stranded together trying to negotiate their passage back to the old country. Those were desperate days. Everyone – management, other group members – had abandoned the Boy. But Luman stuck with him. He was the only one.

He'd always seen something in the Boy the others hadn't. That's why their relationship endured. Certain tittle-tattle merchants had dared to intimate back in the day that the pair might be gay, which only shows how those with minds languishing in the gutter can defame the truth. The truth?

They were blood brothers. Kindred spirits. Well, at least until that acid trip. Joined at the hip they were, for a time anyway.

Sometime in the 1970s they went their separate ways. Luman married and went legit, drove a London cab. The Boy took his own calamitous route. But they still reconnected from time to time. His visits in the last decade had been infrequent and tended to coincide with him needing John to do him an urgent favour. This sometimes left John Luman with the feeling he was being used, a feeling that his wife and son were often quick to echo.

And yet, when he'd heard that raspy voice on the blower earlier that day, his heart had skipped several beats.

The first ten minutes of their reconciliation were understandably tense. The meeting occurred in Two Livers' apartment in Lambeth, a snug, well-decorated hidey-hole for a precinct that had seen better days. The Boy's out-of-the-blue phone call requesting a face-to-face powwow, after more than three years without any form of contact, had left its recipient in a conflicted state of mind. His wife's words, 'It's all a one-way street with that one,' resonated anew. And she was bang to rights with her verdict too. He'd start counting all the let downs and the unfulfilled promises, and his blood pressure would begin hotting up like he'd just been stung by a particularly vicious wasp.

But then his rising temper would hit a brick ceiling and evaporate into nothingness. He loved the man called 'the Boy' deeply: that was the bottom line. Not in a physical sense. Nothing to do with bottoms or any of that malarkey. He loved him like a comrade, a battle-scarred brother in arms.

A while back he'd watched a thing on TV about ancient Rome, and the gladiators back in those times would routinely swear their troth to one another. True, they wore skimpy togas that showed a lot of thigh, but those muscular killing machines were bonded together not by a lust for buggery, but the quest for chivalry. Important distinction, that. Likewise, he and the Boy were bloodied but unbowed warriors still waging war against conformity and 'the man'. True, his soulmate was a flawed entity. But who among us can say we are otherwise? Let he who is without sin make the first judgement call. Otherwise keep it muzzled and affect a jaunty air.

'John, long time no see. How're tricks then, my old mucker?'

'Oh, up and down, y'know. Dad passed away two years back. The wife's doing part-time work at the local Citizens Advice Bureau. I've got a few naughty schemes on the hoof to tide me over financially – small stuff, off the radar, you know what I mean.'

'So how have they been hangin' then? Long and strong, I trust.'

'I can manage a semi these days. Two years ago I was dead from the loins down. The doc said it was brewer's droop so I quit the brandy and concentrated on wine and beer instead. He put me on that Viagra, though, which got things straightened out, if you follow my drift.'

'I do, although I want to stress that I've never had problems down there. In certain less civilised regions of the world, the locals have ended up calling me "the stranger with gonads of steel".'

'You're lucky then, mate. But you always were, weren't you? Lucky, I mean.'

'So that young lad of yours, still in school, I'm guessing? Darryl, wasn't he called?'

'Darren. He's all grown-up and the world's his fucking oyster. He's a dab hand at computer hacking. He can empty a stranger's bank account quicker than breaking wind. Three finger stabs on a keyboard and the readies tumble forth.

'And get this. As well as his extra-curricular activities, he's hellbent on pursuing a career as a drummer. Plays with a death-metal group called Pentagram and a Goth girl who got institutionalised for setting her hair on fire mid-performance. I keep telling him, "Drummers have had their day, Darren. They were the heavy lifters of the music industry. But not any more, son. Machines do that kind of thing nowadays." But he doesn't listen. Said to me one time, "You don't understand, Dad. Rhythm is a calling."'

'That's poetry, John. Don't dissuade the lad. I've always been fond of a proper mad-lad drummer.'

'Don't think you were so keen on Keith Moon that night in the Speakeasy when he threw those plates around and hit your girl full in the face. Deirdre, that was her name. Knocked her clean out, as I recall.'

'Your memory is failing you, mate. I can guarantee I wouldn't have been seen dead with a woman called Deirdre. I've got standards, John. Remember that. You're right, though, whatever her name was, she ended up with a cut lip and the left side of her face swelled up. I made the effort to talk sense to Keith that night but he retaliated by rubbing a handful of warm spaghetti into my chest. He wasn't a true original anyway. All those flash fills, all the loony stunts and bevvied-up horseplay, he stole them from Viv Prince. He was all over the kit like an octopus. Moonie was just following in his brothel-creeping footsteps.'

'Not sure I remember Viv Prince, mate.'

'Sure you do. The Pretty Things. You were there that night at the Wilted Cock, weren't you? You, me, Viv, a couple of girlies, Kenny Lynch and that fey bloke who was getting sodomised regularly by one of the Kray twins? Viv took against the piano player who turned out to be a midget. Tried to rugby tackle the little bugger but the half-pint kicks Viv in the testes and gives him a karate chop.

'Those were the days, eh? But enough of this merry banter, John. I have weightier issues currently pressing down on my shoulders and need your input as a way of possibly lightening the load.'

'I'm listening.'

'Well, buckle up cos your ears are about to receive a raging torrent of bad tidings. Like only this month – the phone rings. Me old mum. Brown bread. Death – it just creeps up on you.'

'I'm sorry to hear that. She was a good, good gal, your mum. Non-judgemental. Not like mine, God love 'er.'

'You're a sentimentalist, John. Sometimes it suits you and other times it makes me want to give you a dry slap. Mothers – you don't want to get me started . . . "A mother's love can be a wonderful thing." I heard that line in a country and western song once. Fucking cowboys. They're either serenading a horse or crying into their beers. I beg to differ. Mothers can sustain you and drain you in the very same instant.'

'You're being a bit harsh, mate.'

'Harsh? I'll tell you what's harsh. Your mother finally pops her clogs, you think you're quids in for a tidy windfall when the will gets read, being her only next of kin and all, and then you find out she's got nothing to bequeath to you but six hundred lousy quid, a chamber pot and a fridge full of jelly.'

'Jelly?'

'That's harsh! That's fucking inhuman. Particularly when you factor in my current predicament. The details needn't be pored over. Suffice to say I owe some very dangerous men a significant sum of money for "services un-rendered". Unless I turn up something like a hundred grand in the coming month, I'll be joining me old mum out there in that great boneyard in the sky.'

'So, reform the Unstable Boys. It's a no-brainer. You're getting this second wave of acclaim from those telly ads and you need to ride the comeback trail. Reunification – that's what the common man and woman want to see taking place. Milk that for all you're worth and you'll be cosy until the reaper comes calling.'

'I hear you, John. Loud and clear. Don't you think I've not thought this through? But I find myself locked in the jaws of a more pressing dilemma, one that requires me to don a veil of invisibility for the time being. Any public appearances and I'd be sorely tempting fate. As we speak, there are young men sporting brutal haircuts and speaking only broken English bent on firing a bullet into my temple. In parts of Russia I'm known as "the sniper's quest".'

'Cor blimey, mate. You don't want to be running foul of the Russian mafia. And neither do I, come to that.'

'Which is why – the less you know about the details of my current troubles the better off you and your loved ones will be, John. Trust me on that. But I need your knowhow to get me out of this jam.'

'Maybe lie low and bang out a quick autobiography. Everyone's doing it. Pay off your Soviet pallies with the advance and you'll be free to re-emerge and take the Unstable Boys out to play the sheds. No more piss-scented nightclubs for you, my son. Glastonbury awaits. Imagine it: two hundred thousand 'shroomed up mud-caked punters chanting your name.'

'I like the sound of what you're saying, John. Those words are music to my ears . . .'

'They did a big spread on the Boys in *Mojo* a few months back. Eight pages long, it was. Did you catch it?'

'I didn't know it existed until you just mentioned it, John.'

'Well, take a gander then.' He reached for a pile of magazines, selected the issue and passed it to the Boy.

'Fuck me, I've not seen these photos of us before.'

'They're very thorough, *Mojo*. They get right inside the nooks and crannies of a story.'

'So why didn't they contact me for an interview then?'

'They probably tried. But you tend to stay hard to get hold of.'

'Oh, right. Well . . . point taken. Wait, who's the fucking slaphead? And what's he doing with his silly slaphead face adorning my fucking article?'

'Hold your horses. That's Michael Martindale, he's only one of the UK's top crime novelists. Plus he's the Unstable Boys' biggest fan. He says so himself in that strip of text below his photo. You should read it.'

'Flattery doesn't sway me these days, John. I could care less. Opinions – everyone's got 'em. They're like belly buttons. Everyone's got one but what use does it serve? None whatsoever.'

'You're not getting the big picture, mate. Listen to this.' John read the whole piece aloud.

I've often dreamed – mostly as a teenager, but even on occasion as a fully fledged adult – that one day my doorbell would ring, I'd open the door and one of the Unstable Boys – either Ral Coombes or 'the Boy' himself – would be standing there. 'I've stories to tell you,' he would say. 'Mysteries to impart.' And I would invite him in and listen ecstatically to his verbal treasure trove of wonder and intrigue. For there is a part of me that is still sweetly imprisoned in a post-adolescent mindset, a sensibility that gets triggered whenever their music is played. Put bluntly, it leaves me giddy and that joyful turbulence has never diminished within me. Most of my dreams have been realised of late but the yearning to interact with the Unstable Boys, to hear their tale and throw back the veil on their lifespan is still alive at my very core, like a palpable urge or a constant lover's prayer. ·

John put the magazine down. 'Now this geezer – irrespective of the state of his fucking scalp – is someone you'd be wise to maybe get networking with. His books sell millions of copies. He's been a regular on the telly. Even got his ugly mug on the covers of the tabloids recently. Wife left him and his kids won't talk to him. He's probably in a right two and eight. Big house, centrally located. He's bound to get lonely.

A bit of company can often brighten the mood. Particularly when that company happens to be his childhood hero who he's already practically begged to pay him a visit. He wants to solve the mystery of the Unstable Boys? Well, there's the man to write your autobiography sorted. And – because he's such a big wheel among the book-reading fraternity – it's guaranteed to be a bestseller. Think about it – he'll be so cock-a-hoop having you as his houseguest he'll be like putty in your hands.'

'John, for a man of limited intellect you are nonetheless a vessel through which genius pronouncements occasionally surface. I'm not being sarcastic. You, my friend, are a man gifted with insight. This scam you're suggesting – it's well plush.'

'So you're sorted then. Sweet. I'm glad I could lend a hand.'

'Not so fast, amigo. I need the man's address.'

'I can't help you there. But Darren should be back in a minute and he'll be able to locate it for you on one of his computers.'

'Good. One last thing. I want you to go with me to meet him. I'm going to do what he wrote – just show up at his front door without prior warning. You'll be there as my manager. You won't have to say much but it would be helpful if you looked menacing from time to time. Not the full Lee Marvin. Just the odd bowel-loosening side glance. Your speciality. Remember?'

'Look, let me be blunt. You're thinking about going in too heavy-handed. You're not out to terrorise the bloke, you want him to help you write this book. And to act as a potential source of bed and breakfast. Be nice to him. Turn on the charm and before you can say "Bob's your uncle", he'll be eating out of your hand.'

'Point taken. I'll make my first visitation all on my lonesome. It'll be more intimate. You know I've genuinely missed you these past . . . What is it? Three years?'

'Have you, mate? Have you really?'

'Well, as much as a man of my nomadic temperament and circumstances can miss another human being at any one time. It wasn't a constant longing, more like an occasional twinge. "I wonder what scrape that mad cunt's currently got himself into." That sort of thing. Affection all the same.

'I feel like I'm on my way back, John. Elvis was born with a million dollars' worth of talent – his manager even said so. Now bear in mind that this was back when a million dollars was a fucking king's ransom. It always felt the same: that my skills were such that great wealth would just naturally be my fate. It's not my fault some low types have influenced me unduly in business matters. The result being that I've been railroaded into declaring bankruptcy more times than Donald Trump. What a role model that man is, by the way! What a beacon of hope to such as I! If a transparent charlatan like Trump can rise to the hottest seat of power in the western hemisphere, it tells me that my future could be as boundless as open prairie skies. The world's gone so mad of late that anyone can pull a con and get away with it. It's a prelude to global anarchy, mark my words.'

The sound of the front door opening and closing interrupted the Boy's ardently expressed soliloquy. John – still half under the spell of the Boy's jibber-jabber – looked up from his chair misty-eyed when his son entered the room. The Boy regarded the new arrival with a degree of alarm. He sported a hoodie and there was every chance that there was a Taser nestled somewhere within his jogging pants.

John – noting his guest's sudden spasm of discomfort – hastened to make the appropriate introduction.

'Darren, son. You remember your uncle . . .'

'Celebrity uncle,' the Boy corrected him. 'I don't usually need introductions. My face is my passport in this world. It's the birthright of the master musician. The last time I saw you, Darren, you weren't much taller than a stinging nettle. Now you're this big strapping geezer. And your dad was just telling me you're mad keen on bashing the old skins – is that so?'

Darren had the air of someone who seemed perpetually underwhelmed by the prospect of being alive. He spoke slowly and without enthusiasm.

'Yeah, I . . . uh . . . tap around the kit from time to time. Snare fills. Rimshots. Paradiddles. You know the drill. I don't need the money. I just like the action. But it's not like it was in your day. Opportunities are fewer. You have to take anything you can get. Like, tonight I was auditioning with this rapper crew out in Brixton. Bloody train wreck. There must have been twenty-seven of the cunts and not a single one of them could string a rhyme together. One of them said it was my fault for not being on the beat so I had to chin him.'

The Boy winced in an attempt to convey empathy.

'You'll find twats like that in any walk of life, Darren. But you look like you can take care of yourself. Seems like you've got good instincts. That counts for a lot.'

John suddenly spoke up. 'He gets it from me, that. Two peas in a pod we are. I only wish, son, you could have been a young man back in the sixties. Me and this mad lad here, we saw it all and did it all too. The full fucking banquet.'

Darren puckered up his face into a look of disgust.

'Old timers bigging up their golden years – spare me please. Why don't you make yourself useful for a change, Dad? We're out of beers and the offie shuts in twenty minutes. You'll just have the time to put the odour-eaters back in your brogues and hobble on down.'

The remark left John visibly stung. He left the room without a word. When the front door closed two minutes later, Darren turned to the Boy and spoke in a measured, almost hushed tone.

'No offence, mate – but I'm not going to listen to bollocks in my own home. Who do you think pays the bills here? If I wasn't feathering his nest regularly with readies and my old mum wasn't cleaning up his messes, he'd be living in a tent in a fucking layby somewhere.'

'I see your point, son ... I mean, Darryl ... no, Darren. Like I said, I can see you've got a good head on those broad shoulders. Quick with your fists too, I'll wager. You see a chance, you take it. You don't mince around like some we could mention – but won't.'

'The point being?' Darren half stifled a yawn as he spoke.

'I'm looking for an expert, a man of parts, a wingman. Your father once fulfilled that role when he wasn't too bladdered. But as you know all too well, there's been a technological revolution taking place that has put folks with no computer skills – like yours truly and your old fellow – at a distinct disadvantage.'

'So you want me to do what exactly?'

'Right now, just one small favour. My immediate future depends on me locating an address here in London. I can give you the owner's name. Apparently he's quite well known.'

'And what's in it for me being your wingman?'

'Well . . . the joy a human heart can receive from selflessly helping a wayfaring stranger. Isn't that enough?'

'Talk figures, not bullshit.'

'I can't give you more than a ballpark sum. But I might be looking at a million, maybe two. And that could just be the starter, the hors d'oeuvre.'

'And my percentage?'

'You don't waste time, do you? More front than Woolworth's. I like that. That's why I'm going to be so generous. How's ten per cent of the action sound?'

'You're taking the piss, surely?'

'OK, fifteen per cent.'

'Wrong answer. And don't be cheeky.'

'Twenty.'

'Twenty-five.'

'Now you're taking the piss.'

'Look, you can take it or leave it.'

'If I'm handing over twenty-five per cent, you do understand I'll need you to do more than just find an address?'

'Yeah. First things first, I'll go grab my laptop. I'm already starting to feel sorry for the bloke you're after.'

The Boy then spoke in a low, conspiratorial voice.

'One thing before your old man comes back – do you have easy access to a shooter? Something untraceable? A tidy little weapon?'

'Anything is possible in my world. I know a lot of people who would feel naked leaving the house without a piece in their pockets.'

'You're a proper bad boy aren't you, Darren? Guns in your waistbands – you and your mates strutting round the local discos like Billy the Kid. Your bravado reminds me of something the great Bo Diddley once said. You should know about Bo Diddley. He invented his own rhythm, which you'll never do, irrespective of your skills behind a drum kit. And he could beat a man to death with his two bare hands – though to be strictly accurate, I don't believe he ever did. Anyway, we were in a hotel room and this third guy – drunk as a cunt – he just pulled out a gun and started waving it around. He wasn't trying to be intimidating, he was just pickled in the head and showing off. Bo Diddley slapped the guy in the face – boff! – and disarmed him in one svelte grab. Dislocated the bugger's jaw. Then he said something that has stayed with me ever since. Pearls of wisdom. He said to the guy, "There are two kinds of bad guys in this world. The pistol wavers. And the pistol whippers. Which one are you, pee-wee?"

'So, Darren, you've been talking a good game. But I don't see any exit wounds or duelling scars on that upper torso of yours. That tells me you're not battle-tested like me. I'm asking – as one tricky customer to another – are you a pistol waver or a pistol whipper? I need results, not braggadocio.'

'You're in luck, aren't you? Results is my middle name. Actually it isn't – it's Brendan. But it should have been.'

'Always the joker, ain't you? Young people these days – awash with cynicism. Shiftless and way too mouthy as well.

Michael Martindale is the name, so get weaving on the matter at hand, please. It's time for the old dog to teach a young pup like you some tricks. I'm old but I'm still spry. And I tend to come into my own when the time turns to hunting season. Find me a prey or a scam, and I burst into life. I become almost radiant.'

He glanced at Darren who seemed suddenly lost for words. Bingo. Time to move in and go for the kill.

'Have you ever felt radiant, Darren? Thought not. Stick with me, son, and you might just get a glimpse at the real big time. Now, press your buttons and shift your mouse or whatever you call it. Eyes on the prize. There's a man out there who's dying to be taken to the cleaners. He just doesn't know it yet.'

CHAPTER 7

Dusk in early autumn can be a gloomy time even for those living in good homes boasting exclusive London postcodes. The summer had barely registered its presence on the nation – apart from a freak three-day heatwave. And then it had turned back to grey skies, dank, damp weather and a curfew of darkness at around 6 p.m.

Michael Martindale felt that gloom more keenly than most as he sat alone in his study listening to the silence surrounding him on all sides. Normally he'd have put on some music to pep up his flagging mood, but he felt so utterly deflated he didn't have the energy or inclination to make the journey over to the CD player. A bottle of wine – half-consumed – and a glass were placed close by his left elbow. But he wasn't drunk. He wasn't even woozy. Certain liquor can effortlessly lift the spirits, but other vintages can take you in the opposite direction if you're not vigilant about your intake.

It wasn't the drink curdling his mood, however. Something else had unsettled him. A book. Damien, his agent, had sent

him a copy of the first novel by Barnaby Wainwright, the
twenty-something playwright who'd made such a splash
with his play about Margaret Thatcher and Jimmy Savile
meeting in the afterlife and plotting to dethrone Lucifer. All
the critics had gone into hyperbole mode. Both the playwright and the actor playing Savile won Olivier Awards.
Wainwright's name was suddenly on everybody's lips.
Interviewed on television he was given to provocative
pronouncements delivered with a waspish wit. The camera
instinctively loved him and Michael just as instinctively
hated him. He was too self-assured. He was too inexperi-
enced in the ways of the world to be spouting off about
grown-up matters. And he was far too good looking. The
thick black hair hanging just so. The infuriatingly prominent
cheekbones.

And, worst of all, he was becoming far too prolific for
Michael's comfort. Evidently one of those 'Renaissance men'
wannabes. Wainwright yearned to do it all – mount plays,
direct films, paint and sculpt and have exhibitions. And write
novels. He'd come up trumps on the latter ambition by
getting *The Swelling Stain* published by the same company
that handled Michael's tomes. They were all over the book
like a cheap suit on a dwarf and their hype was paying off. A
quarter of a million sales in just one month. No. 1 on the
Amazon fiction charts.

These statistics felt like pins in his heart, because the work
in question was a psychological thriller that horned in on his
territory while gently lampooning the genre and expanding
on its stylistic possibilities. Damien had urged Michael to
read it, and after a sulk he'd capitulated. He'd hoped it would

reveal itself as shallow and unskilled. But it hadn't. Instead it had held him spellbound. That callow pretty boy had a startling gift for prose, plot line and character development, and the twist at the end was a real brain-spinner.

It left him in a turbulent humour. Part of his brain registered that he'd just consumed a top-rate piece of writing and had been duly stimulated by its impact on his senses. But another part – the place where his ego resided – was horrified. This young whippersnapper suddenly posed a palpable threat to his own career. He hadn't seen the reviews but he could imagine them. 'Wainwright's daring prose and blazing imagination have reinvigorated a genre that has lately been run into the ground by the likes of Michael Martindale.'

Damien had sent it to him because he figured it might spur some literary activity, Michael tapping the keys again. This only enraged him further, although his rage invariably took the form of solitary silent seething. The people he'd made millions for were getting worried about their cash cow. That's how he saw it. Trying to pit him against this new Prince Charming – that was their strategy. OK, so he hadn't written anything for months. Projects had been suggested but he'd turned them all down. Fuck 'em all. That was his response to the gathering storm.

If only his publishers and agent weren't so money-hungry and so zealous. The whole business made him feel cheap – like he was in a boyband who'd just been given their marching orders by the record company. He was a writer, damn it. And he had eight million readers to back up his claim. And eight million readers couldn't be wrong. Didn't Elvis Presley once release an album with a similar title?

It was then that the doorbell rang. The sound – like grumpy wind chimes – made him stiffen in his seat. He wasn't expecting company and only a select few were aware of the address. He slipped on the moccasins his wife had bought him many years back; they were both comfortable and comforting, relics from sweeter times. Warily he approached the front door. He kept the chain attached and peered through the door crack. No point in setting oneself up for a potential home invasion.

The human shape – male – was at first bizarre to behold, almost hobbit-like. It was hard to gauge his age. Spindly and small-boned, he wore drainpipe trousers, Cuban-heeled boots and a sort of Edwardian frock coat. His hair – medium-length and still abundant – stood up from his scalp like Rod Stewart's in the immediate aftermath of an electric shock. His eyes twinkled but the rest of his face looked distinctly lived in. Then the figure spoke in a nasal tenor that was both solicitous and mocking.

'Evening, squire. How's it hanging? As you can see, I've answered your call.'

'I'm sorry but you must be mistaken . . .'

'Maybe. But maybe not. Is your name perchance Michael Martindale?'

'Well . . . yes, it is. But I don't know you from Adam.'

'Adam Faith or Adam Ant?'

'I beg your pardon?'

'Adam Faith or Adam Ant. Which Adam are you confusing me with?'

'You've lost me, I'm afraid. What exactly do you want?'

'Oh, it's not so much what I want as it is what you want. That's your signature on the open letter in this periodical.'

Triumphantly, the Boy brandished the copy of *Mojo* that he'd pilfered from John Luman's apartment.

'You were virtually pleading with me to pay you a visit. Being the good Samaritan that I am, I felt compelled to respond. Getting your address wasn't easy, I'll tell you that. Costly too, though we needn't talk further about that. So . . . Has the penny dropped yet? Or do I have to break into song to convince you?'

'Oh God!' Michael suddenly realised who it was lurking on his doorstep. He stood there dumbfounded for close to a minute. Thoughts spun around his brainpan like gravel in a tumble-dryer. Then he said it again. 'Oh God!'

'Not quite, though I appreciate you spotting my resemblance to the Almighty. Others have noted the likeness as well. But I'm a humble sort at heart. A mere troubadour. Put here to write songs. Not right wrongs like your so-called saviour. I'll be frank with you. I'm not really a believer. But before this conversation strays any further into the metaphysical, when are you going to invite me into your abode? I'm freezing my knackers off here.'

'Of course.' Michael seemed to be suspended in a dream state. He struggled to form whole sentences. His trembling hands – why were they shaking so? From some premonition of imminent danger? Or the giddy thrill of expectation? He unhooked the chain and flung the door wide. As the Boy entered, Michael didn't know what would happen next. The evening had taken a profoundly unexpected turn.

Meanwhile his new guest was sizing up the premises with a noticeably impish gleam in his eyes. In the muted lighting of the salon, Michael saw him more clearly and let it fully register that indeed this was his childhood hero come to visit. At first, he felt like a wish-granted child on *Jim'll Fix It*: excited yet bashful and tongue-tied all in the same instant. His eyes couldn't prevent themselves from gawping intently at him. There was a Dorian Gray quality about the man. From certain angles he looked ageless, but his shipwrecked pirate's face and the insolent expression were ever so slightly grotesque to behold. And yet the crow's feet humanised him. He was held hostage by the Boy's very presence, ripe and ready.

From his side of the room, the Boy had already cast his verdict on 'the famous writer'. The cunt needed to go to a gym. And invest in hair plugs. He'd seen some sorry specimens in his time but this guy took the biscuit. All that money pouring in and he still looks like a human beanbag. No discernible personality peeping through so far, either. Still, mustn't grumble. His gaff is well tasty – right up his alley. He could see himself spending many happy hours here. Happy, lucrative hours. Best rein in the sarcasm and turn on the charm.

'Nice spread you've got here, squire. Though you've let it go a bit, if I may be so bold. Plates piled up in the sink. Ashtrays unemptied. I don't see a woman's touch in these premises. Single man, I'm guessing?'

'At the moment, yes. Separated. I was married – still am. But she doesn't . . . It's a long story.'

'It always is.'

Michael became uncharacteristically intense. 'My family have turned against me. That's the long and short of it. My wife won't even respond to my emails. My two sons won't pick up my calls. They've ostracised me completely. I'll be candid with you – it's been a lonely time. My agent found me this house, but it's not home. I feel like I'm in exile in a plush prison, counting the days when I can begin living again.'

This final confession was underscored by a theatrical flourish of the hand. But then he composed himself. 'I'm sorry. The wine's made me too melancholy. It can have that effect. But then again . . . Where are my manners? Can't I get you a glass?'

'Don't mind if I do. No man should drink alone. Women, neither. Makes 'em broody. It only encourages the bad side of the brain to run rampant. You start thinking strange thoughts and the next thing you know you're spread-eagled on some roof with an automatic weapon trying to pick off random strangers on the street. Solitude and alcohol make for rum bedfellows.'

'I couldn't agree more.'

'Loneliness is such a drag. That's a line of a song from the old days. Jimi Hendrix. Died in his own vomit.'

'Did you ever see Hendrix live?'

'See Hendrix? I only fuckin' played on the same bill as Jimi Hendrix. I smoked dope with the man and fucked the same women. He once gave me a suede poncho with fringe beads hangin' all over it. Just like that. Said, "Hey man, you look like you could pull this look off." Made me look like a pregnant squaw but I thanked him anyway.'

The Boy was now on terra firma. He'd been granted the opportunity to transform himself into 'the raconteur', a role he felt he excelled at. He could see it in his listeners' faces when he spun forth anecdotes from the golden age of rock

– that look of rapt attention. And that smile of sweet surren-
der had completely overwhelmed the facial muscles of his
slapheaded host, who beheld him with true submissive
ardour. The Boy encouraged the sense of devotion coming off
the guy like bad body odour. He was limbering up to start
playing this sucker like a harp.

There followed a stream of tall-tale telling that – fortified
by several glasses of *el vino* – ran for almost one whole hour
without interruption. Many well-loved music icons and
celebrities from the late twentieth century were namechecked
during this fanciful monologue, some in circumstances that
would prompt libel suits against the narrator were his words
to be leaked into the public domain. Michael sat there lapping
up the scandalous balderdash, giggling and guffawing at each
and every indiscretion. And yet there was an undeniable
mean-spiritedness about the Boy's reminiscences.

Apart from the likes of Diddley and Hendrix, he had few
kind words to say about his fellow artistes. He roundly
ignored whatever talent they might have possessed and
concentrated on itemising their many human failings.

Thus John Lennon was rebuked for his tendency towards
flatulence. One of Deep Purple was ridiculed for his problems with athlete's foot. These were shabby tales – titillating
at times, yes, but just as often straining the bounds of credu-
lity. The Boy had told such stories for so long now that his
anecdotes had kept snowballing over the years from a few
measly flakes of truth into monstrous constructions of salacious misinformation. Or, if you prefer, lies.

Which was odd because the Boy had indeed lived a wild
and eventful life dotted with celebrity faceoffs and unhinged

anecdote-worthy encounters. But he didn't really remember that much. The key events, sure – but not the details.

For example, he could still conjure up the image of him and Jim Morrison urinating against a palm tree somewhere on Santa Monica Boulevard. This genuinely happened. But everything else – how he and Morrison had first met that night, the location, what they spoke about, how the encounter ended – was lost to him. He'd try to relive the evening in his head and all he'd come up with was the sound of piss hissing on to the sidewalk coupled with Morrison's crazy laughter.

So he embroidered his past with flights of pure fantasy – and his listeners couldn't tell the difference because they didn't want to. They yearned for it all to be true and were more than willing to suspend disbelief in order to bask in the glow of his scattershot revelations.

The Boy kept spinning his yarns and intently watching his host become more doubled over with laughter. He was waiting for the next stage to proceed, the magic words to get uttered. And here they came. Betwixt frantic gulps of air to sidestep the laughing fits. 'You should really write a book, you know. This stuff is priceless.'

Game, set and match.

'Funny you should say that. I've been – shall we say – toying with the idea? A single volume with nothing and no one spared. A treasure trove of tall but true tales and rapier-witted insights into the cultural landscape of the past fifty years. I'll be honest with you – over the decades I've been inundated by scribes begging to capture my words in print. But I sent them all packing. I need to collaborate on the telling of my saga with someone of rare insight and impeccable writing credentials.

'I read your piece in this journal here and I thought, hold on, this bloke is clued-in to what makes me and my music tick. I like his attitude – respectful yet penetrating. Maybe he can help me get my own life and thoughts finally pegged down on to the printed page for posterity. So Michael, any thoughts? Or maybe you're too busy. I know you're in heavy demand. New cases to solve and all that.'

'I . . .' Once again Michael's gift of the gab failed him. His mind was reeling – the wine and all that scuttlebutt had scattered his thoughts to the four winds. He felt merry – very, very merry – a merriment tinged with mild hysteria. A strain of unfettered exhilaration was also coursing through his central nervous system and up into his brain stem. For the first time in months he felt truly elated. His sack of woe – the burdensome shame and recent public humiliation – suddenly didn't even register in his thoughts.

He attempted to articulate actual words, but only got as far as 'I'. His throat felt dry. But he wasn't parched – the wine had seen to that. It was inarticulacy. He wasn't thinking straight. He wasn't thinking at all. A voice from his adolescent past spoke up in his place.

'I . . . I . . . I'd be honoured,' it said.

CHAPTER 8

When Ral Coombes had started his daily marathon hikes around Amsterdam, he'd just put one boot in front of the other and taken in the view. There was no sense of direction to these walks, never a fixed destination. It was just aimless floating. He never knew where he was going or how he was going to get back, but he'd somehow manage to return safely and endorphin enhanced to his new home by eventide.

One day, after he had been in Amsterdam for a few months, he found himself on a tiny side street, which housed a large health-food store taking up three floors of the street's main edifice. In the same building's basement, music was being piped out at a significant volume. Ral didn't recognise the song or the act but he nonetheless guessed the era it had been plucked from. It was late 1960s psychedelic rock. The frequent feedback squalls, the primitive echo-drenched production, liberal use of a wah-wah pedal and those quaint faux-abstract 'trippy' lyrics were all the evidence he needed. The effete manner in which the vocalist sang also clued him into concluding – correctly – that the song was of English origin.

Curiosity compelled him to descend the metal staircase
to the basement's door. It was a record shop – that much
was already obvious – and as he entered it, he was struck
by a powerful aroma: the scent of old vinyl mixed with
incense and pot smoke. It made his sinuses tingle with
recognition. Because it was the scent of the 1960s – his
1960s. In a flash he felt at home inside this dark candlelit
room. It was in places like this that his youth had been
spent, soaking everything up until the odours and sounds
had become part of his very DNA. Specialist record stores
had been his chosen places of worship as a teenager. Now
he'd stepped back into that once holy space. But was the
magic still happening? In this world, spells can all too
easily be broken.

For a while, he stood absentmindedly leafing through the
stacks of old vinyl record sleeves that had been placed for
perusal in various racks. An old guy – easily as ancient as him
– was behind the counter chairing an animated discussion
with three young men sporting long hair and extremely tight
trousers. The debate was in Dutch, so Ral couldn't make out
what was being said, but the old guy frequently changed the
music coming from the speakers, picking specific records and
then lecturing his visitors assertively about their different
qualities. The guy's devout obsessiveness made Coombes
smile. He'd met his type before. Come to think of it, he'd
been his type before.

They even looked similar. Same gaunt faces. Same suspicious eyes. Same receding hairlines with what hair remained
tied back in unkempt ponytails. The big difference was the
moustache, a flamboyant growth of facial foliage that sat

atop the record store guy's upper lip like something possessing a life all of its own.

Though Ral spent over an hour in the shop, he never spoke to its proprietor. When he returned two weeks later for a second visit, again, no dialogue passed between them. Instead they'd thrown each other cautious glances from time to time.

It was during the third occasion he'd stepped into the premises that actual contact was established. There was no other clientele, just the two of them. The counter man's eyes wouldn't stop boring into him. He looked strangely excited. Then he said it. 'I know who you are,' and pulled out several records from one of the shelves directly behind him, arranging them across the countertop. They all featured Ral: every Unstable Boys album, all the old 45s, some with picture sleeves, even the doomed solo album he'd managed to record and get released in the early 1970s. The guy in the shop pointed to the cover of one record that featured a prominent photo of Ral at the age of twenty and then pointed the same finger at Ral himself.

At first he was astonished because he'd rarely been recognised by strangers. His fame – such as it was – had occurred way back when his hair was thick and lustrous and his face less furrowed and careworn. He'd been a different person then and, as he'd aged, he'd changed so much that when he caught glimpses of his younger self he'd instinctively recoil.

So he was more than a little taken aback by having his identity outed. At first he remained silent, unsure of how to react. But his eyes couldn't help scanning the plethora of discs laid out before him on the counter.

To his astonishment, several of them were recordings that
he didn't even know existed. There was a live CD apparently
recorded at a Californian venue sometime in 1967 that he'd
never seen or heard of before. Another CD contained a
collection of BBC radio sessions mostly from the same era:
again, no one had thought to consult him about its release.
Even more surprising was the pirate CD from Japan that
claimed to feature tracks from Ral's aborted second album
sessions, tracks that must have been retrieved from tapes he'd
long believed to have been destroyed in a fire.

So he just stood there with a look of dazed incredulity,
saying nothing, his eyes feverishly scanning the counter's
contents. The man behind the counter kept waiting for him
to speak up. Finally he did. 'Where do you think the money
goes?' he said. The Dutchman looked bewildered. 'These
records I helped write and arrange and play on. These records
that were the product of blood, sweat and tears – mostly
mine. And screaming bloody madness. And what was the
end result? Broken friendships, broken promises, shattered
nerves and a bunch of recordings you have absolutely no
control over whatsoever.

'So I ask you again. Where do you think the money goes?
Not to the musicians – that's just a straight up fact. No,
instead it goes to all the crooks and petty swindlers, the liars
and wrigglers and gigglers, the deal makers and breakers
who make the world of rock such a wonderful place to be
railroaded into.'

Ral then pointed a finger at the photo of his juvenile self
on one of the sleeves. 'That guy is dead,' he said to the
Dutchman. Then he turned on his heels and exited the

premises, making a clattering noise on the metal steps as he did so.

Two days later he returned to apologise. He knew he'd overreacted the moment he'd vacated the premises. Melodrama really wasn't his thing. But his precious anonymity had been violated. And it had shaken him up intensely. Not to mention those bootlegs and pirated CDs he never knew even existed.

But he shouldn't have vented his spleen at the shop owner's expense. He seemed like a nice guy. So he returned to make amends. The fellow was over the moon when he did so. 'I thought I had offended you,' he said after the apology had been made. 'Believe me, that wasn't my aim.' He then proceeded to deliver a rapturous soliloquy on the merits of Ral's musical output and the effect it had had on his life.

His name was Pieter and he proudly stated he'd been involved in the music business back in the 1960s, as a roadie for Golden Earring, the Netherlands' best-known rock act. He was in raptures about a concert the Earring and the Unstable Boys had performed in 1968 that Ral couldn't recall.

He then asked Ral if he'd do him 'the honour' of visiting his apartment, which was just two minutes' walk away on an adjacent side street. When Ral accepted, Pieter bounded to the door of his shop and began locking it, placing a sign in Dutch on the glass window to indicate that the premises were closed for the time being.

As Ral might have predicted, Pieter's home was part mini-museum of 1960s and '70s rock and part old hippie's mancave. A four-room apartment on the third floor that offered an attractive view of the surrounding area, particularly around dusk, the place was a mess. The ashtrays hadn't been emptied and the remnants of yesterday's takeaway meal were stuck to a plate on the living-room table. Ral stood in the main room for a while, absorbing the tightly packed clutter of old records, old books and old memorabilia. The walls were festooned with old psychedelic posters too: it was as if the man had turned his living quarters into one endless all-encompassing acid flashback.

'I'm guessing you're a single man,' Ral had remarked deadpan after taking in Pieter's chaotic surroundings and accepting a seat. The Dutchman vigorously concurred. Women had 'cursed' his life with their interfering ways. 'They can be beautiful but oh so devious . . . their agenda is to catch a man, and then wrap him in chains and slowly bleed his spirit dry. They ensnare you with their physical gifts and then before you know it you're spending your life arguing tooth and nail about the correct position of a toilet seat. If that's what great romance boils down to, then I'm better here all alone with my boxes and my bong.'

As he said this, Pieter grasped a large green tube and lit it, letting his lungs take three strong pulls on its contents before exhaling a mighty plume of smoke that hovered tentatively just above the two men for some minutes. Thankfully they were sitting on an actual sofa. Lying on one of those bean-bags would have played havoc with Ral's back. Again, alarm bells were getting ready to ring in his head. It had been a long, long while since his last encounters with those who followed the ways of the wacky.

Like many of his generation, he'd smoked pot fastidiously throughout his twenties and early thirties, but then around the age of thirty-six he'd started getting sudden nasty panic attacks that he eventually realised were being caused by his weed/hash inhalation, which he promptly curtailed. Other nastier drugs were in the mix until they too were curtailed, and for eighteen years – apart from one month on Xanax prescribed by a local GP to cope with his son's death – he'd been clean if not exactly serene. The longer he'd stayed free of their impact, the less he thought about them. It wasn't that hard. But he'd made a point of no longer socialising with active drug users as there was no sense in letting temptation muddy his resolve in keeping to a straight and narrow path.

And now here he was in an eccentric stranger's room somewhere in a foreign city rife with drug abuse, watching this man suck manically over and over again on a green glass tube that smouldered incessantly, pouring out reams of unfiltered pot smoke that were guaranteed to give Ral a contact high just from breathing in the same vicinity.

He said nothing at first. He was steeling himself for a panic attack. But none came. This was interesting. He could feel the stuff start to seep through his blood and into his brain. The music being played in the background suddenly started sounding more vivid. The posters on the walls began gently undulating before his eyes. And all the while Pieter was rattling on ten to the dozen.

In another time and place this strange scenario would have been his idea of hell on earth. Old hippies, worn vinyl, stale reefer fumes and the whole sleepwalk of nostalgia – what was he doing in this preposterous twilight zone? And yet – and yet – he liked it here. He felt no discomfort. His new acquaintance was cranky, true, but he was also accommodating and strangely personable.

So far, only his choice of background music was questionable. Too many obscure vintage stoner jams with vocalists braying on about the astral plane. So Ral spoke up, requesting records from an earlier epoch. He was suddenly seized by the long-suppressed desire to listen again to the songs of his youth that had stirred him to become a musician in the first place. 'Do you have any Jimmy Reed?' Ral only had to ask and Pieter scurried off to crouch down and rummage through some cardboard boxes until he'd rebounded with a vinyl copy of *I'm Jimmy Reed*, placed it on the turntable and cued up the needle.

As the first bars struck up, the whole room seemed to breathe a sigh of relief. The battering ram rhythms of Pieter's psychedelic playlist were suddenly banished by Jimmy Reed and his three-musician cohorts leisurely playing the same three blues chords over and over again, while Reed vocalised over the changes, employing lyrics so simplistic they seemed to just roll out of his mouth without the first hint of forethought.

He and his bandmates sometimes sounded inebriated during their performances but never incapacitated. None of them were virtuosos and musical sophistication was clearly not their forte, but together they shared something ultimately more precious. They'd somehow managed to take the most rudimentary musical ingredients and weave them into something so exquisitely effortless sounding that the effect was utterly hypnotic. But the source of their timeless appeal was mostly to be found in the grooves Reed's quartet were able to conjure up with such thoughtless ease.

Back in the day, musicians referred to grooves as 'pockets'. 'So-and-so was really in the pocket last night.' You'd hear it said all the time, particularly in smoky jazz clubs. Jimmy Reed's music had pockets so deep they contained whole universes you could live in quite happily.

'High and lonesome – be on your merry way,' he was singing and those words, the light, ingenious voice crooning them and the ramble-tamble dynamic percolating underneath worked their magic on Ral like a fairy-tale hero's kiss on a sleeping princess. The music was stimulating him again. It felt unsettling for a split second. But the bewilderment soon morphed into exhilaration, a state of spiritual giddiness.

He decided then and there to up the ante. Impulsively he reached out for the bong and took two healthy sucks on the mouthpiece. More smoke billowed everywhere. Ral felt a long-dormant sensation rise up his spine and neck and then attach itself snugly to the back of his brain. He felt no pain and he felt no panic. He felt moulded to the moment.

After that, the hits just kept on coming. Ral would name a once much-loved record from his distant past and Pieter would hunt it down and play it for him, grinning manically all the while. 'Buddy Holly's "Valley of Tears",' he'd say and, two minutes later, the song would be playing and Ral would be smitten anew with Holly's forlorn voice from beyond the grave and the eerie phantom of the opera organ accompanying it. All of a sudden the lyrics shook him in a way he hadn't felt before. They spoke of broken hearts exiled from joy in the valley of tears. He knew that place.

No use in succumbing to gloomy self-absorption though. Time to change the mood and up the tempo. Bring on the barbarians and the show boaters. A feisty old guitar-slinging blues instrumental was urgently needed, if only to keep the spirits in the room moving in an upward trajectory. Something by Freddie King perhaps. 'The Stumble' or 'Hide Away'. They'd always been able to bust things wide open.

But Ral then remembered a record in the same vein that he'd been particularly smitten with as a youngster. 'You don't possess a copy of Jade Harris's "Knuckle-Dustin' Time" by any chance?' he enquired of Pieter who for the first time that day had gone blank and slowly shaken his head. But then he sat behind a laptop computer – one of three in the room – and after two minutes of pressing keys and typing in the song and the artiste's name the track started playing. The sound quality was far from perfect but its essence was still there for all to marvel at. Like its title suggested, this was mean-eyed, menacing, rambunctious music.

As an extended electric guitar solo – which is what it was, albeit with a drummer and bassist desperately trying to keep up – it was an astonishing tour de force of fingers-on-fret-board gymnastics and all-purpose sonic mayhem. It sounded like Harris had turned up in the studio, refused any rehearsal with his rhythm section, recorded the instrumental in one tumultuous take and then – taking his guitar and the bassist and drummer with him – promptly exited the building in order to execute an armed robbery of a nearby bank.

Pieter was so visibly impressed his rheumy eyes were almost popping out of his head. 'Who is this guy?' he asked incredulously.

'Jade Harris was a black guitar player from ... Illinois, I think. Maybe New Orleans. He came along around the same time as Buddy Guy and Otis Rush started making records in the early 1960s. Mostly instrumentals. He wasn't much of a singer but his guitar playing made him someone that all the top-shelf string benders of the day were more than a little intimidated by.

'He was the only guitar player I ever saw who gave Hendrix a serious run for his money. He didn't have Hendrix's ambition, mind you. Hendrix knew how to package his skills for mainstream consumption. Jade Harris most certainly didn't. And he couldn't get beyond playing blues. So career-wise he was pretty hemmed in to little league cult status.

'I got to know him for a spell. The Unstable Boys were playing a week-long residency in a nightclub in San Francisco and he was booked as our support act. It was ridiculous, really: this virtuoso second-billed to a shower like us. We were all staying at this hotel down by the waterfront. One night he just showed up in my room. I think he'd heard there were drugs available and came to investigate. We ended up smoking some good reefer together.

'At first I was thrilled to be in such close proximity. But he was a very bitter individual and made it abundantly clear that he was most unimpressed by the white rock acts he was saddled with supporting. I honestly think he would have preferred to have been making his living through some form of criminality – burglaries, pimping. He talked more respectfully about felons he'd known than he did about any musician, alive or dead.

'In fact . . . Oh man, this truly shook me. We were in my hotel room and I had this tape playing as we spoke, very much in the background. Then after a couple of minutes he said, "Hey man, turn that off!" I asked him if he wanted to hear some different sounds and he looked at me and said, "I don't like music."

'I thought he was just kidding around but he was as serious as cancer. He didn't like hearing it and he didn't like playing it either. He found no pleasure in his artistry. He would have rather used his hands to feed coins into a slot machine than play.'

'Maybe Jade was . . . jaded?' Pieter offered.

'That was certainly part of it. But see, being born with God-given talent brings with it an obligation – to hone that talent to fruition. If you short-change it or squander it, you're automatically throwing yourself into darkness. God-given talent in godless men – that's often a recipe for a life ripe with catastrophes.

'At the time, his comment left me thunderstruck. My feelings for the guy went from awe to pity in a heartbeat. I felt genuinely sorry for him. To lose your love and passion for music – that sounded even worse to me than getting a limb amputated. And yet many years later I found myself facing the exact same predicament. Music – my music and everyone else's – was no longer uplifting. My own stuff sounded twee and shallow – the rantings of a self-absorbed young man afraid to assume any form of adult responsibility. And everyone else's music just depressed me, the good output more than the bad because the good stuff made my own efforts seem even more pathetic.

'So I stopped listening to it. I'd still hear it when I was out in public being piped through a public address system in a department store or in an elevator, say, but I'd never seek it out.

'You'll probably find this hard to believe, Pieter, but this is the first time in ages that music has drawn me in and given me pleasure again. I remember reading that some famous musician after a personal tragedy said, "My soul went dead to music." Jade Harris had the same thing happen to him for whatever reasons. And so did I.'

Ral had taken five measured draws on the bong. The way he'd suddenly lunged for the thing was at first a mystery to him. Was he opening Pandora's box and old psychic wounds? Warnings about pot being a gateway drug rattled in his mind. But then he thought – fuck it. His decision to get high again was based on pure impulse. But it had done the trick: it had brought him out of his gloomy shell.

Ral suddenly felt a compulsive need to talk about his personal circumstances to his new Dutch compadre. Pieter sat transfixed as his honoured guest unburdened his soul. The dead son, the crazy wife, the mind-boggling windfall that paid for his retreat to Amsterdam – all these subjects and more were spoken of at length. He remained dry-eyed throughout the monologue, detailing his travails as if they'd happened to another man – a close friend, perhaps. Pieter was deeply moved by the confession.

'You have suffered enough,' he said finally. 'You need to live again. Too much solitude. If you need a friend you know where to find me.'

'Thank you,' Ral replied in all sincerity.

Friendship wasn't something he'd cultivated much in years gone by. Phone numbers got lost, correspondence remained unanswered. This reticence was all part and parcel of being an only child, he guessed. That concept known as 'splendid isolation' – he understood both its pros and cons. And the French guy who wrote 'Hell is other people' – he had a point too. But his issues were more deep-seated. He hadn't been a good friend in the past. He'd let people down. People he'd cared about.

That needed to change if he was going to keep breathing. And no time was more propitious than now.

Ral's rejuvenating sojourn at Pieter's psychedelic shack had provided him with something of a lucky break, albeit one he would remain blissfully unaware of ever having transpired. While ensconced in the crazy Dutch guy's apartment, he'd received a visitor at his own current residence.

Trevor Bourne had turned up there at around 8 p.m. totally unannounced in the hope of scoring an investigative scoop by door-stepping a bona fide rock recluse. He'd got the address from the phone number a 'source' had supplied to him. He needed to act fast and pin down his quarry, even pester him – if necessary – into being interviewed on camera and dictaphone. The clock was ticking now. The race was on. The documentary required the participation of Ral Coombes in some form and so the time had come to find him and coerce him back into the spotlight. It was time to assume a new role: part investigative journalist, part bounty hunter.

He needed to go to Amsterdam personally. Martindale was particularly insistent about that. So he made the trip, checking into a four-star hotel and hitting the minibar and room service facilities with all the gusto of a man who knows his bills will be paid by somebody else.

Suitably liquored up but still capable of walking in a straight line, he left his hotel to set out on foot to his quarry's current hidey-hole. The drink in his brainpan emboldened him without unduly inhibiting his mental faculties – a win–win combination. The phrase 'Dutch courage' danced in his mind briefly until he dismissed it with a smirk. He just knew he felt prepared for whatever might transpire in the coming hours. He needed to get the old codger to trust him, to let him enter his property and win him over.

What if he didn't even open the door and instead shouted 'Bugger off' in a voice etched with the threat of violence? Could he brass it out – just stand there, wait and tactfully cajole his way inside, armed only with his questionable gift of the gab? Time alone would tell. One thing was for sure, though. It was going down.

Only it wasn't. At 7.55 p.m. he found himself at the entrance of the apartment block he'd been reliably told housed – among others – the elusive butterfly aka Ral Coombes. The front door required no key – you just pushed and it opened. Before him stood an office where the building's concierge – a bellicose big-boned older woman with a thyroid condition and an aggressive approach to verbal communication – was standing by her desk and eyeing him warily. 'What you want?' She enunciated the words in English with a vigour that was authentically intimidating. From that moment on, her mean mouth had switched to incomprehensible Dutch, and Trevor was thrown abruptly off his game plan. He tried to put on a brave face and explain the circumstances of his visit, without mentioning the journalistic quest aspect of course, which inevitably involved bald-faced lying.

Ral Coombes was an old friend. 'Actually we're blood relations. Of the distant sort. He would be most disappointed to know that I'd visited but was refused entry.'

Nothing. 'Is not there' was all the old crone would say. Finally – after he'd tested her patience sufficiently – she bade him follow her into an old elevator and punched a button with the number 3 on it. They'd walked down the hall with its different odours seeping from each apartment until she planted herself in front of a particular door. The concierge banged on it vigorously with her meaty fist, making a hellish racket in the process. No reply. She did it again, this time so violently that it was a wonder the door didn't splinter.

Still no response. The pair then listened in silence in order to pick up possible sounds of someone lurking furtively behind the door. Nothing. The place was empty. Trevor asked the concierge if she had any idea when her tenant might be homeward bound. She shrugged and said something that sounded like 'he keeps strange hours'.

He thanked the concierge for her help – even though he instinctively detested the old bat – while making it as clear as he could that he'd be back in a couple of hours in the hope that his 'beloved relative' would have returned from his nocturnal assignation.

Finding himself at a loose end and feeling temporarily deflated, Trevor Bourne then repaired to a coffee shop on an adjacent street to the apartment to rethink his strategy. He'd promised himself that he wouldn't indulge in any of the hash or grass-based confectionery available at such an emporium, at least until he'd completed his professional commitments.

Those goodies could be relied upon to catapult him into the sweet spot but they could also muddy his thinking and take his eye off the prize, make him sloppy and focus-frazzled. Plus he'd been drinking and drink and drugs – even pot – rarely mixed well. The last place he needed to find himself in right then was an alleyway retching up his evening meal all over his shoes.

But Trevor was weak and after almost two minutes of indecision, he capitulated and ordered a space cake. It tasted good and his stomach seemed able to hold on to it without the threat of sudden regurgitation. He sat there and watched the way his surroundings were starting to swim before his eyes.

The faces of the other customers changed each time he tried to focus on them, not just their expressions but their skin tone and bone structure. He got the distinct impression that he was hallucinating, seeing things that might not actually be there at all. But another part of his brain was calmly telling him to chill out and go with the flow.

It was at this point that Trevor made a new friend. His name was Pedro – he was part Spanish and part African, or so he claimed – in his late twenties, a freewheeling spirit who'd chosen Amsterdam as his home away from home for the usual reasons. After some minutes of abstract chit-chat, Pedro mentioned that he had some cocaine to sell and Trevor was immediately all ears. A few well-measured lines of Peruvian marching powder might just be the tonic to bring him down from the spacey place he was currently floating around in and redirect his steps back to his urgent professional duties.

The two men retired to the coffee shop's toilet area where the Englishman handed over 60 euros in banknotes to his new amigo and received in return a minuscule white paper packet containing roughly half a gram of what he was assured was unadulterated flake straight from the tundra of Bolivia. The transaction completed, Pedro disappeared off into the night, leaving Trevor to inhale a significant quantity of his purchase behind a locked door in one of the three cubicles.

Although he would have ardently told you otherwise, Trevor was no connoisseur when it came to drugs in powder form. Some forty seconds after his first snort, he felt his nasal membrane go numb and his heart start to palpitate recklessly. He said to himself triumphantly, 'Ah-ha! This is the real thing right enough. Let's go crazy!' But in strict point of fact it wasn't the real thing at all. The numbed sinuses had been caused by traces of novocaine while the palpitations were caused by a form of speed. In other words, he'd just inhaled a somewhat dubious cocktail of powdered 'cut'. Nothing life-threatening but still pretty much guaranteed to give whoever used it an uncomfortable few hours with high anxiety taking centre stage over those longed-for high times.

Focus, for God's sake. Eyes on the prize and all that motivational malarkey. Trevor manoeuvred himself tentatively from the coffee shop to the street outside. The fresh air hit him like a bitch slap. It was now almost 11 p.m. Surely the bugger would be back in his lair by now. So he began putting one foot in front of the other, moving in a direction that he believed would lead him back to the apartment and its odious concierge.

He was no longer able to walk in a straight line. Instead he weaved chaotically along the pavement, causing oncoming pedestrians to step out of his way. He wasn't thinking straight either. He kept looking for familiar signs – the building was only two streets away – but couldn't for the life of him remember exactly where these damned streets had intersected. Soon enough he was lost. But what the hell! He was stoned in Amsterdam. The red-light district sparkled seductively before his glassy eyes. Time to bring some class to these dyke-fingering inbreeds.

Sometimes he walked and sometimes he staggered but as long as he stayed in some form of forward motion he felt confident that he could retain his balance. It was when he paused to stand still that the dizziness manifested itself most worryingly. His vision was now blurred to the point where colours seemed to be bleeding into each other, like the picture in an ancient colour TV screen about to self-destruct. A woman was gesturing to him from behind a long window-pane. She seemed fit. But her skin was green. Part of his brain recognised it was just an optical illusion caused by drugs and the green neon ceiling lamp lighting the woman from the head down. But still. She'd looked like some bimbo alien out of *X-Men*.

He next found himself lurching through an arcade of women seated in individual showrooms. They blew kisses at him, thrust their hips suggestively and boasted in broken English of their sexual skills. Trevor looked around at one point and saw three other males lurking in the same vicinity. Two were middle-aged businessmen – Germans from the sound of them – out on the razzle.

The third was a far more brutish-looking entity. He never spoke so Trevor couldn't verify his nationality, but he looked like a species he was all too depressingly familiar with: the unreconstructed, ill-educated, knuckle-dragging criminal-minded northern English prole: wife-beater, shaved head, Humpty Dumpty physique.

The guy was staring at one of the women in the windows shimmying suggestively before him. He was a big lad and in different circumstances – with a skinful of hard liquor in his bladder, for example – he could easily have turned into a raging psychopath. But Trevor looked closer at his face and saw that no trace of belligerence lurked there. Instead his expression was almost beatific, like a child in a nativity play. He stared at the prostitute as though she'd materialised from a fairy story and not the sin-soaked streets of Amsterdam. He must have been overdoing it with the space cakes, skunk and magic mushrooms. Still, anything that can keep the wrecking classes docile and unthreatening is a major boon to mankind. So let's bring on yet more sensory befuddlement.

Trevor found an unoccupied cul-de-sac and snorted some more faux cocaine straight from the packet – a messy and somewhat wasteful procedure that left a faint white residue around his nostrils for all to see. He had to get back on the trail of the person he'd been sent here to find. But, for the life of him, he suddenly couldn't remember the guy's bloody name. Nor could he recall his address. Jesus, he couldn't even call to mind the name and location of the hotel he'd booked into earlier.

Whenever he'd found himself on the horns of a work-related dilemma in the past, Trevor had asked himself the question: what would Hunter S. Thompson do in such circumstances? If he was sober at the time, he'd opt to do the exact opposite of what he imagined his teenage role model's course of action to be. But if he was intoxicated, he'd embark on a pattern of behaviour that could end very badly for him. It had happened before and it would happen again.

He was moving – sloppily – away from the arcade down a street running adjacent to a canal. A party was going on somewhere close by – loud music, high-spirited yellings and screamings. And women were still lurking in shadowy windows and doorways with their come-hither smiles and scanty clothing. He needed to get his mind back on track and continue his quest for . . . whatever his name was. But the night was playing tricks on his already fickle resolve, leading him astray, distorting his vision and diminishing his sense of professional obligation. He felt a distinct erotic charge rising up within his loins. He hadn't had sex since that night when Jess . . . banish that thought!

So he was in a somewhat vulnerable state of mind when what was about to happen began to take place. He found himself suddenly face-to-face on the pavement with a young woman wearing only a bikini and high-heeled shoes. She had coffee-coloured skin and giggled when she spoke. Another girl with the same dark skin colour stood at a slight distance from the bikini-clad temptress, grinning enigmatically. They seemed very friendly. And easy on the eye.

Trevor generally didn't frequent prostitutes. Something about paying for sex rankled his sense of vanity. But then the bikini girl – her name was either Vanetta or Vanessa – had uttered the magic words. 'Let me suck your cock. I'll do it for

free.' At last – someone in this city who spoke half-decent
English, Trevor thought to himself. Then he cast his glassy-
eyed gaze over her physique. Ample-breasted. A sizeable
derriere. Some excess flesh around the lower torso and waist.
A face like a doll. Not too much make-up.

Why not?

They ended up walking down a long alleyway that
connected with yet another side street rife with the scent of
stale urine. They entered a dimly lit building with minimal
furnishings. There were three of them – Trevor, bikini girl
and her silent, grinning companion. He was starting to feel
his libido twitching urgently within him. He'd never been in
a three-way.

But the other girl wasn't there to participate in any sexual
activity, he soon realised. In fact, why she was there at all was
something of a mystery. She sat in the corner of the cramped
room they were now inhabiting, leaning against the wardrobe and looking bored while he and bikini girl started to get
better acquainted. She'd placed one hand on his crotch and
stroked the genital bulge in his trousers while giggling incessantly like a naughty girl. At first the giggling had sounded
oddly arousing to Trevor's chemically befuddled mind. But it
quickly became irritating. Why couldn't she just pipe down
and use her mouth instead to accomplish what she'd promised him – oral gratification?

It was then that he felt the sharp pricking sensation
against his cheekbone. He'd closed his eyes in readiness for
the first caresses of intense sexual contact but opened them
just as the piercing pain had announced itself. What his
eyes focused on was a sight so scarifying that it was little

wonder that Trevor instantly vomited on to the room's lino-leum-covered floor. A man was holding a knife to his face. He was a big man – tall and lethal with lightning quick gestures and movements. Eyes like untended tombstones. Trevor didn't dare look him full in the face for fear he might soil himself.

'So what you doin' with my woman, white boy?' he barked. 'This my gal.'

He pulled bikini girl alongside him and fondled her body with his free hand. She was giggling again – as was the second girl – and their tinny contemptuous laughter sent him tumbling to a low place he'd never been before. On many occasions in the past, he'd felt compelled to tell himself that he was living through hellish circumstances. But those circumstances hadn't really been hellish – they'd been more relationship roadblocks or career missteps. Nothing in the 'valley of the shadow of death' variety.

This, though, was the real thing. Hell in all its hellish, kill-ing-floor grotesquery. Those damn drugs! This wouldn't have happened if he'd just said 'no'. Panic-driven thoughts skit-tered around his skull like meth-lab rats. He felt impossibly vulnerable. Any thoughts of escaping were futile. Melodrama be damned, he was splayed out on death's very threshold. This realisation then prompted a torrent of inner-directed questions urgently requiring answers he didn't have. How violent and painful would his end be? How many knife wounds would suffice before that final breath could be drained from his punctured lungs? And where would his corpse be buried? Would he even be missed? Would anyone actually investigate his disappearance? His father? Possibly.

But would he genuinely mourn the loss of someone he'd routinely disparaged as 'a waste of food'? Debatable.

And then there was sweet Jess. Would she lie awake at night pondering his loss and cursing herself for leaving him a broken-hearted hostage to the cruellest of fates? It would be nice to think so. Nice but unrealistic.

He was trying to reconcile himself to whatever dire fate awaited him. But his guts were too full of dread to comply and he was shaking all over and not in the way Johnny Kidd and his Pirates had once sung about. One thing he was certain of: he really, really didn't want to die. Pain and humiliation he could just about withstand – to a degree. But termination of his life was an absolute deal breaker. He was too young to die. He'd yet to really make his bones in this world. All that potential haemorrhaging out in blood-red spurts onto the grime-caked floor of a subterranean knocking shop. It couldn't end that way.

Fortunately for Trevor, his drug-addled consciousness had mistaken a pimper's shakedown for a potential murder scenario and so his life was spared. His pride on the other hand took a terrible hammering. The knife-wielding brigand indicated to bikini girl that she should relieve Trevor of his trousers, which were already unzipped and sagging around his thighs in anticipation of what he'd come for in the first place. This she did, giggling all the while. The other girl was still giggling too. The heartless harridans.

Having been handed the trousers by his trifling doxy, the thug emptied the contents of the pockets onto a table. He then did likewise with Trevor's jacket. Rifling through what lay before him, he pocketed the wallet with both cash and cards, the mobile phone, watch and passport. He also located the tiny packet of faux cocaine and, dipping a long fingernail into it, then brought the bump of white powder up to his left nostril and snorted vigorously. The effect it had on his sinuses further aggravated his already foul and obstreperous mood. He made a spitting gesture and, scrunching up the packet and its remaining contents, threw it towards a bin. Trevor meanwhile kept trying to brace himself for the worst-case scenario. But he couldn't prevent his heart thundering within him like galloping horses trapped in a forest fire.

And then it changed. He was brusquely directed at knife point into a tiny side room which turned out to contain only a sink and a toilet that reeked of foul odours – a mix of faecal matter and cheap disinfectant. He was wearing only a shirt, some boxers and his socks. The door then shut behind him, followed by the sound of a key turning. The floor was damp and whatever vile liquid lurked beneath him was soaking into his socks. Then he heard the giggling voices recede in volume. Another door – this time more distant – was opened and shut. Then there was silence, punctuated only by the random drip-drip-dripping of the tap in the sink.

It took him close to four arduous hours to kick that door open: no easy task when you're in stocking feet and still semi-paralysed with bilious dread. But the hinges were weak. Otherwise he might still be there.

Everything around him was shrouded in darkness. Using his hands and feet to guide him, he felt his way from one black space to another. There was no source of light whatso-ever. His frantic grasp duly fingered what might have been a doorknob. He turned the object in his hand and felt something clicking. He pulled it forward hesitantly and a dim shaft of light appeared before his eyes. Moving toward it, he almost fell down the flight of stairs.

Another door separated him from freedom. It opened without difficulty – just a turn of the wrist – and he was out in the open again with the fresh air spiking him back to reality. Yet what had just transpired had been real too. Or had it? What was going on? Why had his life taken this terrible turn? Oh Lord – those wayward drugs: never again.

He stood in the alleyway trying in vain to get his bearings. He needed to move before his assailants returned so he started walking. But the pavement felt hostile when being traversed without shoe leather protecting the soles of his feet. There was also the distinct embarrassment of being witnessed in public without trousers.

As he walked – head down – the severity of his predicament began to eat away at him. He had no money, no credit card, no passport and no mobile phone. All the relevant data relating to his work schedule in Amsterdam – addresses, phone numbers, etc. – had been stored on that wondrous contraption, not to mention all its other essential uses. And now it had been stolen from him. He felt as bereft as a newly orphaned child. His eyes were starting to moisten. It was all too much to take on board. He couldn't even sit down in a bar, order a calming beverage and sort through his sack of woes until some genuine solutions had been arrived at because he had no money, and even if he did, the lack of trousers might weigh against him getting served.

And so he walked – what else was there to do? The rogue cocktail of substances he'd ingested earlier were still swilling around inside him but their once-all-too-potent effects were gradually thinning out. Night was ending, the darkness lifting and the sky above announcing itself as a foreboding shade of grey. Somewhere a hotel was waiting for him. With a bed and a bath. But he still couldn't remember its name or the address. Meanwhile, people were looking at him oddly. Oh sweet God in heaven, please make this torment cease.

He finally left Pieter's apartment at 6.45 a.m. The sky above was overcast – it would probably rain today – but Ral, whose moods were often influenced by the weather, was still feeling good. Good and giddy: a combination he'd not felt propping him up in aeons. The music – and the pot – had reopened pleasure centres within him that he'd thought had long closed down. And though he knew all too well that it was just a fleeting sensation and that soon enough he'd be back in the doldrums, he wanted to keep the afterglow smouldering for as long as possible.

The music – more than the pot – had reawakened something within him that had once been so precious it had defined his very existence. And then one day its power to nourish and enchant him began to abate until he was all but deaf to its virtues. But now it had returned to lift his spirits at a time when all hope seemed to be lost. The final record he and Pieter had listened to was still playing in his head: Miles Davis's *Kind of Blue*. Healing music. A soul massage. A gentle two-chord piano vamp of Bill Evans's from the album's last track had lodged itself inside his brain as he walked and was playing in rotation. It dovetailed exquisitely with the leisurely pace of his promenade.

It was then that he noticed the strange apparition coming towards him. A youngish man prowling the same pavement had clearly been the victim of calamitous circumstances earlier that night. His lack of trousers and shoes suggested as much and the stricken look in the eyes further underlined it. He was mumbling to himself too. Lost and undone, Ral thought judgementally. Then he realised – there but for the grace of God go I.

The hapless soul sounded like he might be of English descent and Ral decided to approach him and offer assistance. But the man's lack of coordination told him in no uncertain terms that it would be a futile gesture. Meanwhile John Coltrane's sax solo was starting to pipe seductively through his cerebral cortex. He felt that heavenly uplift still stirring within him, the embers still burning. And so he left his unfortunate fellow countryman to his ongoing journey through bedlam and continued on his gentle way towards home, hearth and some much-needed bed rest.

CHAPTER 9

The Boy sat there sipping his host's wine and surveying his opulent new surroundings. Luxurious, he thought to himself. He was on his best behaviour. Which was providential because, as he'd be the first to tell you, he was known far and wide as an incorrigible over-the-line stepper. A law unto himself. An out-of-the-box thinker. 'I've pushed more envelopes than fucking Postman Pat,' he was fond of remarking. People would laugh but he was always deadly serious. He saw himself as one of the immortals. Unfortunately a sideways glance back at his post-Unstable Boys career would tell any interested parties a very different story.

The man they called 'the Boy' had grown up in the era of barmy show-offs such as Screaming Lord Sutch and so felt duty-bound to always amp up the zany and fantastical when caught in the public gaze. But without good music to shore up his act, his antics soon grew tiresome and desperate. One week he'd be heralding the formation of a new group that he'd be fronting. The next he'd jettisoned his new playmates and – having secured a healthy advance from some gullible

record-label boss – decamped to somewhere far away like
Australia for six months to pursue indolent pleasures without fear of reprisal.

UK-based record companies soon learned to avoid him
like the plague and the nation's managers and agents promptly
followed suit. So he'd widened his net. He still had a certain
cult cachet in parts of Europe. He'd trawl around these
regions and drum up some kind of support. He'd work with
pick-up bands. Of course, he never paid them. He believed
they should feel privileged just to be breathing the same air
as he did.

For a while in the mid-1980s it was all very hand to mouth.
But opportunity knocked one evening in Zurich. Her name
was Serafina and she was loaded. She witnessed him playing
a show in a beer-soaked club that had terminated with the
singer assaulting the drummer's cranium with a faulty mike
stand. 'You're a very dangerous man,' she'd purred at him
coquettishly after introductions had been made. 'Dangerous
things attract me. Untamed things.'

And so it had begun. Serafina Rothstein, heiress to her
rich daddy's publishing empire, jet-setter, 'bonne vivante' and
a no-holes-barred dissolute woman, had found a new beau
and the Boy had found a new avenue to lead him ever closer
to the high life in which he so yearned to bask.

She'd spirited him away to her snowy chateau in the
mountains and he'd offered up no resistance to the abduc-
tion. A sexy time was had by the pair. They were never love-
struck but they shared a connection because they were alike
in many ways: moody, self-fixated, easily bored. The early
months of their 'courtship' had their share of fleeting, tender

moments; they were well suited in the sack. But to call their liaison a 'torrid love tryst', as Serafina did in an interview for a Swiss daily (one of her father's many publications) shortly after they'd first hooked up, would be stretching the truth to unacceptable proportions.

Beyond a certain animal attraction, they were linked together by what they represented to each other rather than who they really were. To the Boy, Serafina represented wealth and security, log fires, haute cuisine cooking, above all shelter from the gathering storm of recent career mishaps coming home to roost. To Serafina, her new love interest was just the latest in a long line of rock-related fuck puppets she'd dated. She'd once been engaged to the singer of a Belgian combo with cheekbones to die for who ended up overdosing. The Boy was his latest replacement, someone she could take with her to casinos. And when the mood in the room grew less than festive she could say, 'Do you know my companion here is a famous singer? He knew Elvis Presley.' And all the rich fuckers would prick up their ears and want to hear more.

Of course, the Boy would oblige; three glasses of vintage wine in his belly and he'd effortlessly slip into his raconteur schtick. It mattered little to him that the story he was telling so compellingly was a complete fabrication. He'd never known Elvis Presley. He'd never met Elvis Presley. He'd never even seen the man from a distance performing on a stage. But who ultimately cared? It was all a performance. Another mad caper. Something to provide a fleeting respite from the stultifying boredom of lush life.

Generally speaking, he felt quite cosy in his new alpine landscape, so cosy in fact that he went so far as to propose marriage to Serafina – the only time he ever popped the question. The proposition was made not out of romantic impulse – the truth be told, he was becoming irritated by the woman's nutty company – but through a more pragmatic desire to glom on to her fortune.

Serafina had issues. She liked drugs too much. She'd broken her hip while getting out of the bath one evening and her physicians had prescribed these new-fangled megadose narcotics to ease the pain. She loved how they made her feel – all light and airy – and decided to place herself under their influence whenever possible. When the doctor started to diminish the dosage, she contacted other physicians in the area until she'd located an alternative source. When that dried up, she turned to the black market. Shady individuals with darting eyes would suddenly turn up to the chateau at strange nocturnal hours, bearing packages and leaving with envelopes of cash. Serafina would always be in bed. As she became more and more deranged the Boy became more and more alarmed.

From his vantage point, things were teetering towards the intolerable. He had not been put on this earth to be anyone else's nursemaid but that's exactly what he'd become. The woman couldn't even make it to the toilet unaided. And the mad stuff that came out of her mouth, the talk about seeing dead people and witchcraft: it turned his stomach.

One night she further boosted the chemical cocktail already bubbling in her bloodstream by consuming a bottle of vodka and duly lapsed into incoherent ranting. The Boy could stand it no more and had locked her in her boudoir – having removed all alcohol from the room – to stop her from drinking, rampaging and causing more drama. He'd acted from good intentions. That was the irony. The one time he tried to be good, things turned out so badly.

Serafina Rothstein died on 11 January 1999 – aged forty-four – in her bedroom. Cardiac arrest. It happened the same night he'd locked her in, though of course he neglected to mention that at the inquest. Foul play was soon ruled out but the death was still heavily probed by the media. A rival Swiss daily then broke the story that drugs had been found secreted in the unlikeliest places throughout the chateau. The Boy was further incensed by this revelation. The bitch had been holding out on him. And when an anonymous source was quoted speculating that the Boy had been one of her suppliers, he really hit the roof. First of all, it was a bald-faced lie. He'd – on occasion – joined his lost love in consuming certain substances but he'd never 'supplied' anything. The gall – to imply he was 'her dealer'! Why didn't they go even further into the realm of pure fiction and refer to him as 'her plumber'?

On a more pressing note, the media-authenticated insinuations meant that literally overnight the Boy suddenly became persona non grata in the region. His latest gravy train had been savagely derailed. Serafina's family were particularly vehement in their condemnation of his 'degenerate influence' on the woman they were burying. He was barred from the chateau, came back one evening only to find padlocks on the doors. He couldn't even get in to retrieve the valuables Serafina had bestowed on him during their good times together: the diamond tiepin, the emerald cufflinks, the gold necklace, the several tailored designer suits.

Then he discovered that the apartment she'd bought for him in some upmarket Zurich enclave – he'd convinced her he needed to build a recording studio there in order to make his next album and she'd fallen for the ruse – had been repossessed by Serafina's brother and sister. They'd also frozen all her finances, making the credit cards she'd once given him worthless. And while all this was unravelling, her rich daddy – still alive despite several heart scares of his own – was muttering dark oaths and plotting acts of retribution. A deeply vindictive man, he chose to blame the Boy for his spoiled-rotten daughter's demise and made several phone calls to 'certain parties' who were known to administer savage beatings to complete strangers for the right kind of payday.

Fortunately for our man, no such unpleasantness transpired. He'd taken the hint and vanished by the time the hit squad came looking for him. But where could he go with no money and only a car – another of Serafina's gifts – containing roughly half a tank of petrol?

Frantically he'd leafed through his trusty little red notebook, the one he always kept in one of his pockets. It was full of names, addresses and phone numbers of potential exploitees stretched out across the globe. He needed a mug punter quickly – a good old boy who yearned to fraternise with a bona fide rock legend and who would be only too happy to foot the bill and provide suitable accommodation in exchange for simply basking in his aura. It was when he came across the name and address of one Jean-Claude Messman that he felt salvation might be at hand.

He dimly recalled the man. A fat, shapeless peasant-type with a face the colour of beetroot and serious body-odour issues. He'd been one of those fans – 'You're my biggest hero' – all that airy waffle. Knew his entire back catalogue. Even quoted lyrics. The Boy would have normally brushed him off after some superficial banter but perked up when the guy had invited him to 'come and stay anytime' at his place in some secluded little village deep in the Alps. Hideaways were always convenient to have at your disposal when one lived life impulsively at the roll of the dice. That was why he'd scribbled down his name and address and that was why he was driving to that same address now. 'Any port in a storm' was the mantra of that moment. He didn't even phone ahead to see if the guy was on the premises.

The journey there was a peril-packed white-knuckle ride: 150 miles of bad road, a blinding blizzard, ice all over the tarmac. When he finally skidded into the little village of Val d'Isère, his petrol tank was empty and his nerves were unsteady. Desperation and hunger were starting to eat away at him and he felt himself becoming stroppier by the second.

Fortunately his arduous trip had not been made in vain. Jean-Claude was indeed in residence at the given address and welcomed the Boy into his abode with an ardour that born-again Christians might summon forth were St Peter to materialise from out of the mists of antiquity and pay them a house call.

Adoration was the only word fit to describe Jean-Claude's feelings for the Boy. It could be touching to observe, from a certain distance. The rotund little bar owner radiated real joy whenever the Boy would launch into one of his soliloquies recounting past exploits, even though – his grasp of the English language being tentative at best – he barely understood half of whatever came out of his hero's mouth. But the Boy could do no wrong in his eyes and Jean-Claude made it abundantly clear to him that he was welcome to stay in his family's house with meals and bevvies free of charge for as long as he cared. He even went so far as to exile his younger brother – generally regarded as a simpleton – to the garage while the Boy took over his room in the house itself, a draughty wood and concrete edifice that backed on to the bar, one of only eight buildings that made up the village's minuscule high street.

The Boy feigned being grateful for a day or so but quickly tired of having to keep up the pretence and reverted back to his basic nature. His recent cruel reversal of fortune continued to rattle his cage. He'd been so close to the big score – so close. And then the bitch had pegged out on him. The greedy cunt. And then her old man and those sniffy siblings – spiteful greed-heads, the whole damn family. Negativity roiled around inside his skull day and night.

It found an outlet in mistreating the other inhabitants of his new Alpine retreat. The first casualty was the dog, Jean-Claude's beloved red setter Milo. The Boy didn't like animals and always made a point of never sharing accommodation with four-legged creatures. In less than seventy-two hours after he'd first set foot in the building, he managed to torment the animal into fleeing the premises for good. A few well-placed kicks and a steady outpouring of corrosive bad vibes spurred the bewildered pooch to abandon its formerly tranquil home. Dogs are more sensitive to bad hombres than most humans. Sadly his grieving owner stayed blind to the same warning signs. Jean-Claude traipsed around the

immediate vicinity for several evenings plaintively calling
out Milo's name. But the dog never rematerialised.

Then there was the wife. Yvette was her name: skinny,
brassy, a cigarette always ablaze between her fingers, smoke
rings floating just above her dyed blonde hair. Rarely smiled.
Seemed perpetually underwhelmed by her surroundings,
dissatisfied with her lot in life. A bit of a moaner.

At first she and the Boy had tolerated each other.
Communication between them was always respectful but
invariably strained. But then one night when Jean-Claude
was out dog hunting, they'd shared a bottle of some potent
wine and Yvette had become tipsy and began broaching intimate subjects. When she imprudently informed the Boy that
she and Jean-Claude no longer had sex due to her husband's
'condition' (unspecified), the Boy saw no reason not to offer
his services there and then. Yvette was so drunk she didn't
question the urge. They repaired to the bedroom and coitus
was begun only to be abandoned before a mutually satisfactory conclusion could be reached. The Boy had penetrated
her in a previously undisturbed orifice and it had hurt like
billy-o. For a week afterwards she couldn't sit down without
the aid of a cushion.

During that same week, relationships deteriorated in the
house. Arguments raged nightly between the married couple.
Once or twice the Boy had to knock on their bedroom door
and tell them to vent their discord at a lower volume. Then
she moved out. Went to stay with her sister who lived somewhere in the south of France. Before leaving, she informed
Jean-Claude of her infidelity and warned him in stark terms
that his idol – the Boy – was 'evil incarnate'.

Jean-Claude begged her to stay but wouldn't hear of jettisoning his beloved Boy from the home and hearth. The very notion was unthinkable. And so he sacrificed his own family in order to squander his future to the pipedream of fake rock 'n' roll camaraderie. Three months after his wife stepped out of the frame, his bar burned down. The house was gutted – and so was Jean-Claude.

This last mishap had nothing to do with the Boy, by the way. Faulty electrical wiring caused the blaze. Still, it was high time for the wandering lad to move on to pastures new. A Japanese promoter had got in touch about him doing some live work over there. It would be low-key, off the radar, but the money sounded promising. Maybe while he was there in the land of the rising yen he could sweet-talk his way into doing one of those big-budget adverts and gaining a fat payday from simply being filmed caressing a bottle of liquor or mouthing the name of some fruity-scented perfume.

And so he left the little village much as he'd arrived there – furtively, without ceremony, in the dead of night. He avoided saying goodbye to Jean-Claude. Amazingly his portly patron had never cottoned on to his true nature. Even after his own wife had denounced the man and accused him of cuckolding his sorry arse, he still beheld him like a young God. Maybe the guy was a homo, thought the Boy. It happened to him a lot. Men would attach themselves to him like fucking limpets sometimes. Somewhere deep within him he knew it was a bit off to steal away without bidding farewell to his latest benefactor but a larger part of his core being was revolted by sentimentality. Why waste time – and words – on expressing feelings you don't even have in the first place? Human beings could be so daft.

The twenty-first century had by now dawned. Its first years found the Boy's always precarious fortunes plummet to an all-time low. Things got so lean he'd periodically return to his mum's old gaff where he'd gorge on jelly and ruminate glumly on his lowly status in the business of show. That big score he'd long dreamed of was nowhere to be found. The gigs had dried up and the record industry was becoming obsolete in the face of internet piracy. In desperation the Boy had let himself be lured over to Russia in order to record with a techno DJ.

At first he'd imagined his collaborator – they'd only spoken once by phone – to be just another potential pushover: a vodka-swilling potato-headed rube with a shaved scalp just begging to be exploited. But he realised he'd miscalculated when they came face to face. His stage name was Ivan the Terrible, he had the physique of a man mountain and made no secret of being deeply embroiled in organised crime. The recording sessions did not go well. The Boy had felt intimi-dated – a rare sensation for him – by Ivan and his entourage (a rowdy pill-popping bunch who liked to fire loaded guns in the air when sufficiently jacked up) and therefore was unable to give of his best.

This did not sit well with Ivan and his henchmen. They jeered at his struggles to vocalise and mimed cutting his throat. Things got progressively uglier. At one point, the Boy was hung by his legs from the rooftop of a very tall building and soiled himself in terror. It was via such tactics that the Russian mob managed to coerce him into signing away all future publishing and performance royalties from all his previous recordings, including the Unstable Boys. At the time he'd put pen to paper his back catalogue had not been worth much. Royalty statements were infrequent and offered only paltry three-figure sums when they reached him. Being separated from such measly cash injections would be inconvenient for the Boy – not to mention unfair – but he preferred it to being peeled off the pavement and placed in an unmarked grave.

But then those old Unstable Boys tracks had suddenly been cherry-picked from obscurity in 2014 and it had snowballed from there. This sudden second wave of mainstream acceptance placed the Boy in a personal theatre of conflict. The renewed interest thrilled him but also drove him barmy. Those old Unstable Boys tracks were suddenly generating a whole new revenue stream. Thousands were accumulating in various accounts during the months that those old songs were getting maximum TV and radio exposure. That big score loomed large in his thought processes once again. But oh the cruelty of kismet: he couldn't collect on the windfall. A bunch of Russian thugs were profiting from it in his place.

And worse was to follow. These same Slavic brigands had decided to yoke our luckless vagabond to a management contract that would have proven dramatically disadvantageous to his future cash-flow situation. It was slavery pure and simple and his would-be slaveowners were uncomfortably precise about the penalties he'd face were he to rescind on the deal.

A kind-hearted woman in the gang's employ took pity on him and ferried him to the nearest train station before he signed the contract they'd drawn up. When – after five days and nights of gruelling travel made even more onerous due to lack of funds – he finally arrived via Eurostar at King's Cross station, England had become a different landscape to the one he'd left behind when he'd embraced the ways of Europe. It felt distinctly inhospitable. The recent news of his mother's death had further shaken him. That old safety net was no longer there to catch him when he fell. The woman herself? Good riddance. But the sanctuary she'd always offered – even though he'd generally loathed being in that musty old firetrap of a house – was something he now strangely missed.

The gloves were off now. No more pussyfooting around. He was too old to be nickel and diming his way around the Eurotrash circuit, too old to be hounded by blood-drinking Russian sociopaths who were – for all he knew – still hot on his trail. Too old and too impatient.

His philosophy had been a little too cavalier back in the day. He'd felt he could cash in anytime on his million-dollar potential like a bunch of chips scored at a roulette wheel. He'd been in no hurry. A little too leisurely perhaps. But that giant payday had never quite fallen into his lap. Adventures he'd had aplenty but the money proved more elusive to keep a hold of.

Now he was closing in on his seventies with no pension plan to back him up in his twilight years. That big score, it was now or never. This time there'd be no mistakes. He'd fished out his rod, reeled out a line fat with bait and one more time – perhaps the last – he'd landed a catch. A big catch. A game-changing catch.

On the face of it, his new quarry resembled just another shapeless sweating sycophant like that Swiss tosser he'd shacked up with aeons ago – the one with the stroppy wife with the bad case of haemorrhoids. But this new joker was a real prize. The slackest of the slack. Malleable as plasticine. And rich as Croesus. The kind of clueless bugger who was just begging to be taken to the cleaners. So – let the naughtiness commence.

But tread softly at least at the outset. Vibe your intended victim out. Get inside his brain right up there in the attic and root around, cause a little disturbance. Spot his weaknesses and play on them accordingly. Be chummy but also be sure to inject a subtle side order of menace into your repartee. Keep him smitten and yet unbalanced.

It was close to midnight and the Boy's recent litany of scrapes had been relegated to the furthermost recesses of his mind. He was feeling no pain, no remorse. The wine had helped but the physical surroundings were what had really sealed the deal. The Boy loved luxury. He'd spent too long in pokey little rooms bereft of quality furnishings. Now he was back where he truly belonged – in a deluxe house with classy drapes, spacious floors, Persian rugs everywhere, even a fucking bidet in the bathroom. Class up the arse.

And all he had to do was converse from time to time with this scribbling clown who owned or at least rented the joint. The first moment he'd set eyes on the dude, all his instincts had told him, 'You'll be able to drain this mug like a fucking vampire.' And he'd been right – deliciously so.

He was seated before him at that very moment beaming like the fucking sun king and asking stupid questions. He'd already started taping their conversations in readiness for the tome they were to collaborate on together. (A title had been mooted – 'Unstable But Still Able' – but the Boy preferred it simply be called 'Legend'.) On the coffee table was this chintzy little dictaphone that was recording everything they were saying even though it looked more like a wafer-thin bar of chocolate than the hefty Grundig tape recorders of his youth. A tiny red light shone from it. It had unnerved the Boy at first – that something so small could be so ingenious at capturing his every half murmured syllable. But he did not let it cramp his style. Two stiff drinks were all it took when the time came to loosen his tongue. He'd sip and scrunch up his face and pretend to discorporate into an inner space, a mind vault where his many ragtag reminiscences were stored.

Michael Martindale observed the transformation with unabashed glee but generally displayed a reticence for asking probing questions, preferring to let his subject ramble on to his heart's content. The job of a ghost writer – and this was what Michael had taken on the moment he rashly agreed to the project – involves specific journalistic and interviewing skills that he quite frankly didn't have at his disposal. He was out of his depth in more ways than one.

The Boy fed him his usual blarney. Some of what he said was based in truth, other scenarios he detailed were plucked from fictions he'd concocted long ago and never bothered to delete. An arm-wrestling contest with Wilson Pickett? Why not? Anything to keep the credulous spellbound. Of course, Wilson Pickett could have ripped his arm from its shoulder blade like a man picking apart a chicken bone. But somehow, the line between fact and fake had become so blurry that it didn't really matter any more.

Trump was right. Facts are fake. You make up your own reality as you go along. The Boy had known this practically from birth, mark you. He'd been a pioneer at slippery living, rule bending and consequence avoidance. Lately, though, it had felt like the stars – the ones in the sky, not earthbound celebrities – had turned against him. He didn't hold much with astrology but Serafina had been deep into all that stargazing business and had managed to persuade him that cosmic forces were casting poisonous vibrations all over his destiny. It had sounded most unpleasant, like a bunch of demonic school children egging your car while you sat inside the vehicle, powerless to respond.

Talking of cars – the great crime writer Mr Bankable perched there before him couldn't even drive. All that money and he didn't even have a nice fast flash motor to show for it. The Boy tried to imagine the movers and shakers of his youth – the Michael Caines and the Terence Stamps – without a set of slick wheels under them and laughed like a drain.

It was time to strike: the man needed to be needled. Just baby steps – nothing too harsh. But this overpaid scribbler needed to learn that basking in the aura of classic rock survivors came at a price. He felt duty-bound to nudge the social dynamic into more of a master-and-servant direction. In order for his ruse to work, he needed this fucker right under his thumb. Don't let him think you're equals. Let your alpha male side off the leash. A few bite marks won't go amiss. Just don't draw blood. At least not at this stage of the game.

'No disrespect, squire, but I have to say I'm a little disappointed you don't have a big flash motor parked out front, being the man of means that you are. Cars complete a man, I reckon. Give him something to grip – the steering wheel for one – and of course the gift of mobility. They're like your very own moving bubble. Trains and buses can't compete. They can't take you door to door.'

'I never passed the driving test,' Michael replied a touch defensively. 'When I turned eighteen I took some lessons. I think it was during the third one that I reversed into a stream. The fellow giving me the lesson – it was his car – called me a "bloody bugger" – I'll never forget that. Told me never to attempt driving a car again. Said it was for the public good. I took him at his word.'

'Point taken. But a gent of your stature – well, it's almost mandatory that you have a flashy set of wheels parked outside your castle and moat. It lets the neighbours and the hoi polloi know who they're dealing with.'

'I never thought of it that way.'

'You need a driver? I know a man. You don't want to be bothering with those Uber blokes. Vipers in the grass, they are. Rank opportunists.'

'Well, I do have a regular driver . . .'

'But do you really know the man? He might be a secret drinker. Or one of those self-medicators. Perhaps he's got relatives who kidnap famous folk and cut off their fingers one by one to secure a ransom. Have you thought of that?'

'Frankly, no.'

'Of course you haven't. You're living a life of luxury after all. But take it from one who's been there, done all that and still has the scars on his back to prove it – fame and fortune are double-edged swords, my friend. For all the adulation there's a wagonload of envy that rolls into town when your lucky star starts to ascend. Old acquaintances suddenly turn hostile. Vile innuendos start making the rounds ... It's not all slaps on the back. Knives can be poised there too.'

Of course, this struck an immediate chord with Michael who took the opportunity to unburden himself on the matter of his recent tabloid roasting to his new best friend.

From his point of view, it had all been a dirty set-up. He'd been targeted by jealous media hacks who resented his uncanny knack for knocking out award-winning fiction while they were still stuck behind desks nursing perpetual hangovers. These wretched, wretched people had colluded together to lampoon, vilify and demonise his very existence. He'd been knocked off his pedestal only to land in a snake pit of smut and vile chicanery.

This is what had really happened. He was at a Waterstones in Doncaster signing books and doing a Q & A. About one hundred people lined up to have their copies of his latest opus personally autographed. One of them said her name was Fiona. She was a trim-looking young lass and complimented him lavishly. Called him her favourite author. Said she was a writer too, albeit an unpublished novice, and asked for advice. One thing led to another and Michael ended up inviting her to his hotel for an evening meal.

Alcohol entered the picture at this point: gin and vermouth – a risky combination. He remembered parts of their conversation – the early parts. But after that things got a little sketchy. Somehow they managed to vacate the restaurant area and made it up to his suite. Primal urges may have been stimulated, a certain amount of fondling and groping may have taken place. But no penetration. No oral. Not even a hand job.

Unfortunately the fondling and groping had occurred in front of an unshaded window. 'Fiona' had planned it that way. Her boyfriend – an unscrupulous tabloid photo hack – was outside in the bushes with a high-powered lens on his camera capturing the moment for posterity. And that is how easy it can be to fall from public grace these days. He found out later that 'Fiona' (real name: Avis Thorpe) and her fancy man had pocketed ten large apiece from the *Daily Star* who ran the shots on its front page a day or so after the incident took place.

The exposé had cut him to the quick. His wife and sons had turned on him and basically shoved him out of the family homestead like an old rubbish bin. Three months had gone by and he still remained unforgiven. And the beastliest aspect of the whole sorry saga was he hadn't done anything to be truly ashamed of.

'You mean you never even got your end away?' the Boy had interjected with a note of genuine incredulity in his voice.

'Just so,' Michael had retorted plaintively.

'But I bet you wanted to,' he fired back.

'Well . . . um. Yes and no.'

'Come on, mate. You're among friends. You can unburden yourself around a man of the world such as I. Be candid. You wanted to shag it.'

'My libido is almost certainly less, shall we say, demanding than I imagine yours to be.'

'Spare me please, Sigmund Freud. You brainy types, you get locked away in your ivory towers. Meanwhile your old wedding tackle is down there wilting on the vine. When some good-looking piece of totty finally shows up, you lose all proportion. You need to be taken in hand, my son. Get those inhibitions all stripped away. I know some ladies blessed with quality skills for just that sort of thing. They're only a phone call away. They'd be just the tonic for you and me both. You might be surprised to learn this but I've had my share of heartache and vilification too. Did I ever mention Serafina to you? The love of my life?'

There followed an abridged version of real events with the Boy duly inflating his role as the concerned suitor. His description of first finding the corpse must have been gripping because Michael looked distinctly moist around the eyes at its conclusion.

A bond now linked them. They'd each spoken of deep feelings with a candour that most other humans would shy away from. Michael felt that way, certainly. What a big girl's blouse he was turning out to be, thought the Boy. For him the evening had gone splendidly. Like a chess master he'd moved his pieces around the board until he had his opponent hemmed in and one sweet step from utter capitulation. And the beauty of it was – the dope didn't realise he was being taken. One of the world's top creators of sleuths and crime solvers and he couldn't see what was happening under his very nose.

They chose to end the night on an upbeat note. Michael wanted to show a DVD of some American sitcom to the Boy, some show with 'enthusiasm' in the title. He liked a good giggle as much as the next man and so agreed to giving it the once-over. At first, he couldn't understand the fuss. The main character was some bald-headed plug-ugly rich dude called Larry – a sort of more abrasive Woody Allen. The running joke was centred on his lack of social skills but right off the bat, he was underwhelmed by the punchlines.

But then just as he was starting to doze off, a new character materialised. A lanky black dude in a wife-beater and skullcap called Leon. Now this was more like it. Leon was a motor-mouthed ducker and diver who'd busted into Larry's rarefied world and set himself up as some kind of life coach to the man. The dialogue that passed between them was priceless stuff: they were like a hip-hop Laurel and Hardy.

Leon had these braggart's sayings. 'I brings the ruckus' was the one that stuck out the most. Michael would double up with laughter every time he heard it said.

Meanwhile his new houseguest was looking at him with one gloating eye and at the big plasma TV screen with the other. Somewhere in that devious little brain of his, the ruckus was already brewing.

CHAPTER 10

It was two hours past midnight, a half-moon hung like a sickle in the sky above starless Amsterdam and silence reigned supreme in the frugally furnished apartment. Ral Coombes, its occupant, had fallen into slumber while seated fully clothed on the living-room sofa. His head was slumped forward and his neck muscles were starting to tense up when the banging commenced. He woke with a start. The commotion was coming from his front door. Someone kept knocking. Oh Lord – had the mad neighbour rematerialised? Gingerly he unlocked the latch and readied himself for whatever lurked behind it.

His eyes widened when he beheld the figure on his doorstep. Suddenly he was face-to-face with a woman who'd lately been the object of a significant aggression. Her face was bruised and she was holding herself in a lopsided way that indicated she was suffering significant pain in her ribcage. There was a visible welt on her upper thigh where her stockings had been ripped.

'Jesus Christ . . .' Ral exclaimed in shock.

The woman locked eyes with him and said in a deep Eastern European voice dripping with weariness and terrible discomfort, 'Jesus Christ had nothing to do with this. Unfortunately I'm desperately in need of the kindness of a stranger. I need ointment, bandages, anything to stop the pain . . . I'm sorry. I didn't know where else to go. I live on the next floor. I saw your light was still on from the outside of the building. We passed in the hallway once or twice but never spoke.'

He remembered a woman in a hoodie – tall, athletic looking – that he'd caught sight of entering and exiting the building. Always in a hurry. Her hooded form had suggested to him that she too probably craved anonymity. But then he'd put her image out of his mind just as swiftly as she'd walked in and out of his world.

But now came this dramatic introduction in full damsel-in-distress mode. There was only one option: invite her in and indicate the medicine cabinet (left well stocked by the apartment's previous occupants) that contained an abundance of panaceas and first-aid-kit essentials (all bearing Dutch brand names so Ral was basically clueless as to what they contained).

She'd been seriously kicked and thumped but the aggression hadn't propelled her into a state of shock. There was no hint of lingering hysteria in her demeanour. She rifled through the cabinet methodically, muttering to herself in some indecipherable language – Russian? Latvian? – although she spoke English well and without hesitation. For a moment, Ral wondered if she'd spent time in the UK or the US. A tube of disinfecting lotion was enthusiastically applied to the leg wound and the small cut under the eye. It must have stung like a motherfucker but she barely winced. She then consumed a large number of what Ral hoped were medium-strength pain pills.

'You're maybe wondering what happened to me tonight that caused this . . . unfortunate turn of events.' She looked at him knowingly. 'Or maybe you already have your own suspicions.'

Ral knew next to nothing about this person – she hadn't even told him her name – but he didn't need to possess clairvoyant powers in order to place her as a streetwise prostitute. Her come-hither dress code and inch-thick smeared make-up were the unmistakable uniform of the fallen woman. Still she obstinately refused to play the victim card, even in circumstances where the opposite was clearly the case.

The pills were starting to have their effect, loosening her tongue. Slowly the pain in her side seemed to recede. She asked if there was any alcohol in the house – 'A stiff drink would be medicinal right about now.' Ral said no, he didn't imbibe, but offered her a thimbleful of the grass Pieter had pressed on him instead, a gesture she readily took him up on. The smoke made her more feisty.

'You think I got beaten up? You should see the other guy. For real! Thought he could take me over and pimp me out. Think again, little man. These marks . . .' she gestured wildly at her bruises, 'are nothing compared to the wounds I left on his worthless bones. He's never going to be able to piss straight again.'

She seethed for a while before becoming calmer and more reflective.

'You must forgive me. I've had many hard times and in adversity it is easy to lose one's humanity. You have shown me real kindness tonight, stranger, and I will not forget you. What is your name?'

'Ral,' he replied. He hadn't said much so far. Hearing his own voice, he registered that he was speaking in a child-like whisper. He needed to assert himself more in the conversation.

'And yours?' he asked.

'Well, that all depends.' She gave a shrug and then a smirk briefly lit up her bruised face. 'Some days I'm Petra. Other days I'm Simone. In my line of work, it's good to be flexible with one's identity.

'But I sense you're the kind of man that I don't need to wear a mask around. So ... Magda. That is the name I was born with. Although it says something completely different on my passport. What can I tell you? Life for me has been complicated. As I sense it has for you, my new friend. You look like a painter or a musician. Am I right? Some kind of artist, anyhow.'

'Why would that be?'

'Because you're damaged and you wear that damage in your face. And damaged people – if they're able to survive and still behave righteously – have wisdom to impart.'

'That's a bit rich, coming from someone with a black eye and a possible fractured ribcage.'

'Hey – what's that phrase you have in English? It takes one to know one. But you didn't answer my question ...'

'Oh right. Well, I was once a professional musician. But then I retired.'

'You retired? You mean you stopped performing on stage?'

'More than that. I stepped away from music altogether. I stopped playing it and I stopped liking it. There was no enjoyment factor any more.'

'I can relate to that in part. I feel the same way about sex. But at the same time I've got bills to pay and no rich sugar daddy to pay them.'

During his years as a travelling musician and later when he fell into drug addiction, Ral had encountered a number of women who'd been forced to turn to prostitution as a way of paying their bills. He'd got to know them – almost always platonically – and had noted that in most cases the women concerned were ashamed of their circumstances and in denial about what they were doing. Magda by contrast was brazenly candid about her lot in life. It was oddly refreshing.

Meanwhile those pain pills must have been strong stuff because within an hour of taking them she triumphantly declared she felt no pain whatsoever. There might have been some form of stimulant in them because she talked a lot and her eyes would get very intense. But the weed was reining in her manic side sufficiently so he never felt uncomfortable in her presence. He made a mental note to tread gently around her and not ask her questions about herself, even though he wanted to hear the answers more and more.

Like her age. Her body was still supple and toned. She'd obviously been putting in the hours at some local gym. Her face was temporarily too disfigured to offer clues pertaining to her exact lifespan. She could have been in her mid-thirties but something about her general demeanour made her seem at least a decade older. That was the price to be paid for exposing yourself over and over again to the rank side of human experience. You think you can flit around it but it still ends up seeping into your bones until you turn vampire-like in the sense that you look ageless but not in a remotely healthy way.

And yet she was still an attractive woman. Age and experience had left their mark but had not as yet withered her. She was still a head spinner. But he couldn't bring himself to think of her in a sexual way. Her bruises were too visible. And his own libido had closed up shop for quite some time. She was dressed in a short, low-cut, blood-red dress, boots, torn nylons – but her appearance failed to spark even a tentative erotic charge from within his dormant loins. Most men might find this a disturbing condition to be saddled with – sexual impotence by any other name. But Ral at this stage of his life was less alarmed. To him, his lack of libido was a godsend more than an affliction. It made life less complicated and relationships less messy.

Magda sensed Ral's asexual quality as soon as they'd started talking. She'd long grown used to the lustful way men tended to stare at her – the look that instantly told her they regarded her as a worthy sexual conquest but not someone worth expending real affection and tenderness on. So Ral's English reserve and chivalrous intentions were enchanting to her. She'd rarely spent quality time with a decent man. Most of her clients were perverts with wives who evidently refused to get engaged in the kinds of hardcore sexual activities their husbands were paying her to perform. In the streets, men undressed her with their eyes. Lately she'd forgotten that good men actually did exist somewhere in this sin-caked universe.

So she asked him to tell her about himself and after a prolonged silence he obliged. He recounted his backstory in an even voice that shunned any hint of melodrama. He brushed over his origins, chose his words sparingly when discussing his Unstable Boy tenure (Magda hadn't heard of the group but became excited when told about the tracks on the recent ad campaigns) and acknowledged his wife's illness without volunteering much in the way of detail.

It was when he spoke of his son's death that Magda began crying. In between gulps of air she spoke about her daughter. It was a sorry tale. An unwanted teenage pregnancy. Discovered too late to be aborted. The baby orphaned out. Mother and daughter briefly reunited when the daughter turned eleven – mother adored the child, calling her 'the light of my life'. The child seemed well adjusted, her foster parents well meaning. Her school grades were high. All seemed well but then at age fourteen something bad happened – Magda never discovered what exactly – and her daughter suddenly turned into a troubled teen. Drugs entered the picture and her daughter fell into fast company. Soon enough she was railroaded into taking up her mother's line of work. Then she disappeared.

Magda had not been in contact with her now for over nine months. She hoped for the best but feared the worst. The fact that she was currently residing in a different country meant that she couldn't start up a search party in the region of Latvia her daughter was last seen. She also had an outstanding warrant for her arrest, so couldn't return to the area. A daily stream of phone calls had so far uncovered nothing. The uncertainty of it all made her visibly shudder when she spoke.

'Have you ever felt cursed?' she asked him.

Ral pondered the question before replying as calmly as he could.

'Yes, I have. Maybe I still do. Things tend to fall apart around me. They wither and die. A part of me tells me I'm not to blame – it's just fate playing its hand. But another part keeps insinuating that I had a hand in their demise, that I'm in some way guilty. That would be bizarre, mind you. I wasn't raised a Catholic.'

'Listen to yourself. Don't ever think those victim thoughts again. Don't even entertain them. Open your mind to self-pity and you're doomed. I'm a fighter, not a victim. Not a hooligan. Not a barbarian. A warrior. And I have always prevailed. It's a hard life, true, but I don't spend my down time weeping about my lot in life. I save my tears for my daughter. She's the one who's causing me all my sleepless nights.

'Do you know,' she continued animatedly, 'I've often thought musicians and prostitutes shared similar traits? They're both essentially there to seduce and bring pleasure to whoever makes up their audience. And the best of both species have genuine healing powers. A good prostitute can glue back together a broken man like a good song well sung can comfort a broken heart.'

Ral spoke up this time. 'Another similarity you forget to mention – both musicians and prostitutes are perfect prey for unscrupulous thieving scumbags like your aggressor tonight...'

'You make a good point. But I'm guessing there are also significant differences between the two professions. Sex workers can bring fleeting joy to their clients but often end up feeling spent and soiled by the experience they've put themselves through. The musician by contrast leaves the stage to applause all aglow with an inner rapture. That's what I have always envied about your breed. The connection they manage to make with others feels pure and untainted by shame.'

While the words spilled out of her mouth, her eyes were darting around the room in search of something that evidently wasn't there.

'You say you're a musician and I sense you're probably quite gifted. You have a musician's hands – long, elegant fingers. But what puzzles me ... there are no instruments here. You have nothing to play.'

'But I already told you, I became disenchanted with music.'

'But how could you let that happen? Because you got ripped off? That's not reason enough. For a real musician to stop playing music it must be like trying to shut out the sound of their own heartbeat. You play or you decay. It's not a part-time hobby. It's a full-time calling that needs to be daily nurtured.'

Straight after this pronouncement she rose abruptly from the sofa and walked unsteadily towards Ral's front door. 'Wait here,' she told him, 'I'll be right back.'

There followed the sounds of four-inch stiletto heels clattering along the uncarpeted hallway floor, a lift being summoned, then a key turning in a lock some distance away. Three minutes later she'd clattered back. As she stepped around the door, Ral could see she was holding an acoustic guitar in her hands. Why exactly was that? Was she about to initiate a hootenanny session on her host? At first, he regarded the instrument with a degree of alarm.

Magda meanwhile brandished it triumphantly.

'One of my clients – a regular – took me to his place for the usual. He was drunk and he became verbally abusive. He refused to pay me, then he passed out on the bed. I went through his clothes and wallet – nothing. So I took the guitar for services rendered. He claimed to be a musician too. But he played to me one night and it was unbearable. I'm confident I did the world a favour relieving him of what in his hands became an instrument of torture.

'Anyway, I'm giving it to you.'

Ral was stunned. He really didn't know what to say. He should have been grateful – the guitar itself looked like an expensive model. But it was stolen and he certainly didn't need the instrument's rightful owner tracking him down and alerting the authorities. More than that, the very presence of the instrument in his living space spooked him. He felt it staring back at him like a long-neglected wife. *'Embrace me, you fool.'* He didn't know if he was up to the task.

Magda meanwhile was becoming insistent.

'You came to my aid and so I feel obliged to return the gesture. Use this guitar to reacquaint yourself with yourself. Play music again. It doesn't matter if nobody else hears it. Play for yourself. But play.'

'You're very persuasive. But the original owner, surely he's . . .'

'Don't waste a thought on him. Just play. Play now. For me. Show me what you've got. Otherwise I'm taking it back.'

'But I haven't played in literally years. My fingers . . .'

'What are you scared of? I'm asking you to play me some music, not partake in an orgy or step into a boxing ring. I've just handed over a fine guitar to you. The least you could do is play me something on the damned instrument.'

'Point taken,' Ral acknowledged. 'And please don't confuse my current state of bewilderment with a lack of gratitude . . .'

What to do? Ral began by picking the guitar up and cradling it awkwardly like a thirteen-year-old holding his first female dancing partner at a village fete. The wood looked sturdy and the strings weren't rusty. His fingers tentatively brushed along the fretboard and he was relieved to note that the light-gauge strings would most likely not cut his finger-tips to ribbons.

So he tried for a chord – E major, then E minor. Some retuning was necessary. He struck some harmonies on the twelfth and seventh frets and the bell-like tones told him instantly that the instrument was finely crafted. So he pressed on. Playing the guitar again suddenly didn't seem so much of a challenge. It was like riding a bicycle: you just instinctively fell back into the routine. He struggled through a version of Davy Graham's 'Anji' as a way of exercising his fingers. His finger-picking technique needed practice but the hand shaping the chords experienced minimal difficulty in finding the right frets. Magda looked impressed anyway. She clapped her hands at the instrumental's conclusion.

'See, it wasn't that difficult! Now I want to hear you sing as well.'

She wouldn't take no for an answer. So Ral was once again coerced into recalling something suitable from back in the mists of time. It had been years since he'd done this sort of thing. Once upon a time he'd been able to pull songs out of the air and perform them without a second thought. Old songs with countless verses. New songs in tricky time signatures. Now he cast around in his mind for a selection he could do justice to but kept coming up with blanks. He'd pick a number and then realise he'd forgotten most of its lyrics.

Finally he settled on Leonard Cohen's 'Sisters of Mercy'. Its subject matter felt appropriate: the song's narrator glimpses redemption via a chance encounter with a prostitute. Also it had simple chords and its lyrics had stayed somehow forever lodged in his brain.

Hearing himself sing again for the first time was jarring. His voice had changed with the passing of the years. High notes he could once hit effortlessly now felt tantalisingly out of reach. He had to adjust and change the key to a lower register. So when he finally sang the song it had sounded tentative and mournful – not a winning combination.

Magda called a halt halfway through its execution.

'My God, what a gloomy song. Did you write that?'

'No, Leonard Cohen did.'

'Well, tell him from me that he'd be better served pursuing another line of work.'

'I would but he just passed away. You're too harsh. The man was touched with genius.'

'I don't want to hear any dead men's songs right now. Play me something from the land of living. Do you know anything by the Rolling Stones? They're more my kind. The music of champions.'

Ral down-tuned three of the six guitar strings to an open G and played 'Wild Horses' without once messing up the chords. The lyrics were all there, stored inside and ready to tumble out. And his strange new voice was able to carry the melody without a struggle. Magda closed her eyes and sang along to the chorus. The performance seemed to transport her somewhere beyond the four walls they were hemmed within. At its conclusion she smiled at him tenderly. Ral took it as a sign of encouragement.

Then she noticed the flashing light on her phone. A message.

'What date is it?' she asked, suddenly distracted.

'I'm not sure. November the ninth perhaps. I haven't been paying attention.'

'So you haven't been aware of what's going on in America?'

'You mean Trump? I've been keeping an eye on his progress. But he won't get elected. Americans aren't that gullible.'

'Think again. A girlfriend just texted me. The pussy-grabber is the new President of the United States.'

'So, suddenly it's official: the far right and rabid intolerance are taking over the world,' he said to Magda. 'Immigrants like us are going to need all the survival instincts we can muster in the years to come.'

Magda looked downcast. 'Sometimes it feels like the devil is already winning.'

'But we can't let him do that,' Ral countered ardently.

The exchange gave him pause for thought. 'The devil may be winning/But we can't let him do that.' It might make a good chorus for a song yet to be written.

Dawn was creeping through the curtains. A soft mushroom cloud of smoke hovered over the room. Seated some distance from each other, the two new acquaintances felt a comfort in each other's presence that neither chose to articulate. Their silences weren't strained and awkward. When they spoke, their exchanges weren't trivial. Like that song from his youth that Frank Sinatra had scored a no. 1 hit with, they'd started out as 'Strangers in the Night' – two lonely people together. But somehow they'd bonded. No physical contact whatsoever but a soul connection had been ignited nonetheless. The recluse and the warrior woman: what a pair they made. And what a character she was turning out to be: four-inch high heels on her feet, a stolen guitar and an attitude that could strip paint. What kind of muse was this? Yet she fascinated him. She could be his spur, his audience, his confidante.

After a while, he looked at the clock: 6.45 a.m. No ghostly visitations had transpired that night. No guilty thoughts either. No tears to stifle. By now Magda had fallen asleep on the sofa, fully clothed and breathing noisily, so he turned the lights out and tiptoed to his bedroom. Then he impulsively returned to pick up the guitar.

Safe in his room, he let his fingers stroke the instrument until they slipped into chord shapes. Out in the big bad world, panic was raging. Things were going to hell in a handbasket. But in his snug hidey-hole a sense of stillness reigned. He plucked some harmonics and they sounded like church bells blending with the birdsong outside his window ledge.

Leonard Cohen re-entered his thoughts. His recent passing had cut deep. Wisdom was always in short supply in this world but he'd been one of its most eloquent channellers, a sage, an oracle. One couplet of his in particular now played repeatedly in his thoughts. It was about early morning bird-song foretelling new beginnings.

Finally, he was hearing the birds. They'd probably been out there serenading him with their dawn chorus for weeks but he'd never noticed them before. But now he was fully alert and even accompanying them on a stolen guitar. Something was opening up within him. Even in the midst of global meltdown, tiny epiphanies were still possible.

Then Ral took the line from earlier in the evening – the devil may be winning but we can't let him do that – and completed his first song in over twenty years.

CHAPTER 11

The moment he let his new guest over his threshold, Michael felt his life suddenly transformed. One minute he'd been deep in his cups, then this magical encounter had ensued and zing went the strings of his heart. The troubles that had been beset-ting him – looming divorce, writer's block, the feeling that his lucky star had vanished from the firmament – were temporar-ily silenced. His new chum had banished his host's blues with his cheeky charm, wit, wisdom and bonhomie. He'd fallen victim to an attraction that utterly overwhelmed him. He'd go all girly-eyed as he listened to his teenage hero telling his stories about 'the old days'. The Boy's implausible tales reso-nated in his cranium like a narcotic fired intravenously into the bloodstream. He couldn't hear enough of them.

And when the Boy had coyly suggested the two of them collaborate on an autobiography, it had been music to his ears. At last a project that would break the logjam of his current creative inertia. The moment he heard the sugges-tion he couldn't think of anything more pleasurable to lose himself in.

It made perfect sense to invite him into his new digs because – as the Boy pointed out – he'd be close by when some long-forgotten nugget popped into his cranium and be able to jot it down. A routine was quickly established. The Boy's biographer and his subject would converse for several hours each day and then, having recorded everything, he'd transcribe the dialogue into his computer. It was time-consuming work but he didn't care. It kept his mind away from depressing thoughts. And it felt good to be doing something again, not just dreaming and drifting.

His new pal had thoughtfully introduced him to a pill he'd heard about but had never taken before. He'd said that all musicians have been reliant on them at one time or another, that they keep you wide awake, super alert and ready to take on an army single-handed if the need arose. The effect on him had been stimulating in the extreme. He'd tapped away at those keys, transcribing every word they'd said earlier in the day for hours and hours until his mouth was as dry as a sandpit and his bones were aching. The first couple of times he'd had trouble sleeping afterwards and had felt bad thoughts gnawing at him as he'd tossed and turned in bed but the Boy had come to his aid again with another pill. This had the opposite effect. It switched him off like a light bulb. 'Better living through modern chemistry,' the Boy had called out. It sounded like fun.

Had any psychiatrist worth their salt been commissioned to enter that house there and then and evaluate the mental state of its tenant, they would have concluded (above all else) that Michael was suffering in extremis from the rejection of having been exiled by his family and – temporarily unable to press forward – had reverted back to the state of an excitable teenager still craving a role model to emulate. In short, it was a delayed midlife crisis. They would be right, of course, but only in part.

There was the bromance factor to untangle as well. That was the buzzword currently doing the rounds to define the ageless state of intense male bonding. Men routinely fell in love with one another without any sexual tensions rising to the surface. Of course, they never used the word 'love', they preferred 'buddies', 'comrades' or at most 'blood brothers' – more rugged-sounding terms of endearment. But something deep links likeminded men together in ways that women rarely know even exist.

That was Michael's opinion anyway. And faced with his current circumstances he was sticking to it, come hell or high water. He'd always wanted to be cool but he'd been saddled with the wrong shape and the wrong temperament and the wrong everything to achieve that status. Now he found himself neck-deep in cahoots with a man he'd long perceived to be one of the coolest people on the planet and they were cooking up all kinds of wild schemes together. And as they plotted, he couldn't help sensing that some of the Boy's undeniable aura was beginning to slightly rub off on him. The thought fascinated him. He'd never imagined that charisma could be contagious.

His brain was moving very fast these days. His train of thought was supercharged, bulleting along at a devil's pace, though he sometimes noticed it straying off on peculiar tangents. So this was what living in the fast lane felt like. A mind ablaze with thought and a mouth like the Gobi Desert.

Butterflies in the stomach too. But the butterflies were there not from fear so much as a sense of ticklish exhilaration mounting through his internal organs.

Of course, to accommodate this new arrival in his life, sacrifices had been made. He'd not been in the place longer than twenty-four hours when the Boy suggested that for the duration of his stay he took over the entire first floor. He declared he needed space in order to delve back in his memory for the kind of juicy anecdotes that would give the text they were piecing together that extra push over the cliff.

Michael had felt a tiny bit put out by the request. After all, his bedroom was up on the coveted first floor. The big bathroom too. Not to mention the classy toilet with the bidet. But then he thought he didn't really need them. There was a downstairs toilet with a bath right next to it. The room itself was small and draughty but a bit of spartan hygiene wouldn't go amiss with him. Michael could sleep on the couch in the living room. He'd already passed out on it enough times recently that it was starting to sag in the middle where his body had left its imprint. Still, it was comfortable. So problem solved.

He didn't give it any more thought than that. He never even questioned the imposition.

Every time he gazed at the wiry little man, he was transported in his mind back to ... when ... 1968 ... 1969? Thereabouts. There was a lad back then in his village named Shane Carlisle. Michael had idolised him from afar. Carlisle must have been three years older and an incorrigible deadbeat. Smoked cigarettes around the bike shed back when he had bothered to attend school. Six-foot tall with longish dark brown hair, a thousand-yard stare and a purposefully loutish way of walking. The local girls all yearned to dally with him. Mrs Dwyer at the newsagent's had even insinuated he'd got a friend of her daughter Mary pregnant. Michael had never dared approach him in all the years they'd lived in the same suffocating region.

But then one day on a bus they'd found themselves seated together and Carlisle had actually deigned to strike up a conversation with him. Brian Jones had just been found drowned in his swimming pool and Carlisle was visibly upset by the news. A die-hard Stones fan, he spoke of Jones's death with a tenderness and tristesse that Michael had never imagined existing within him. He listened mostly to the monologue with hushed respect. But also felt emboldened to toss in a couple of comments that would indicate to his travelling companion that he too was a bit of a Stones aficionado. He'd never forgotten Shane Carlisle's face when he'd said that the Stones had lost the plot a bit on their *Satanic Majesties Request* album. 'Too fucking right' were the words out of Carlisle's mouth but the look in his eyes – the look that said 'respect due' – that exact moment had been the most exciting instant of his otherwise sheltered and unexciting young life.

He never knew what happened to Shane Carlisle. He made enquiries once when he went back to their old stomping ground but no one seemed to know: said he was long gone and had left no forwarding address. Sometimes in his dreams he'd be back on that bus and Shane Carlisle would be next to him and he'd feel that same fleeting connection with something magnificent and wild. But lately a new bad boy had taken Carlisle's place on the bus.

The Boy was Shane Carlisle at an altogether higher volt-age. This was kismet, something life altering. Michael felt like he'd found his very own big brother and guiding light. He was that smitten.

Unfortunately others in his circle failed to see his ongoing adventure in a favourable light. His agent Damien Greene – normally a pair of sympathetic ears – had reacted with horror to the news that his client was ghost-writing a has-been rock singer's memoir instead of beavering away on a work of crime fiction. Rock books generally appealed to a niche demo-graphic, unless the author was someone with real clout such as Bob Dylan who'd also taken the time and effort to pen the text all by himself. Michael kept agitatedly explaining that the man's story was 'unique', 'mind-boggling' and used other frankly inappropriate adjectives, but the pages of transcript he'd provided as a taster of things to come were unprintable, to be blunt. Anecdotes abounded, famous folks made saucy cameos on practically every page, but the narrator was far too cavalier and scattershot with his opinions and any self-respecting publisher would wince at the number of potential lawsuits lurking in the text.

Nonetheless he'd assured his client that he'd do his level best to find his latest project a suitable home. Just don't expect a six-figure advance. View it as a labour of love. Get it out of your system and then return to what we all love you for – the contemporary whodunnit.

Michael's ears heard what had just been said. But it's debatable whether he was actually listening. Those speedy pills – he'd taken one just prior to this meeting – were stimu-lating one side of his brain while shutting down the other side, though he was blissfully unaware of the fact. The agent noted the symptoms – the stammering and copious sweating, the twitching in one leg. He couldn't sit still and he couldn't shut up long enough for simple common sense to permeate his thinking tackle. And when he began heatedly formulating a special TV project he had in mind to reunite this waste of time, food and breath of a singer and his geriatric combo, the agent had regarded him with the utmost apprehension, as though he was weighing up whether to call the men in white coats.

Yet what did this ignorant young pup know? He was only thirty-nine, a babe in the woods. He'd not even been conceived when the Unstable Boys and their glorious singer were putting a steel-toed booted dent into youth culture. So how could he even get a glimmer of what was happening here? History was about to be made.

Still, he knew that when he got back home and told the Boy that 'the big payday' he'd imagined their project netting them from a publisher's advance wouldn't be nearly as big as expected, his guest would be deeply disappointed. 'I'm not doing this to get a suntan,' he'd exclaimed during one tetchy interlude in their interview sessions. 'I'm pouring my guts out here to entertain and educate the masses. This stuff is worth millions. Make sure your agent man gets us the wedge we deserve.' But his man had just told him not to expect more than £50,000, which meant £25,000 for the Boy. A piddling sum by today's economic standards. He'd gladly forego his own 50 per cent though, so that the Boy could pocket fifty grand straight off the top. Maybe that would placate him.

He didn't want the Boy to become angry. That was imperative. Because when the Boy got angry and turned his ire in Michael's direction – it had happened on one or two occasions of late – he'd been left scared and scarred. The invective had been unsparing, the tone verging on the demonic. He'd felt humiliated, like a child given a good dressing down by a new stepfather. He still craved the Boy's company, mind you. Nothing changed on that score. The interviews were coming to an end soon. But Michael didn't want his subject to slip away yet; he'd become too embroiled in his day-to-day existence. How would he be able to tap into the vicarious thrill of reliving scenes from the golden age of rock 'n' roll without this silver-tongued fully qualified survivor to feed him the plot lines? And how else would he have access to those pills he was now taking daily? No, it would not be wise to alienate the man or sully his mood with sad tidings.

He'd soft-pedal the news by accentuating the positives. He'd set the telly idea in motion, having gone so far as to take the names of three producers who his agent felt might be up for it. And their mobile phone numbers of course. He'd call them each later without the aid of any go-between. The agent had stressed to him that the personal touch might aid in the project's acceptance.

Michael couldn't see why any of this trio of prospective collaborators wouldn't be smitten by the show's premise. The members of a much-loved rock act – long separated in a complicated labyrinth of personal differences – are coaxed into burying the hatchet, taking the stage and proving to their now white-haired baby-boomer peers and their offspring that old dogs can still effectively learn new tricks. It had all the right juicy elements. The drugs and sex would be candidly discussed and detailed when required. The human interest element meanwhile – the reunification factor – would hold the attention of the vast reservoir of mainstream viewers who'd otherwise be left lukewarm by the musical content.

The Boy had been in his bedroom when he re-entered the premises. Music – one of his old records – was blaring away upstairs. In due course he descended wearing only pyjama bottoms. His torso was naked and Michael could still see traces of the old muscle contour. But time had left its disfiguring imprint as well. The stomach was no longer flat. It had become strangely distended as though something oval-shaped and malignant had taken up residence in his gut.

He'd just taken a bath and seemed in an unexpectedly mellow frame of mind. Michael took this as a good omen. And the Boy was keen to hear about his encounter earlier that day with 'your secret agent man'. So Michael seized on the TV special idea, told him excitedly about the three producers he himself would be contacting to nudge the thing into fruition. He even held up the piece of paper he'd written their phone numbers on and waved it excitedly in the Boy's face. The Boy received the news without expression but a coldness crept back into his voice when he enquired about the advance for their book. Michael was trapped. He'd already decided to slip him his half. Surely that would be sufficient.

But evidently it wasn't. The Boy went all ferret-eyed when the potential sum was quoted. 'A lousy fifty grand,' he hissed. Michael waited for the full indoor fireworks to ignite but the

Boy just sat there in silence eyeing him with a look of, well, 'severe disappointment' would be the gentlest way of defining it. It seemed to last forever. Then he broke the silence with a bombshell of his own.

'Your wife was here. Today. Late this afternoon.'

'What . . .'

'You heard me. The missus – your better half – paid you a visit. Rang the doorbell repeatedly. I was preparing for my bath at the time. I won't beat about the bush – it was disruptive. Your visitors need to call in advance, quite frankly.'

'You're telling me Jane came here? Why? And what exactly happened?'

'I found some togs, went downstairs and answered the door. We ended up having a right old chinwag on the doorstep. I invited her in but she declined. Asked where you were, how you were – the usual drill. Then she asked who I was. I was a bit put out by that. My face is my passport, I told her. She didn't seem to see the funny side. So I mentioned our current work together. And the living arrangements, of course. Told her not to worry about you, that you were in rude health – all bright-eyed and bushy-tailed. Then she left.'

'Did she pass on any message?'

'Not that I recall. There was a fellow with her in the car they came in. Distinguished-looking but still full of vim and vigour. Full head of hair too. A dapper-looking gent. I saw no actual displays of physical intimacy pass between them but nonetheless sensed some kind of chemistry at play. Maybe I'm reading too much into something barely glimpsed but I'm also known for my clairvoyant powers. It's for you to make the next move.'

Jane had called around in person after months of not even responding to his countless phone calls, of ceasing all communication. The whole tabloid business and the presumed betrayal it was centred on had left her disgusted, he knew that much. It had been harsh for her too. He'd always recognised that.

But not nearly as harsh as it had been for him. He'd been set up. No major infidelity had transpired. And yet she'd reacted the way she did. No empathy, no acceptance, no forgiveness. Just a deafening silence, a look of rank disgust and a finger cocked towards the front door indicating he was no longer welcome in the premises he'd mostly paid for.

For months he'd yearned to re-establish some degree of contact with his wife and their offspring. But then his mind-set had shifted to new horizons. Life had presented him with a new road to navigate and a new shepherd to guide him on his way.

He knew he should at least call his wife back. But at the same time he was confused. So he did what came most naturally to him in that moment: he sought advice from the Boy. 'I suppose I should ring back,' he remarked plaintively. The Boy wrinkled up his face to indicate his dismissal of the idea. His short tête-à-tête with the woman in question had not been one in which his customary powers of seduction had prevailed. Unlike her soft old spouse, she was clearly no pushover. She could become troublesome and needed to be marginalised or – better yet – given the full heave-ho. So when Michael asked him, he already knew the answer he was going to give and how he was going to word it. But first he was just going to sit there, looking inscrutable and saying nothing. Enigmatic silences made for great theatre. Cult leaders favoured them too. Because when you finally speak, your disciples really listen.

'Jane, I'm really worried about Michael. I saw him today and he's . . . well, he seems to be falling apart, unravelling. He was babbling on – there's no other word to describe his exchanges – and making no sense at all on occasion. He's very pale-looking and agitated. Can't sit still. Frankly, I think he might be on . . . something.'

'Damien, are you saying Michael's on drugs?'

'Possibly. I've seen the symptoms before. Look, Jane, I wouldn't be talking to you like this if I wasn't genuinely alarmed. Something needs to be done. An intervention or something of that order.'

'I actually paid him a visit today. It was the first time I'd attempted to make contact with him since that awful scandal blew up. I don't know what compelled me. I didn't call in advance. I just turned up at his doorstep. Then the door opened and a strange man in a dressing gown appeared. He said Michael had gone out and would be back later. When I asked him who he was, he told me he was some kind of singer and that he and Michael were living together in the house while they collaborated on some "projects" – whatever that means. He invited me in but I declined. Frankly he gave me the creeps.

'Part of me keeps saying, "Well, Michael has made his bed. Now he can lie in it." But I also know how vulnerable he can be. And that creature he's got leeching off him seems to have got his hooks into his malleable nature all too easily.'

'Oh God, the singer. They call him "the Boy" apparently. I looked him up on Wikipedia. He was something to behold in his day, but that day came and went fifty years ago. The fellow's a nasty piece of work by all accounts and short-changed a lot of people in the music industry on his way to the bottom. Recently resurfaced as the voice of that advert for mobile phones.'

'The one for Technokratix? I've actually heard that – six months ago it was inescapable. But that wasn't a new song. It was as old as the hills.'

'Precisely. Unfortunately your husband in his current befuddled condition has mistaken this has-been for some kind of saviour. God knows why. Only a five-star psychiatrist could give you a plausible explanation for the attraction. But the fact remains, I sense Michael is in some sort of imminent danger. If the drugs I'm ninety-nine per cent sure he's taking don't short-circuit his nervous system, that charlatan he's giving food and shelter to will almost certainly be hard at work plotting to relieve him of as much of his fortune as he can get away with. Something ought to be done.'

'What do you suggest? You mentioned something about an intervention. How exactly would that be organised? I'm completely at a loss as to know how to react to all this. I've never been faced with a situation like it before.

'At the same time ... have you ever heard the term "compassion fatigue", Damien? Have you ever woken up one day only to discover that the person you love has started changing into someone else, someone you don't actually like any more? Our marriage began breaking down a long time ago. He became too susceptible to the fools and flatterers stroking his ego. We were both getting on each other's nerves long before the "tabloid betrayal". Then I had to withstand the indignity of being portrayed as the clueless little wife at home darning socks while her husband was out groping some bimbo. I was the injured party, but Michael just didn't get it. From his standpoint he was the victim. He just blindly expected me to provide support, to be sympathetic.

'It was then that I started feeling contempt for him. I banned him from the house because I knew something was well and truly broken between us and that nothing in the world could help put the pieces back in place.

'The point is – this is still a little too raw for me. So he's in trouble? Fallen into bad company? Well, a part of him has to recognise that he chose that bad company before any changes can be made. And he needs to come to that realisation himself. Intervention? I don't know.'

'It can work, you know. Those Narcotics Anonymous organisations swear by them. Many, many lives have been saved.'

'This is too much drama for me, Damien. You talk about Michael like he's a junkie at death's door being preyed upon by some satanic imp. Are you sure that your concern for him isn't just being fuelled by his current inability to give you another fat payday?'

'That's a low blow, Jane. I've always had Michael's best interests at heart. You know that.'

'I do, I do. Sorry – look, let me reflect on this. It's all so bizarre I need to step back. But I'm not going back to that house. Not while that odious little man is on the premises. If Michael calls me, I'll pick up. But he needs to make the next move. And he needs to have a clear head and a full tank of contrition in his heart.'

Michael sat there expectantly as the Boy stayed silent for . . . Two minutes? Three minutes? Hard to say. Time was standing still in the room. A judgement was about to be handed down. He felt his heartbeat start to slacken. That slow-you-down pill he'd taken some fifteen minutes before was starting to work. Jane was there in his thoughts somewhere but things were beginning to get cloudy and a bit indistinct. Thank Christ the Boy was there to point the way. Speak – o wise one.

'I've given this some thought,' he finally declared somewhat pompously. 'And it's my considered opinion that you should give your missus the swerve at least for the foreseeable future. Why rake over dying embers? You're a free man now but you don't see the opportunities. You're like certain criminal acquaintances of mine who keep doubling back into the old penal system because they can't deal with being out in the real world.'

Michael interjected plaintively. 'Not even a phone call? I mean, she was here . . .'

'I'm old school, Mike. Bear that in mind. Almost always been a single man. Women? They're a lovely distraction but they can fence a man in and slacken his stride. Best not get over-involved. "Taste the milk but don't buy the cow." That's my philosophy. Women respect an independent man more. "Treat 'em mean. Keep 'em keen." There's some food for thought for you.'

'So you're saying don't call . . .?'

'Precisely. Let it drift from your mind. You look like you're well on the way already. You love those pills, don't you? Michael? Message understood?'

Michael grunted and then slumped back on the couch he now used as his bed. The Boy stood over him, whispering ever so softly.

'Out like a light! Oh, you're making this so easy for me. So easy. Just lie there in your stupor and watch me go to work on you, my son. You think I'm Little Bo Peep, don't you? Wrong. I'm the big bad wolf come to blow your house down.'

It was all falling into place like a charm. This new mark was like wet clay in a potter's hands. That big elusive score – he could smell it again. It was right under his nose. Time to step things up, move to stage two. The ruckus had already been brought. The Boy was a virus on two spindly legs. The house was already contaminated. By the time he'd finished with it, it would most likely need to be condemned.

CHAPTER 12

It was an overcast Saturday night and the trio of Ral, Magda and Pieter were together in Ral's apartment.

In a matter of days, they'd gravitated towards each other instinctively and become a social threesome. It was an odd mixture of temperaments: Magda was blunt and brazen, Pieter was sweet-natured and easily cowed, and Ral was wary-eyed. Yet together they seemed to complete each other.

Pieter had finally realised his impossible dream. Ever since he'd conversed with Ral in his shop, he'd been dying to show him his collection of old Unstable Boys live appearances from 1960s TV shows now long forgotten. Two years earlier, he'd even edited together and then uploaded to YouTube an hour-plus compilation of the vintage footage; it had already netted over 300,000 views. He was proud of his video homage but nervous about cajoling his new friend into watching the often grainy black and white videos of his younger self, as Ral has made it crystal clear from the outset of their relationship that he felt an overwhelming compulsion to not let his past interfere with his present state of fragile equilibrium.

Pieter had respected that but Magda, as soon as she'd heard him mention that such footage existed and was easy to obtain via the internet, had demanded that it be broadcast at the earliest opportunity on any available computer.

At first, Ral had bridled at the suggestion. 'Not on my watch,' he'd remarked in a hushed tone. 'Oh, listen to the sensitive artist!' Magda – bolshy as ever – had retorted. She liked to push his buttons. Normally someone like that would not have lasted long in his company. But a different dynamic was developing here. Decades earlier, he'd formed his own view of the opposite sex. There were the quiet girls, the English roses, supportive and empathy-ridden, homemakers. And then there were the wild girls. Free with their opinions. Always daring their consorts to throw caution to the wind. Prone to using their sexuality as a lethal weapon.

A rhythm and blues singer called Luther Hancock had once told Ral, 'You take up with a woman like that, think you can change her, sand down those rough edges – you're only foolin' yourself. You can't change people. Devil women. Triflin' Janes. Call 'em what you want. But don't even let 'em near your heartstrings. Let 'em run wild instead. That's where they belong – out in the wild, scratching on the shutters.'

'Magda, has anyone ever called you a devil woman?' He asked her clear out of the blue with Hancock's past pronouncement still in mind. He realised it sounded strange as soon as it had escaped his lips, but he was already quite stoned from just two bong hits.

Magda didn't seem offended. At first. 'I've been called worse than that. Men call women devils when they can't control them. What you perceive as evil is often just a woman exercising her will to act on her impulses. Men try to trap them into fulfilling the role of the dutiful decorative spouse but obviously that's not going to happen and they drift off to some new liaison, leaving their exes broken and bewildered, babbling on about the devilishness of womankind. But who's the real devil here? The possessive, deluded man or the free-spirited woman?'

Both Ral and Pieter remained silent. Magda meanwhile was just gathering steam. She positioned her body at a confrontational angle to Ral.

'You have a nerve asking me that question. I first heard about devils and angels as a child. Fairy tales. Bedtime stories. Then out there in the big bad world I met my fair share. More devils than angels, unfortunately. But such is life – or more precisely, my life. The point is, I know the difference. Devils defile. Angels illuminate and spread kindness. Now, do you know the difference?

'You have shown me kindness and I have shown it back to you in return. How can you accuse me of being a devil woman?'

'I . . . I . . . oh God, you're right. It was a very wrong thing to say. I apologise. Sincerely. The reefer sometimes makes me say things that should really just have stayed in my head.'

'You need a slap from time to time. You're scared of being challenged – scared period. I've known your like. You start out riding some big wave and then that wave comes splashing down and you're left shipwrecked. So you go deeper and deeper into your solitary space hoping to become invisible and to even obliterate your own past from memory. I can sympathise with your sorrow but the lifestyle you've chosen is . . . well, limiting is a gentle way of putting it.

'Isn't it time to come up for air ? We're going to watch Pieter's footage of you and your workmates back in your heyday and you're going to stay right here and absorb it all with us. Some commentary from time to time on your part might also prove helpful. But don't feel like you're being pressured. Just bear in mind that if you try to leave the room during the thing, I might well feel tempted to break either one or both of your legs. Is that devilish enough for you?'

Magda was grinning triumphantly. Ral should have at least bristled but he didn't. He simply acquiesced. That was Magda's thing. She offered you no choice. Normally such behaviour would have driven him to distraction.

'Pushy women are the bane of the earth,' his father had often said to him as a child but maybe that was what he needed – a push. In the right direction, of course. But which direction was that? No matter. Just as long as it meant he could vacate the gloomy mindscape he'd been sleepwalking through for what felt like an eternity.

So Pieter switched on the computer in Ral's apartment and tapped a few keys, dimming the lights while doing so. Ral felt butterflies fluttering around in his stomach and prepared himself mentally for what was to follow. The screen came alive with moving images accompanied by loud music coming from the speakers on either side.

The first images were in black and white and so washed out it made everyone look like ghosts – which in a sense they were. A young man and woman were compering a show called *Beat Beat Beat*. A bland-looking pair, they bantered with each other in an indecipherable foreign language for some thirty seconds before introducing the Unstable Boys, who were on some sort of raised platform behind them.

The music began – it was 'Dark Waters', their first big hit – but it quickly became apparent the group were miming, not playing live and had yet to master the dubious craft of pretend music-making. The Boy threw some sullen poses though and the cameraman wisely kept focusing on him throughout the performance. The drummer managed to snag a single three-second close-up while the bassist hovered ineffectually, tossing his hair out of his eyes from time to time. Ral was initially stunned to see himself at such a young age. His young image was barely recognisable to him now. He gawped at his two or three close-ups and tried to re-enter the mind of the youth whose face he once possessed. It was no easy task.

What had been going on behind that self-consciously moody expression he'd adopted? He tried to delve back into the moment but came up empty-handed. He couldn't remember the show itself – some foreign thing probably slotted in during an already packed work day – and he couldn't place himself in the skin of the man on the screen before him. It was a somewhat desolate feeling but he was used to those and so he didn't flinch.

Magda, meanwhile, was voicing opinions with her usual unbridled gusto. 'Ah, some pretty young boys for me to gaze upon wistfully. This won't be a wasted evening. Look at you! Not bad, not bad.' Ral couldn't help himself smiling. Maybe that's why he was attracted to her company. She bullied him out of his inertia.

Pieter – in his element – was becoming increasingly excitable as the footage rolled on, spluttering out arcane details about the various performances he'd collected and then edited together. Many were mime jobs – *Top of the Pops*, *Beat Club* – but a few captured the group playing live.

One twelve-minute segment – again in black and white with a timecode running under the images – consisted of a single camera operator and soundman chronicling part of a show at London's Marquee Club sometime in early 1967.

To call it 'raw footage' would be charitable. The cameraman was perilously poised between the small stage and a rabid audience and was constantly being jostled so the images had a generally hectic herky-jerky quality to them. At one point it looked like something – a tambourine or a fist? – struck the cameraman and rendered his equipment inoperable for several seconds before refocusing and re-joining the fray. In short, it wasn't easy on the eye and the live soundtrack accompanying it sounded like it was mixed in a wind tunnel. And yet the men who suffered to capture this vintage telly segment (for a short-lived 1960s BBC Two series called *Youth on the Move*) did not do so in vain, because their chaotic 'report' managed to capture something essential about the Unstable Boys. A moment in time was frozen and then spat back out for future generations to chew on.

Miming in a studio, the group tended to look constrained, a bit constipated. Live on stage, though, their core appeal and personal magnetism came alive in no uncertain terms. A Clark Kent to Superman transformation evidently took place. The Boy was particularly impressive in this footage, endlessly goading the front rows while managing to sidestep any violent episodes by elegantly waltzing away just as the trouble he'd incited was about to kick off.

In another scene one audience member – a young man probably still in his teens – clambers onstage and briefly kneels before the guitar player, Mick Winthrop, holding his hands up in prayer before being roughly tossed back into the crowd by a roadie. Winthrop looks completely bewildered by the deification before laughing it off and playing on with appropriate abandon.

It was the season when electric guitar virtuosos were being elevated to the status of holy men. 'Clapton is God' was a common piece of graffiti around London. But Mick Winthrop was neither Clapton nor the Almighty. He was a two-legged work in progress: 'snaggle-toothed Mick' from Ipswich with his jovial air, his encyclopaedic knowledge of old blues guitar licks and his openhearted gullibility. Seeing him in his element – bending strings, fingers all over the fretboard, his gleeful face awash with goonish joy – Ral felt a wounding nostalgia seep into him. Mick would have been twenty when the film was shot. Eighteen months later, he'd be dead. Car accident. Nothing salacious or sordid. Just tragedy in its starkest, most blistering form. A promising young talent snuffed out by a drunk driver. No rhyme or reason to any of it.

When sweet-natured youths die young they leave behind memories that tend to keep pulling at the heartstrings of those survivors they left behind. They never grew old and mean and so shine on brightly within us. Ral felt his eyes moisten. He blinked away the tears before they ran and focused on the footage instead. He'd never seen any of it before – ever. In the late 1960s he'd not owned a television. He had no use for one because he had no time to waste sofa-surfing in front of such a contraption. 'Where it's at' was out there in the wild world, not closeted away in front of a box of moving sound-abetted images.

It was at this point that the fuzzy footage they'd been watching suddenly morphed from grainy black and white to garish colour. It was early 1968 and the Unstable Boys were on *The Mike Douglas Show*, a late-night US talk show with an obligatory music act. Ral's memory was jolted into action when he saw the set dressing they were performing around – a tsunami of balloons – and the recollections started dripping down.

They'd got the gig – a very prestigious slot guaranteeing a wide demographic of viewers across America – only because Jefferson Airplane had pulled out at the last minute. Douglas wanted to talk about the psychedelic revolution gripping young America and had invited an odd collection of seasoned celebs to do just that: sultry singer Eartha Kitt, Dan Blocker who'd played one of actor Lorne Greene's sons on *Bonanza* and Jewish stand-up comic Shecky Greene. After their perfunctory live presentation – replete with an overreliance on strobe lights – Douglas calls Ral and the Boy over to join his other guests on the couch. A debate of sorts quickly ensues on the subject of 'this hippie thing' and young people returning to the tribal ways of times long past.

'Do you guys see yourselves as a tribe?' Douglas suddenly asks the Boy who looks unnerved by the enquiry even while endeavouring to maintain a sulky calm throughout the exchange.

'Listen, mate, we're not redskins. Check out our equipment. You won't find any tomahawks. Or firewater. We're from England. We live in houses not wigwams.'

Eartha Kitt then rounded on the Boy for his 'insulting' comments regarding Native Americans and all hell broke loose from that moment until its merciful termination. Dan Blocker threatened to punch them both out on camera. The Boy sputtered back a few glib phrases that fell flat. Important life lesson: never cross swords verbally with Eartha Kitt. Ral was clearly on some sort of drug that had short-circuited his cerebral faculties. Whenever the Boy and Ral spoke they came off as arrogant popinjays – decorative but spineless.

'We had the Righteous Brothers a few weeks back – a wonderful act. True professionals,' Douglas remarked at the segment's end. 'And now we've got you two limeys – the Self-Righteous Brothers.'

It got the biggest laugh of the night. Living through this the first time had been traumatic enough. Revisiting it again as a mute observer was equally jarring. Ral was only slightly mollified by the fact that his hair had looked really good and his cheekbones super prominent. It was odd: back in the day he'd rated himself as a musician but lacked confidence in his looks. Now what he was watching was tempting him to take the opposite view. He'd been an erratic guitar player but a good-looking kid. He preferred it when it had been the other way around.

The trip down memory lane ended with a clip from another vintage US programme, *Playboy After Dark*, the group's final telly appearance before the big split at decade's end.

It started with the show's host, Hugh Hefner, his then-girlfriend Barbi Benton and Bill Cosby, together in a room full of gyrating, voluptuous-looking women and a few males throwing 'funky' poses, talking earnestly about the sexual revolution. The subject quickly changes to politics. Hef asks Cosby who he'll vote for in some upcoming election. The 'Cos' retorts with a line about supporting anyone who can give America a stable economy. It's a setup for Hef to riff back, 'Well Bill, you'd better not go near a ballot box while this next act are in the room. Ladies and gentlemen, put your hands together for England's very own Unstable Boys.'

The group play two songs live. Ral remembered the affair as something of a fiasco. Mick had just died but there was a US tour booked and a new album to promote so their manager somehow persuaded them to employ one of his other clients – a Mexican blues guitarist called Ace Valdez (real name Hector) – to fill in for the dead guy. There were frequent drum defections – far too many tub-thumpers either leaving or collapsing mid-tour. Ral didn't even recognise the dapper-looking sticksman playing with them on this Hefner slot and had to ask Pieter who it was (the answer: Matt Flookes from Slough, formerly of beat combo the Magnificent Socks; apparently he lasted all of three shows). Only he, the Boy and the bass player remained from the group's initial incarnation and you could hear the wheels coming off the wagon. Too many outside cooks spoiling the broth. The music was up-tempo and feisty but its execution was aimless and muddle-headed.

The show's party decor promoted a happy-go-lucky ambience but the group played as though they'd been booked to perform at a wake. No matter: the cameras lingered lasciviously on the lithesome lovelies and their consorts bumping and grinding instead. And then it ended.

Magda was the first to speak. 'I wonder how many of those dancing girls got drugged and raped by Bill Cosby that night?' she said. 'A thousand curses on him and Hefner's sexual revolution.' Her brow was deeply furrowed and it looked like she was about to erupt into another bout of spleen venting. But then her facial expression softened and she turned to Ral: 'But you guys were good. You classed the place up. The Playboy Mansion? More like Pimper's Central. Was it cathartic for you?'

'Watching all that clutter? Hard to say. I'm still processing it.'

'That woman on the talk show with the voice of a sexy snake . . .'

'Her name was Eartha Kitt.'

'She was deadly.'

'You needn't remind me. I still bear the scars.'

'She really did a number on you two. Cut your singer a new asshole.'

'She did indeed. Mind you, he deserved it. Unfortunately I was sat next to him and got tarred with the same brush. Actually I was more worried about the *Bonanza* guy. He had serious anger issues and was built with all the heft of a white hillbilly Sonny Liston. One of the technicians told us he'd broken a toilet seat in the green room just prior to the transmission.

'Most of the TV cowboys I met had already been put out to pasture by the powers-that-were. Jay Silverheels who played Tonto in *The Lone Ranger* – met him at a party in Hollywood. I even smoked reefer one time at another Hollywood soiree with the little Oriental fellow who played Hop Sing, the wagon train cook in *Rawhide*.

'Wooo, get you, Mister Big Shot!' Magda interjected.

'Yes, well I wouldn't expect you to grasp the significance of these strange encounters. At the age of twelve I would watch these same men every week punching cows when not punching out bad guys and occasionally each other and I would be transported to another more welcoming world. Less than ten years later, I suddenly found myself actually rubbing shoulders and chewing the fat with these same legends. The difference being – they were no longer characters, their roles were drying up, the money was running low and a divorce was pending. And – as it was the late 1960s – they were drinking and drugging too much.

'Yet despite all those factors, most of them still managed to behave like gentlemen. Some of my rock brethren would have done well to cultivate those same qualities when their careers started losing momentum. My former singer springs to mind here.'

'Your singer?' Magda butted in. 'What's the story there? He definitely had something . . .'

'Several STDs, certainly. You can count on that . . .'

'I'm referring to his presence, smart ass. You others just stand there striking moody poses and looking cute but he gets right into the camera's lens and brands his image into the audience's retinas. A touch of the Jim Morrisons about him. Jim Morrison's my hero, by the way.'

'I only met Jim Morrison once,' Ral spoke up. Magda's eyes sparkled at the revelation. 'He and our singer had socialised when we played in Los Angeles but their relationship had been brief and ended badly for some reason. On the surface Morrison and the Boy had things in common. They were singers and they were rabble-rousers. They had a gift for feeding off chaos. They could command the attention of all who beheld them. They had an uncanny grasp of self-projection. But the Boy in reality was a superficial chancer who just happened to excel at loose cannon theatrics. Morrison was a more complicated individual, more a man of substance.

'A raging alcoholic, first and foremost. I encountered him during his last year of still living in Los Angeles, not long before he moved to Paris. I was staying in an apartment owned by our group's former publicist in an alleyway directly off the Sunset Strip. It was after midnight and we were quietly smoking pot and listening to a Beatles album when suddenly there was this ugly noise outside – a sort of simultaneous clanking and rattling underscored by the sound of boots scraping along a pavement.

'That's when the publicist – a woman named Pat, as I recall – looked distinctly alarmed and stated in an urgent half whisper, "Oh my God, everybody, it's Jim Morrison. Turn out the lights. Turn down the music. Pretend you're not here. And don't even think of answering the door."

'The figure outside began beating on the door frame and shouting like a wounded beast. After two minutes of having her door hinges placed under heavy assault, she accepted the inevitable and opened it.

'Morrison shambled into the room in a state of considerable agitation. His first words to us were "You know you're all a bunch of fucking slaves." That was his mantra when paralytic apparently. Everyone in that room – myself included – was unnerved by him. He was a big man. Big and ferociously drunk.

'He kept shouting about how we all needed to listen to some blues, that blues music was the only real music. He staggered over to the record player, ripped the Beatles album off the turntable and threw it against a wall. Then he rifled through the other records piled around the sound system until he'd located an Elmore James compilation. He put it on, scratching the record to bits in the process. Then he sprawled out on a beanbag and sang along while continuing to drink copiously. "You're all a bunch of slaves," he'd say over and over again. Then he stood up, opened his flies and urinated on the carpet.'

'Wow!' A slack-jawed Pieter remarked, clearly taken with the reminiscence.

Magda's brow was once again furrowed.

'All humans are flawed. You doubtless met him on a bad night.'

Ral then added: 'I remember in 1967 he was the golden prince of acid rock, the leather-clad Adonis, the young lord of misrule. His group were number one in the charts and the world was his oyster. But mainstream success disagreed with him. He could have been Elvis, he could have been Steve McQueen, he could have been Clint Eastwood. But he didn't have the ambition or the self-discipline to make that kind of career leap. On the contrary, he was lazy and strangely resentful of having his freewheeling lifestyle regimented by the responsibilities that come with a successful act.

'Being famous quickly bored him. And touring was getting more and more draining and inconvenient. At a certain point musicians who are alcoholics and drug addicts face the dilemma: do I honour my commitments and turn up to play the gig or do I stay sprawled in bed and sleep off my hang-over? He made his choice. He was better suited to a life as a barroom philosopher. He wasn't Elvis, he was Charles Bukowski.'

Pieter was now frantically pressing keys on his computer. In due course the music of the Doors blasted out of the speakers alongside footage of a live concert replete with Morrison in full deranged flow, throwing himself down on the stage and mimicking an epileptic seizure in order to maximise the mayhem coursing through the audience. Ral found the video oddly compelling to watch but bristled inwardly at the sound of the music because it was so much better than his own group's output from the same era.

In the fifteen minute film, Morrison morphed through the stages of his astonishing physical decline. One second he was lean and leopard-like, the next bearded and bloated. Five years had been all it had taken to set that transformation in motion. At the time, five years had felt as brief as the blink of an eye.

Meanwhile Pieter and Magda were mourning Morrison's passing by making toasts with shots of vodka mixed in with the bong hits. 'And this is for all the doomed young poets . . .' Ral blanched when he heard them jabbering away. He could stand no more.

'Your doomed soul rebels! Do you ever wonder if you'd actually have liked them had you crossed paths with them? You portray them as over-sensitive victims but they were just as often ruthless, manipulative, self-interested people bereft of even a shred of empathy. Human beings are complicated – that's the only crumb of wisdom I've managed to come up with in my sixty-plus years on this planet. Not a startlingly original thought, I'm well aware. But there it is. Your man said it himself: people are strange. And performers are a breed unto themselves in the strange department.'

Pieter protested that Morrison was a shaman and cultural guerrilla but Ral quickly cut him off. 'Your mouth is writing cheques that your brain can't cash, Pieter. Tell me this – your shaman, your over-the-line stepper, your chaos bringer – what differentiates that individual from your common or garden sociopath?'

'One breaks taboos, the other breaks whatever they can get their hands on, perhaps?'

'Touché, my clog-wearing compadre. You make a moot point there. But – from my increasingly decrepit perspective – it's gotten harder and harder to tell the two apart.

'Seeing my old singer in all his sneering splendour again reminded me of all the most tainted aspects of rock worship, the way fans mindlessly venerate the most shallow people and perceive a depth and dignity in their characters that simply doesn't exist in real life. The idea of rock – for those who've never performed it onstage – is all about partaking in this mighty rapture of big amplifiers, loud guitars and audience adulation. The reality is having to help move a bulky amplifier or keyboard up three flights of narrow stairs on a rainy afternoon. One perspective is a glorious illusion. The other warns that bad back problems will probably start manifesting themselves when you hit your early thirties. But that's reality for you. Contrary. Mundane. Unromantic.'

'What about the freedom, though?' Pieter piped up earnestly.

'But is it freedom they're advertising or the fever dream of a life lived without consequences? A man works in a bank. One day he cracks up and smashes his computer with all its files to buggery on his desk in front of the customers waiting in line at the till: that man will almost certainly be sacked for his behaviour. Another man plays guitar in a rock band. One night he smashes up his equipment in front of a paying public. He gets a standing ovation instead. See the disconnect?

'It's an act, the selling of a fantasy. Actions spark consequences you inevitably can't escape. Rock mostly wants to hoodwink you into believing you can sidestep calamity boomeranging back at you, that we're here to let the good times roll, live for the moment and not give a tinker's cuss about the consequences. But we all know in our hearts it's not like that.'

Pieter countered with a line he claimed he'd read somewhere, about how we're all flawed entities trapped in a sad beautiful world; but if one focused on the beauty the sadness could be contained. It had a nice ring to it and both Ral and Magda complimented him on the soothing effect his words had suddenly instilled in the room.

In jubilant spirits – and having succeeded in rewiring Ral to his past exploits – Pieter recognised it was an ideal time to take his leave and return to his psychedelic lair. At first it was difficult. The bong hits hadn't mixed so well with the vodka and he was unsteady on his feet, tumbling over the edge of a sofa on his way to the front door. Ral helped him back up, dusted him down and stood at the entrance, guiding the way for his comrade's stumble to the elevator. Three minutes later he could see him out on the street shuffling along. The night air looked to be having a restorative impact.

He ambled back into his flat. Magda was very stoned. Sometimes this became a problem. When highly intoxicated her moods could turn erratic. But tonight she was serenity personified. Kittenish even. And – for the first time in their relatively brief relationship – borderline flirtatious.

'I feel so comfortable right now. I feel weightless. Like a feather. Please let me stay here with you tonight. I just want to float. I'm not looking for a lover. But there is something about you that I crave. Your companionship above all. Two lonely people together. The damage we carry within us dovetails together somehow. I can't explain it. I just let it happen.' And then she was gone.

Ral stared down at her tenderly as she lay spread out on the sofa. She was deep asleep now. The hard contours of her face had relaxed and made her look years younger. She was a beautiful woman with a beautiful body. Any other heterosexual man in his position would have felt some form of libido rush. But Ral's thoughts were elsewhere. He emptied the ashtray, turned out the main light and sat there in the darkness. Another woman was calling to him. Another voice and face were invading him anew.

Cathy Gates had been a professional dancer before becoming Catherine Coombes, Ral's wife. She was part of a trio of gyrating girls professionally known as the Dolly Birds – a downscale Pan's People – who had performed their come-hither dance routines on pop-based TV shows throughout Europe. Ral had been wincing at the sight of his old group miming on a German broadcast from the late 1960s when there she suddenly was with her big kohl-drenched eyes and trim form throwing her limbs around in strict time with her two colleagues to the Unstable Boys' backing track.

The close-up lasted only a second but it left him transfixed. She looked so young and so unspoiled. He scoured through his memory – was this shabby-looking TV soundstage the location of their first actual meeting? Had it all begun there? Probably not. He had a detailed recollection of their first significant conversation in a London nightclub, the Bag O'Nails, the first all-important meeting of minds. And spirits. Cathy was a spirited girl. They would dance together and the dance floor would clear to afford her the space to throw her loony shapes and leggy dropkicks.

When had she stopped dancing? After she hit the hippie trail? Hard to say. Something had changed within her very gradually. For him, it was like watching a light slowly getting dimmer. Yet in that sliver of footage her young face became alive again inside his mind. He felt that sweet summer breeze rustle around his age-weary limbs once more. His lips were poised to whisper a lover's prayer. Then that pure, dear image was involuntarily replaced in his mind by one from the last time he had seen her, when he had flinched. Like Orpheus in the underworld. What was his ghost wife's name again? Penelope? Eurydice? His knowledge of Greek mythology was regrettably limited, he concluded. As was his understanding of womankind.

He looked again at Magda. She was semi-comatose. A faint wheezing sound was issuing from her mouth. It wasn't a snore. It sounded more like apnoea. He checked to see she was breathing properly before moving away to the sanctuary of his bedroom.

The ashtray on the bedside table contained a half-smoked joint which he lit up and inhaled from until it was nothing more than a remnant of hot cardboard between his two fingers. As he lay on the bed anticipating slumber, he felt his heartbeat fluctuating at a slow-fast-slow-fast clip that alarmed him. He felt his body temperature suddenly dipping. There was discomfort in his chest cavity. For thirty arduous seconds it felt like the devil was driving a bullet train through his inner torso. Then the tremors subsided. Once his heartbeat had levelled out again, his head bent back into the pillow and sleep swooped down.

But those tremors were a reminder of something that was already shadowing him. Before he'd left the UK, Ral had been to his doctor's surgery for an annual check-up. He'd mostly enjoyed sound physical health and so wasn't fully prepared for the outcome of the measurement of his heart rate: 200 beats per minute. The speed of a bad techno record. The doc called it 'arrhythmia', said it could prove fatal if not checked. He strongly advised a hospital procedure involving an electric current being fired directly into the heart valve in order to stabilise its erratic beating. And he prescribed some medication that he urged him to consume daily while warning him that improper use could result in sudden death.

So this was going to be the next challenge, he understood. I've buried my son. I've institutionalised my wife. Now I've got to adjust to my own heartbeat revolting against me. Why bother? The electric shock procedure boasted only a fifty–fifty success rate and gave him the chills whenever he imagined it. The pills seemed to agitate his condition rather than placate it.

So when he'd arrived in Holland, he'd pretty much jettisoned his heart-scare concerns. His doctor had issued a severe reprimand, told him he was courting disaster – a stroke perhaps – by ignoring his health issues. Ral had promised he'd find a Dutch physician but had so far failed to do so.

Instead he'd attempted to heal himself. His long daily walks around Amsterdam were one way of making his heart more resilient. He'd made inroads into mastering yoga too. In the months he'd been resident here, he'd experienced no 'episodes'. But now he was living a less healthy existence. All that pot smoke corrupting his lungs and tweaking up his blood supply was not going to be sending his poor old heart any restorative valentines.

Some would say that Ral Coombes was committing slow suicide by wilfully ignoring such primal health issues. He might even have agreed. It was between him and God now. You've wiped out my loved ones. Now it's my turn to feel the reaper's blade against my neck bone. So bring it on. Do your worst.

But he only entertained thoughts that bleak in his lowest moments. For now, he was in a better place, the land of dreams. His wife might even be there in all her youthful splendour. Somewhere within him his heart was already beating in anticipation. Like a ticking time bomb.

CHAPTER 13

The little digital clock next to the upstairs bathroom mirror read 6.33 a.m. Dawn had yet to break and all was silent in the house, save for the distant snoring of his comatose host downstairs. The Boy sat naked on the toilet and waited for nature to pay its call. These were the worst moments of the day for him because they were the ones that told him flatly that he was getting older and progressively more enfeebled. Constipation – he'd never given it a second thought back in the day. Bowels like pistons.

He'd read somewhere that people generally spend between twenty to forty minutes a day toiling in the shitter. What were they doing in there? He'd simply step into the cubicle, drop his slacks, sit down – boom! Get back up and wipe his bum. Back out the door. In total, no more than three minutes flat. If they'd actually timed him, the results would have probably made the *Guinness Book of World Records*.

Nowadays, though, the process had become a lot more time-consuming. He didn't like squatting there with his face all scrunched up, huffing, puffing and straining like some old grumpus. It was undignified. And it put a nasty strain on his heart. Images of fat Elvis Presley keeling over inevitably surfaced. If the King himself could be struck down by this same depressing condition, then he needed to be doubly prudent about not getting too 'backed up' himself.

Eighty per cent of it was diet. He'd read that somewhere too. More likely, been told it. He didn't read much. He was currently eating a lot of cheese. Apparently it can clog up the colon and cause blockages. He'd have to change his eating habits. Easier said than done, mind you. Prune juice, sushi and vegetarian cuisine? He'd rather eat wallpaper. That healthy stuff was for nibblers. He wasn't a nibbler. He was a devourer.

Still no movement down below. All quiet in the hole. It was disconcerting. He'd eaten a big feast the day before and had expected its evacuation to be a textbook undertaking. But his intestines seemed to be on strike. All that good food was now lodged inside him, hardening by the second and proving stubbornly unreceptive to the idea of moving on out. He needed a good purging.

But how could he relax his innards sufficiently to effect the expulsion? His stomach was as swollen as a woman's belly five months into pregnancy. Bad diet was a source of his sorrow, yes – but not *the* source.

It was that prick downstairs, the feckless fuck, the ghost writer. A measly 50K? Who did he think he was dancing with? Freddie and the fucking Dreamers? The bare-faced cheek of it. Any one of his anecdotes could effortlessly outrank all the fictional serial-killing scenarios he and his overrated kind were getting rich off. His tales were real. Theirs were mickey-mouse macabre fantasy twaddle. The public would know the difference. They were ready for his book, ready to lose themselves in his salty sagas about ducking and diving his way into global infamy. They just didn't know it yet.

It was necessary to locate a true visionary in the world of publishing, someone who could see the real potential of his memoir, pay its author accordingly and then feed it out to the lucky masses. He'd thought Martindale was a big wheel in that world, someone who could lead him to that elusive pot of gold at the end of the rainbow. He'd trusted him, even befriended him – in his own withholding way. But the man turned out to be like that Otis Redding song 'Mr Pitiful'. He should have tumbled that he was shacking up with a rank tosser when he'd confessed that his outed infidelity hadn't even involved penetrative sex. The guy was a born patsy who'd somehow gotten lucky and gotten rich and successful off feeding a formula. He wasn't just asking to be taken to the cleaners: he was begging. 'Drain me,' his eyes kept pleading at the Boy.

So be it. A measly 50K? You are taking the piss, Mr Martindale. And piss-takers are persona non grata in my manor. Liberty takers. Slippery customers. I will have my revenge on you all.

As he felt his blood pressure rise, something loosened up in his sphincter. He gritted his teeth and took a deep breath. Two difficult minutes later, he heard the resounding splash. One mission accomplished. He wiped himself clean and went to put some clothes on.

He tippy-toed downstairs and while Michael Martindale slept on, rifled through his jacket and coat until he'd located his wallet. The thing was literally bursting with different credit cards and he would have swiped one in a second if he'd known the pin. Instead, he took some loose cash – two twenty-pound notes, three tens and a bunch of coins. That would suffice to get him where he needed to go in taxi fare and back again.

A new caper was about to be unveiled. But first the Boy needed co-conspirators well versed in the art of entrapment. He knew just where to find them too. An hour later, he'd cabbed it over to Johnny Two Livers' place. His old mucker had answered the door with difficulty, prompting the Boy to comment on his predicament as they walked to the living room.

'Jesus Christ, John. What's ailing you, old son? You look like a stale pasty. Where's the two-legged tower of strength I used to pal around with? Over in Rotherhithe they used to call you "Hercules Unchained". Or "Herc" for short. Remember?'

'Memories are all I've got now, mate. There's the telly too, I suppose. A few cans of lager of an evening. It's the hernia what done it, what clipped my wings, so to speak. I'm not the man I once was. Sorry to disappoint you but that's just how it goes.'

'It hurts my heart to hear those words, John. We had some times, you and I. Didn't we? But – to be perfectly frank – it was young Darren I was hoping to bump into. He and I need to discuss a business venture I've got lined up.'

Johnny Two Livers started to shout his son's name but the youth was already in the living room – he walked stealthily: maybe it was the trainers he wore – and was regarding both of them with a stony glare.

'I heard the words "business venture" in conjunction with my name just now,' he hissed at the Boy. 'Perhaps you can be more specific.'

'Indeed I can. And will. Maybe some privacy would further aid our dialogue.'

'Dad, why don't you go to the toilet?'

'I'm not feeling the urge, son.'

'Go there anyway. You never know, something might leak out. Your old mucker here needs to unburden himself to me on a matter that I'm guessing may well involve the kind of criminal hanky-panky that you'd be better off not partaking in.'

'It's cold in there.'

'So put on a scarf and wear some fucking mittens.'

John shuffled out of the room balefully. Just moving one leg in front of the other appeared to be sending a jolting pain up into his lumbar region. When he'd receded out of earshot, Darren pointed a finger at the Boy and began laying down some ground rules.

'Number one: whatever this is, the old man doesn't get involved on any level. He stays out of it altogether and if you try to involve him, we'll be having harsh words, you and I. He's useless to you now anyway. Look at him.'

'You don't show much respect for your father, do you?'

'And you do? Pull the other one, grandad. You'd throw him to the lions in a second. At least I'm not leading him into harm's way. He's a pathetic old sod but I do care about him. I doubt you'd understand that.

'Look, my dad's days are done and, to be blunt about it, it's all in the past tense for you too. The nights are getting colder.

The future is uncertain. You're feeling vulnerable, maybe even wounded. You're desperate for that magic windfall. So how can I help you? And, please, don't insult my intelligence by lying to me.'

So the Boy ran down his plan. Darren stayed silent, listened, shook his head once or twice when certain details were mentioned, but didn't laugh in his face as he'd been half-expecting. This younger generation, you had to be a mind reader to work out what might be lurking in their thoughts. He knew he didn't like the kid. He had an attitude about him that was galling to rub up against. 'I'm the future, you're the past. Get used to it, grandad.' Bloody insolence. He'd not inherited that haughty air from his dad. John had always been – what's the word? – deferential. A rock. But his offspring was devious and tricky. Obviously the apple had fallen far from the tree.

But right now the Boy needed him. For his heist to come up trumps, he was reliant on Darren's extensive computer-hacking expertise. Without it, it would all come to nothing. So he took the youth's sarcasm in stride. Even the 'grandad' jibes, though he flinched inwardly when he heard the disrespectful little prick referring to him thusly. Sometime in the future he would have to teach him some manners. But for now he kept his temper tamped down.

The kid had listened intently to what he was proposing. He'd not told him everything, of course. Just that a big score awaited them if Darren turned up that evening at his current digs and hacked into a computer in search of large funds to pilfer. Oh! And bring a camera. One of those mobile phones might do the trick.

He'd expected Darren to be more nosey about the scheme or to turn all weaselly on him and start strong-arming his way into sharing the projected proceeds fifty–fifty or some similarly unsatisfactory arrangement rather than their previously agreed 25 per cent. But he'd stood there eyeing the Boy silently for a good minute. After that he'd simply said: 'OK, then. Where and when is this going down?' The Boy told him the time and place and it was sorted.

There was nothing left to say for now. The Boy bade him farewell and buttoned his coat. Darren, though, had one final question to ask him.

'This Martindale geezer – why are you doing this to him? He's been housing you and feeding you, after all. What's your beef with the guy?'

The question stopped the Boy short. He had to think about it. Invent a grievance or simply tell it like it is? He opted for the latter.

'Because he's an ugly little man and ugly little men don't deserve to be lucky or get rich and famous in my world. Does that answer your question?'

'In a manner of speaking,' Darren replied. But by then the front door had already opened and shut.

Across town, cub reporter Trevor Bourne was at home feeling forlorn and still licking his wounds. That Amsterdam fiasco had put him through one hell of a time. He could fill a book on the whole wretched saga – and probably would if nothing else showed up on the horizon workwise. His failure to locate the Unstable Boys' elusive musical architect had meant that his participation in the TV docudrama was very much up in the air. He'd spoken to Michael Martindale after first inventing a credible fiction to account for his failure and subsequent humiliation. He'd been mugged by crackheads, he told the crime novelist. The area Ral Coombes currently frequented was rife with them. Perhaps the guitarist had joined their weaselly ranks. He had history, after all. That would also explain his incommunicado status.

Martindale had seemed to respond as though his explanation was plausible. But then he'd said something off-kilter. 'I hope the Boy won't be disappointed. He hates to be disappointed.' The remark had tripped Trevor's wires. It was a further sign that all was not well in Martindale's mind. He sounded distinctly out of sorts. And he'd not offered him any alternative employment on the project. That was the real pisser. He had yet to send his Amsterdam expenses in – a king's ransom – and shuddered thinking about how they might not even get reimbursed. It was then that his newly purchased mobile suddenly rang – an increasingly rare occurrence.

'Brian Hartnell here, Trevor. You remember surely. We spoke on the phone. The Unstable Boys. That piece in *Mojo*. You ended up basing your story mostly around my quotes.'

'Of course, I remember. How goes it, Brian?'

'Mustn't grumble, as one of my old clients, the Small Faces, used to sing. We were only in business together for two short weeks, mark you. Eyes bigger than their bellies, those four.'

'I never knew that.'

'I'm a dark horse, Trevor. With hidden depths. But enough about yours truly – I'm calling to pick your brains this time.'

'So pick away.'

'I remember you were angling for Ral Coombes's address over in Amsterdam and I gave you his number. Have you paid him a visit or attempted to get in touch? If so, what happened?'

'I actually went to the address but he wasn't in his apartment. I tried to wait around but got brutally mugged by a gang of Dutch hoodlums and had to abandon my mission.'

'I'm sorry to hear that, Trev. Mind you, the fellow you were stalking, he's a regular will o' the wisp. He should have been a magician. He can make things vanish into thin air. Particularly his own good self. His old singer has a similar skill for making himself scarce. He's off the radar too right now. And that presents me with a problem.

'Earlier today Roger Thornton, the chairman of the Brit Awards, called me up. He said his organisation was in a quandary. They were set to give their lifetime achievement statuette to Dido but she was off recording somewhere in the Caribbean and wouldn't be able to attend. So someone suggested the Unstable Boys instead. It makes sense. Those adverts are still fresh in everyone's mind. So Roger rang to sound me out on the prospect. Would they reunite for the event? That was the hot topic. I told him it was extremely unlikely.

'Then he asked if only a few of the original members might attend and maybe perform a medley of their best-loved work with an all-star backup crew. Noel Gallagher could be the guitarist. Dave Grohl might be persuaded to play drums. He also pointed out something I'd been previously unaware of: Universal now own the rights to the Unstable Boys' back catalogue and are planning to re-release it all with previously unavailable tracks and outtakes added on. The Brits' telly broadcast would be an ideal way to promote those re-releases.

'But here's the problem. The bass player's on board but he's obviously insufficient. They need the Boy to be there as well. But he's gone to ground. Obviously he needs to be informed of this development. I was wondering if you had a clue as to his current whereabouts.'

'I do, actually. The last time I looked, he was residing at the crime novelist Michael Martindale's Berkeley Square maisonette . . .'

'What? The geezer who got rumbled by the tabloids recently?'

'The very same. His recent travails have prompted a sort of belated midlife crisis, I reckon. He's put his own career as a successful novelist on hold in order to immerse himself in the Unstable Boys' messy saga. It's utter madness really. He dreams of reuniting them too. On television. That's why I became involved. I was supposed to help enable his silly scheme into becoming a reality. But so far I've come up short.'

'Are you still in touch with Martindale?'

'Sporadically.'

'Then can you pass on the information I just gave you? The Brits schtick? Tell him to inform the Boy. I'm guessing he'll rise to the challenge, the nasty, narcissistic little man. Never could resist the big spotlight. He needs to just call Roger Thornton and reassure him he'll turn up in a kosher state. It could be a night for him mending many fences in this industry, Trevor. A night to make right all the wrong moves of the past.'

'Are you planning on attending the Brits yourself?'

'No. I'll doubtless have something more important to do at that time. Like taking a leisurely bath while smoking a cigar. I'll probably glance at it on the telly.

'That Boy – he'll do something rash on the night. He's just wired that way. "The singing sociopath", we used to call him. Behind his back, of course. "There's a bad 'un for you" they'd all remark. And they were all right. I warned Roger. But he's desperate for a replacement act and he's not exactly spoiled for choice.'

'I'll phone Martindale right now with the news. He'll probably be over the moon. His main aim in life currently seems to be massaging the Boy's ego and feeding him praise, projects and glad tidings.'

'Tell me one final thing: Martindale and the Boy, are they the only residents of this house?'

'Correct.'

'You mean, it's just the two of them? Now that is cause for alarm. You don't want to be left alone with the Boy for too long. He's like something out of those Greek myths – half man, half snake. You need to warn your employer to keep his valuables nailed down. And his wits keen!'

'I'll certainly try to . . .'

'And remember – I'm just the messenger here. This is the full extent of my involvement; I'm just putting the word around. I'm happy to sit back and receive my percentage of the royalty cheques but I refuse to get back in the fray. So don't call me if and when things go tits up. I wouldn't go near that Boy with a barge pole. You're all playing with fire just having him in your midst. My advice? Wear asbestos gloves at all times.

'And on that note, I'll be taking my leave. Ciao, bambino.'
Then the line went dead.

Twenty minutes later, Michael Martindale received the
call from Trevor while in transit from a meeting in central
London with a TV production company. He'd done his
level best to sell them on the idea of his Unstable Boys
reality docudrama but could sense the disappointment in
their head honcho – his name had been Matthew something – who'd evidently been expecting something more
crime-related.

He'd left Matthew's office feeling distinctly deflated and
even the speedy pill he'd taken just prior to the encounter
had yet to lift his spirits. The lack of enthusiasm these TV
Johnnies – he'd seen two other producers, both dead ends –
had exhibited continued to befuddle him. But then again,
everything these days seemed to befuddle him. And what
was he going to tell the Boy? That the powers-that-be, the
tastemakers just weren't interested? He'd blow a fuse. That
had to be avoided at all costs.

So when Trevor called and told him about the Brit Awards,
he felt a terrible weight suddenly removed from his shoulders. Now he had some real good news to pass along. He
relaxed internally – a rare sensation of late.

The pills weren't doing what they'd done when he first
took them. He recognised that. At least a part of him did.
But a bigger part still took them unquestioningly. And his
body wasn't responding well to the regime. His stomach
ached, his stools were uncomfortable to pass. He thought
he'd even glimpsed blood in the toilet bowl after one particularly arduous session. His bones ached too. Thank God for

the slow capsules. They could really shut you down. Sweet oblivion. Self-obliteration. Same difference.

When he turned the key in the lock and walked inside his house, he instantly noticed something different about the interior. It started with the smell. The air was alive with the odour of women's perfume. Not one of the classier brands. Some dodgy fragrance probably bought from a market stall. It made the insides of his nostrils itch somehow.

Adjusting his glasses he espied where and who it was emanating from. Three figures were occupying the couch that now doubled as his bed. The Boy was positioned in the middle, grinning mischievously. Two women bookended his frame. They spoke in very loud voices and seemed a little too 'merry' for his comfort.

'Here he comes, girls – the great crime writer,' announced the Boy to his two companions. 'I told you all about him, didn't I? He's a real catch, this one. Mike, mate – let me present Tracey and Irma. Two old acquaintances. Two women of the world. Say hello to our host, ladies.'

'I know you,' Tracey piped up. 'You got caught in the *Daily Star* getting your willy wet, didn't you?'

'I ... uh ...'

'I think I saw him once on the telly,' Irma added, talking about Michael like he wasn't even in the room.

'And did he hold your gaze, my sweet?' the Boy saucily enquired.

'Not really.'

'Oh well, we can't all be ablaze with personal magnetism, now can we? That's my department, girls. Michael here is more your court jester type. My court jester currently.

He's gone up in the world, I reckon. So Mike – what's the news?'

'I bring glad tidings.' Michael was desperately trying to lighten the mood in the room as he spoke. The Boy's sarcastic tone and the two harpies at his side were causing him to twitch. 'One of my work colleagues just called to inform me that the Unstable Boys are set to be up for a lifetime achievement award at next month's Brits ceremony. It's practically in the bag. You just have to turn up, give a speech and sing a couple of your old songs in a kind of medley. It'll be televised. Massive viewer ratings are guaranteed.'

The Boy couldn't hide his elation. His face lit up like a depraved jack-o'-lantern.

'Did you hear that, girls? Your wandering Boy has returned to claim his throne. Back in the big leagues. Back where I've always belonged. But Mike, old love – who's going to be my backing group on the night? I don't want a bunch of fucking cowboys donkeying around behind me. I've got standards . . .'

'Your old bassist will be there . . .'

'What, that tosser?'

'Well, it's an award for the Unstable Boys and they want as many of the original members . . .'

'Hold on. I flatly refuse to share the same stage with that ingrate Ral Coombes. I don't work with druggies. Like I say, I've got standards.'

'Well, Ral Coombes is currently completely unreachable so the chances of him actually making the reunion are – to put it mildly – extremely slim.'

'Good. The bassist I can just about stomach seeing again. He was a dull bastard. But inoffensive. Still, let's face it – a singer and a bassist do not a group make. Who's going to play the other instruments?'

'They're talking about an all-star line-up. One of Oasis on guitar. A Foo Fighter possibly behind the drum kit . . .'

'Fuck that. I don't need these younger fuckers jumping on my bandwagon. I want someone with form fingering the fretboard. Jeff Beck or Jimmy Page. And why not get Viv Prince out of retirement to bang away on the drums?'

'I'm sure you can discuss those kind of issues with the organisers. They're very excited to be working with you . . .'

'As well they should be, Mike. As well they should be. Oh my – this news has gone all to my head like necking back an entire bottle of champagne in one extended glug. The possibilities . . .

'A party is definitely in order. A good old high-spirited knees-up-mother-brown ding-dong. Fortunately I must have been given the gift of vision to somehow foresee this providential turning of events. Because Tracey and Irma are here and another reveller is due to arrive at the premises anytime now.

'And of course you're here too, Mike, aren't you? Or are you? You're been looking very peaky of late. You've been forgetting to take your vitamins, haven't you? Bad living can lead to attention deficit disorder. Your brain starts going and it'll be all over for you, son. It won't be your looks that'll keep you afloat.

'But tonight we celebrate. This little bash is as much for you as it is for me. Consider it my going-away present to you.'

'But who's going away?'

'I am, Mike. Destiny calls. A new career path awaits me.'

'But the book isn't quite finished ...'

'Oh it is, Mr Ghost Writer. You just don't know it yet.'

'But ... This is all so sudden!'

'Quite. But that's the way the world turns, old son, when you're a born adventurer like me. You wanted to know what it was like living in the moment. Now you know. It's, uh, transitory. Fleeting. And it's not for the faint of heart.'

The doorbell rang and the Boy sprang from the couch to respond to its alert. Darren had arrived – right on time. He was wearing a hoodie that kept his face shaded and had previously arranged with the Boy to be referred to by a different name when introductions were made. He didn't want any incriminating evidence or too-talkative eyewitnesses to finger him afterwards.

'Mike ... girls ... meet ... uh, Rocko.'

'Ooh, some young blood in the house. Whoopee!' called out Tracey who was now very drunk.

Irma – equally pie-eyed – added: 'Show us your face, darling. You look more like a mugger than a houseguest in that hoodie. Don't he, Trace?' And they both giggled throatily.

'Girls, girls!' the Boy countered. 'Rocko here is a friend of a friend. Treat him respectfully. Don't be getting cheeky. He may be a youngster but that's no reason for lippy trollops like you to besmirch his character. A mugger indeed. Don't listen to 'em, son. But say hello to our host, Mr Michael Martindale. You know of him, right? The famous crime writer. You told me you read one of his books.'

'Which one?' Michael interjected.

'The one with that deejay bloke, the Breeze. I forget the plot line.'

'Did it hold your attention?'

'Sort of. Took it on holiday to read in Ibiza. Don't recall finishing it, though. Does that answer your question?'

'The younger generation, eh, Mike,' the Boy jumped in. 'They don't sugarcoat their outlook on life. Blunt to a fault. But I can't say I blame them. Look at what they've inherited. Life's a constant struggle for them.

'Take Rocko here. His home computer's packed in and he urgently needs to get it back operating. He asked me if he could come round and use the one here – yours – to get things back on track. I said yes. Maybe I was rash. Too open-hearted. After all, it's not mine to loan, is it? It's your equipment. But knowing you as I do, I just reckoned you'd say yes. A good Samaritan like you, Mike.'

'Well, he can use it here, I suppose. But he can't take it out of the house.'

'Hear that, Rock? Why don't you take that laptop on the table there and go into another room, set it up and do your business? He won't be any trouble, Mike. I can vouch for him. While he taps away, we can get this party well and truly started. Leave the old-timers to bask in some well-deserved naughty fun, Rocko. Here, Mike – another special going-away present.'

He handed over two vials of pills. 'The blue capsules slow you down. The black ones speed you up. You know the routine. And here's a special surprise for you: the party pill. Hold on to your hat when this little baby starts dropping down your neck. Go on, be a devil.' He practically forced the tiny pink object into Martindale's mouth. The latter didn't appear to object. He sat there like a dazed bedridden child being spoon-fed medicine by its mother.

Darren observed the interaction with mounting concern. He didn't want to be caught up in a crime scene involving a dead body. Get the job done and get the fuck out, he told himself.

He'd located a small room with a table and reading light adjacent to the salon. It suited his needs. He plugged in the laptop and hit some keys. Then he hit some more keys. In due course, Michael Martindale's accounts and private correspondence started showing up on the screen. He found a pen and paper and scribbled down the codes and all other relevant data.

Certain of his current accounts contained no funds whatsoever but one in particular was flooded with cash: over two million squirrelled away in some offshore bank scam. So the great crime writer had been fiddling his taxes as well as fiddling about in the tabloids. Darren wasn't surprised. Nothing surprised Darren.

The noise from the party room was escalating. It made for an irksome din. Squealing laughter, squealing voices, the odd garbled scream. He didn't want to go back in there but knew he'd have to. Then that thudding sound had started up and he'd leapt up to investigate its origin. He stood at the door and peered inside. Irma and Tracey had stripped down to their undergarments and were staging a mock fight on the couch. One of them had the other over her knee and was spanking her buttocks with gusto. You could see the crimson-coloured handprints on her wobbly flesh.

Michael Martindale meanwhile was splayed out on the floor in a sort of foetal position, a look of stark terror in his eyes. The Boy was standing over him like some all-devouring entity from a bad 1980s slasher movie.

'Time to show the ladies what you've got, Mike,' he harangued. 'Cometh the hour cometh the man. That's your actual Shakespeare, that is. Well, your hour has come. Feast your eyes, you lucky dog. And for Christ's sake, fill your boots this time. Can you believe it, girls? When the *Daily Star* nobbled him for infidelity, he hadn't even consummated the dirty deed.'

'Maybe he's a fruiter,' remarked Tracey in her infuriating accent.

'Now that would be a turn-up for the books, wouldn't it Mike? I have to say I've never warmed to the homosexual community. I'm not what you'd call a bender-befriender. Still, live and let live, I say.'

Martindale was being pinned down by his houseguest who seemed fully in his element. His eyes were pleading with helplessness. His mouth appeared to be attempting to articulate words but a creepy gargling sound was being summoned in their place and a thick line of drool was forming around his weak jawline.

Darren could see he was having difficulty breathing. And he also noted how the Boy seemed to become increasingly stimulated the more his victim convulsed before him.

Before he could intervene, Martindale lost consciousness. 'What did you give him?' Darren demanded of the Boy.

'Mike wanted to go on a real psychedelic trip. But he never had the nerve to set the experience in motion. I told him he needed a push over the cliff. He was uncertain at first but my powers of persuasion inevitably won him over. Look at him – the poor lamb.'

'But he's just passed out. You don't pass out on LSD . . .'

'Who said he'd taken LSD? It's one of the new breed of mindbenders he's on right now. I've forgotten the name. It's a chemical cocktail apparently. A little bit of everything. Like punch for druggies. Obviously it packs quite a kick. Mike here is not gifted with a strong constitution and has fallen once again into his customary stupor. But that only makes our job easier. Did you bring the camera?'

'This phone will suffice.'

'I'll take your word for it. Now, ladies. Stop your tomfoolery, get over here and help me strip this sorry specimen down to his birthday suit.'

'You didn't mention this before,' Darren remarked.

'A good gambler never reveals his ace card until he's playing his hand.'

'But what's the objective?'

'The objective, my young accomplice, is to get him naked and spread out on the couch with Tracey and Irma here cavorting over him. And for you to take some compromising snaps of the scene which I can then use to threaten him with if he comes looking for the money we're about to siphon out of his accounts.'

Darren saw the logic of it. But something was sticking in his craw. The longer he stood there, the more the whole scenario disgusted him. He felt something he'd rarely felt before shift within him. It might have been the first stirrings of a moral compass.

But more vexing still was the sense that his partner in crime was pure poison to all he got close to. He'd known this for a long time. He'd seen his father – a giant of a man in his day – reduced to the status of rock star's flunky by the odious little prick. When he was nine, he'd had to abandon the hope of getting a bicycle for Christmas because his dad had given away all the cash he saved that year in order to bail out his beloved Boy. And for what? Not even a 'thank you'. He'd hated the smarmy ponce then and he hated him with all his heart now.

Those frightful women were being ordered around by the Boy who was now desperately trying to position them around Martindale's nude comatose form in suitably scandalous poses. But it didn't look remotely convincing. Martindale just lay there like a corpse. Darren was starting to feel sick. A wave of revulsion was cresting up inside him, triggering a spot of heartburn.

That's when the Boy made the mistake of getting bolshy with Darren. 'Take the fucking snaps then, pee-wee,' he shouted. Nothing that inflammatory, granted. But it was enough.

'You've got to be joking, old timer. Your man there is so obviously in a coma that no one's going to believe this is anything but a nasty little setup job. And those plug-ugly bints aren't helping make it more credible. Where did you find those two by the way? At an anniversary wake for the Kray twins?'

'Watch your mouth, son.'

'No, you watch your mouth, grandad.'

'You're talking like a big shot, kid. You've been watching too many gangster films. I've heard the dialogue before. Where's the action, though?'

It was then that Darren pulled the gun out from his waistband and said: 'Right here.'

The Boy froze. The trollops froze. Michael Martindale stayed unconscious.

Darren then laid down the law. The photoshoot was to be abandoned immediately. The trollops were to put their clothes back on, grab their handbags and hasten to the nearest cab rank. The Boy was to go upstairs and gather his possessions, then depart from the house and move into a hotel for the foreseeable future. Darren gave the Boy a mobile and said he'd ring when the accounts had been hacked and funds siphoned away somewhere undetectable. The Boy wasn't on board with this new change of plan. But with a gun in his face, he wasn't in a position to argue. So that's how it went down.

At first Darren had viewed the proposed heist as business as usual. But something about the victim's face – the mute horror in his expression – had tilted his agenda. He was a thief, yes. But he wasn't a predatory animal. Suddenly it turned from being simply about money to being about revenge. He wasn't going to fleece Michael Martindale. He was going to crush the Boy instead.

Darren pressed many more keys on the laptop computer. He left Martindale's accounts untouched, save for a covert £10,000 withdrawal – he considered that expenses. He also chose not to follow the Boy's request to download all the text Martindale had been working on pertaining to the Boy's ghosted autobiography.

Before he left the premises for good, he checked in on Martindale. The bastards hadn't even covered him up before they left. His nude form lay there awkwardly positioned, inert and breathing somewhat raggedly. Darren found a couple of blankets and spread them over him. He then bent down and listened intently to his breathing. It sounded laboured as though something heavy was oppressing his diaphragm. He turned him on his side and noticed the breathing become less constricted. Once he'd ascertained that Martindale would survive the experience, he stole away.

CHAPTER 14

The Boy spent the hours after leaving Michael Martindale's house at gunpoint in a state of mounting agitation. He was so near to his goal and yet still unable to grasp the prize and bask in the triumph. The Brits' invitation – that was a blinding stroke of luck. But the Boy was unsure how to respond to it as he'd just masterminded a rip-off of – hopefully – major proportions and knew in every atom of his being that he'd be better served by making himself well scarce in the coming weeks.

How was Martindale going to react when he discovered he'd been robbed blind? Was he even still alive? He'd looked like death the last time he'd glanced his way. Sad cunt.

And if he was alive, would he even tumble to the fact that he'd been scammed? Years ago an industry acquaintance had told him about Sting's accountant ripping off his client to the tune of several million pounds. Sting was so rich that the dwindling of his wealth hadn't even registered with him until one of his business entourage pointed it out. Now Sting – whatever you reckon of his music – was a canny Geordie lad. Michael Martindale by contrast was a spineless southerner.

He'll never notice, the Boy wanted to believe. And even if he did, he wouldn't take action. He'd be too ashamed.

No, the one he had to worry about was that pesky Darren. Just thinking about that fucking delinquent made him feel all feverish inside – and not in a torrid Little Willie John sort of way. His temples pulsed, his ulcers – he had two in their early stages – complained and his hip was flaring up again. He'd been supposed to have hip replacement surgery after that stupid business onstage somewhere in Bosnia when he'd got into a physical dispute with a large amplifier. But he'd never had the time or opportunity.

Now he'd have both leisure, resources and the money to get the best surgeons on his case. If only the scumbag would call. He'd handed him the mobile and said, 'Wait for the call.' He'd even shown him how to operate it.

So now he was tucked away in a nondescript room in a low-profile central London hotel, twiddling his thumbs, necking backpain pills and tabs of Maalox and playing the waiting game. Patience had never been one of the Boy's virtues. He'd long made it a rule never to stand in queues. But now he was being held hostage. By a fucking juvenile to boot. Wonders would never cease.

He knew where the real blame lay: the fucking techno-logical revolution, that's where. A bloke in a pub had explained it to him one night. First came the agricultural revolution. Then came the dark satanic mills of the industrial revolution. Now we're all engulfed in this technological revo-lution mindset.

But the thing is – the first two were brought in gradually so that your Joe Public could properly assimilate. This technological upheaval, however, had happened virtually overnight and it was extremely complicated for old hands like the Boy to keep apace. He'd tried to work a computer on several occasions over the years. But each time he'd got discouraged and given up. He knew he was being foolhardy not persevering but you can only work with what you've got. Being computer-savvy just wasn't on the cards for him even if it meant turning his back on the future as a consequence.

He could always find enablers to press those keys for him when the need arose. Most of them had been obliging schmucks. Not Darren, though, he'd definitely broken the mould. Computer geeks toting guns? That was a turn up for the books. Kids these days – what a shower. They'd kill you for a pair of trainers. No loyalty. No chivalry. Desensitised by video games and internet porn. A lost generation.

Finally, it rang. A little red light flashed on, accompanied by a burping noise that alerted him a call was incoming. He pressed the button on the left. The waiting was over.

'Darren, I've been . . .'

'Who's Darren ? I'm not called Darren. My name is Rocko. Remember?'

'Oh . . . OK, I see . . . Rocko. So how goes it?'

'It goes where it goes, usually. And then it gets gone.'

'I beg your pardon . . .'

'You'll have to forgive me. I'm fond of making the odd abstract pronouncement.'

'Well, now's not the time for playing silly buggers.'

'That's rich coming from you, that is. You've been playing silly buggers your whole life. Playing them for cunts. Like you played my dad.'

'Don't bring John into this. You said so yourself.'

'But unfortunately he did become involved and I'll tell you how. I was sat at that computer with all the commotion going on in the next room. I'd ferreted around on the web and got access to several interesting sites. One in particular was full of juicy stuff to pick from. If I'd put in a couple of extra hours, I'm sure I could have cherry-picked a cool million or even two and sent it sailing off to a private account I may – or may not – have at my disposal. But here's where it gets interesting . . .'

'I'm all ears.'

'I'm sat there thinking: on the one hand, it's a nice score. That's my entrepreneurial side stepping up to the plate. Big money – the thought, the smell, the luxury. It's enticing, to say the least.

'But then I looked around at the people I'd fallen in with and said to myself: "Even two mill isn't worth this kind of botheration." That's when the old man stepped up. Not literally. Call it a ghostly presence if you like. I felt his spirit in the room. And I felt his suffering too. Suffering that you brought to him.'

'Hold on a second . . .'

'No, you hold on. Hold on and hold tight. This might get bumpy. Now where were we? Ah yes, my old dad. Be honest with me. Did you ever actually like the man? I know you needed him from time to time. But did you ever care about him? Did you ever tell yourself, "John: here's a good stout-hearted fellow and I'm proud to have him as a friend"?'

'Where's this all going? What's it leading to?'

'You'll see. I saw last night by the way. Quite an eyeful. Enough to have bad dreams for the rest of my life.'

'OK, things got a little out of hand, I'll admit.'

'A little out of hand? If I hadn't been there, that Martindale would be dead now. You are one evil bastard and I don't use that word lightly.'

'Maybe it was a little too rock 'n' roll for a youngster like yourself.'

'Rock 'n' roll? That wasn't rock 'n' roll. That was sadism and extortion. Get your perspective straightened out. This isn't the seventies any more, Jimmy Savile.'

'So . . . How does this tale of yours conclude?'

'With a young man at a crossroads. Does he take the loot or grow a conscience? I looked at the agony in Martindale's eyes and fate made up my mind for me. It was the same mask of pain I'd seen plastered over my old man's boat race whenever you'd been in the vicinity and on the ponce. That's when I realised that screwing you over as royally as possible would be a greater reward than simply a big fat payday.'

'Is this some kind of joke?'

'Depends how you interpret the punchline.'

'Which is?'

'That you come out of this empty-handed, my old love. At the last minute I refrained from robbing your man. He'd suffered enough just having you biting into his neck. I didn't swipe the text file with your deep thoughts all printed out either. Bollocks to that. And double bollocks to you, you sad deluded decrepit waste of oxygen.'

'You devious . . . dirty . . . ungrateful . . .'

'Now, now. Language, please. A civil tone should be adopted if you want me still listening.'

'Aaagh! You're no better than that lame brain who helped conceive you. Small-time operators, the pair of you. A couple of bush-league tommy tosspots.

'You think you can betray me? Listen, junior, they've just given me the key to the kingdom. The Brits have invited me – me – to accept a lifetime achievement award. Next month, I'll be back on the telly doing what I do best – enthralling the nation with my uncanny stagecraft. I was thinking of asking you to be my drummer on the night too. Oh well, you've blown that gig, haven't you? Just think, I'll be serenading millions while you're down in some poxy cellar playing fusion jazz to two junkies and a three-legged dog.'

'Play drums with you? Get over yourself, old timer. Your day is done. End of subject. And don't even think of re-establishing contact with me or the old fellow.'

'I've got friends, y'know. Real desperados.'

'Oh, pull the other one. You don't have any heavy-hitters in your corner any more. You've made too many enemies. Don't be a silly billy now. Just wave your magic wand and vanish from all our lives. For perpetuity. Big word, that means "forever". I read books, me. They help broaden the mind. I'd recommend you do the same but a little bird keeps telling me your options are getting narrower by the second.

'In conclusion, let me ring off with this final thought: good riddance to bad rubbish. Break a leg at the Brits.'

Then the line went dead.

The Boy was steaming when he left his hotel room. Bullheaded. Fit to be tied. Eyes darting everywhere. He'd made the call to Roger Thornton. Turned on the charm. Acted all placatory. Roger wanted to see him immediately to iron out the details. The big time was still there within his grasp. And the information he'd just gleaned that no robbery had in fact taken place chez Martindale meant he had nothing to fear about going public again. In a way, that Darren had done him a favour.

Not that he was in a forgiving mood. The prick was a dead man. Once he got his clout back, all the bad boys would be hanging around him like groupies again. Fame and criminals go together like Martha and the Vandellas. He'd get a couple of them to do the dirty deed and they'd jump to the task in their eagerness to remain in his entourage.

He pressed the red button that summoned the elevator. He'd rarely stepped out into the London streets during daylight hours since he'd returned to the city. But the promise of fat ratings and career redemption had emboldened his resolve to lose the cloak of invisibility.

'Ding' went the lift. He pulled back the door and moved inside. It was a tight spot. Another bloke was standing in it. He looked familiar. A face from the past, possibly. Possibly not. Another ship passing in the night. Another tiny drop of drizzle on the great windowpane of life. He was wearing a very pungent cologne. He'd breathed in that odour before. Smells sometimes triggered specific memories but the Boy couldn't place the pong. His mind was set on more grandiose concerns.

Another 'ding'. Another opened door. Two dudes standing in the reception area started walking determinedly towards him. The guy in the lift was right behind him so he was effectively sandwiched in between three unknown assailants. At first, he thought they were cops. But then the one behind him said something to the other two in what sounded like Russian and his heart and head sank.

While the Unstable Boys' reunion ceremony was awaiting its go ahead, their musical architect was sat in an Amsterdam café unaware that it might even be taking place. No one had alerted him. But then again, as he was practically impossible to contact this wasn't surprising. Staying off the radar had its perks. It spared him from saying 'no' were the request to get transmitted.

He liked the ambience in these coffee houses. He'd never felt comfortable in pubs. People drinking to excess rattled him and sparked warning tremors in his bones. Look around any bar and you're bound to clap eyes on some poor devil going through some Jekyll-to-Hyde personality switcheroo. Alcohol was too unpredictable.

But pot – when consumed in a room full of strangers – promoted a sense of conviviality. Smoke would be inhaled silently. Heads would roll back. Conversations would dangle. Time would stand still. Eyes would furtively scope the room, seeking out kindred spirits. Glances would be exchanged. A shared complicity would be woven forth. 'We're all in this zone together.' The old beloved home away from home effect.

He'd just nibbled a portion of space cake and was waiting for the stuff to work. Normally he'd forego consuming canna-bis orally, as it interacted with the brain differently from when you smoked it. It was trippier. More of a gamble. A glimpse at nirvana or a screaming panic attack. It was all in the roll of the dice.

But he was lonely and feeling reckless. His new pals had lately gone to ground. Pieter was somewhere in Spain attending his brother's funeral and comforting the widow and offspring. He didn't know when he'd be back. And Magda? Not a sign or a sighting in over a week now. He'd asked the concierge. The old broad hadn't seen her either. Every night he'd tapped at her door and received no response. He was becoming increasingly worried by her absence. What if she'd been abducted? Put to death? In her line of work, anything might happen.

So he was looking for comfort in a coffee house. No big thing. He stared around him. The clientele were almost exclusively youngsters. One old dude in a Grateful Dead T-shirt was off in the corner. A mature-looking woman in frameless glasses sporting blonde dreadlocks that didn't suit her was also present. Nobody was shouting. Spirits were high but they weren't shrill. The woman even passed Ral her joint. He inhaled and felt suddenly queasy. There was too much smoke in his lungs and in the room. Fresh air was required urgently. He made it out onto the sidewalk and felt his chest pounding.

And that was when he caught sight of him. The beautiful teenage boy with the floppy hair and baggy T-shirt on the skateboard. He stood there transfixed. It couldn't be. And yet there he was. His dead son had been brought back to life before his very eyes. There was no time to question the vision. He was speeding further away on that infernal board by the second. He had to give chase.

He started running frantically. Thoughts and feelings skidded around in his brain like a slapstick circus act. Maybe he didn't really die. Maybe that lorry collided with some sort of roadside debris instead of an actual human form. Maybe the coffin I bought and saw being lowered into the ground didn't contain a body. Maybe my son simply asserted his independence and stole away to Amsterdam where we'd be fated to meet again. God – let it be so.

He was still too far ahead. Ral tried shouting his name but his voice lacked reach. He'd gotten out of shape. In the past month he'd abandoned the long bracing walks and commenced polluting his lungs and engaging in a more horizontal lifestyle instead. He was getting cramps in his legs and his breathing was becoming strained and shallow. But he wasn't going to slow down.

As he continued running, a song started playing in his head.

'Sally go round the roses.'

It had been a hit back in 1963. A black girl group the Jaynetts were the credited singers. He'd heard it a lot on Radio Luxembourg. Never owned a copy of it though. Why were its nursery rhyme cadences running riot through his brain now? The way inappropriate music infiltrates our souls at key moments in our lives will forever remain a mystery.

'Roses, they won't hurt you.'

Enough with the roses. My son is there before me. Lord, give me the strength to catch his gaze. Let us be reconciled.

'Saddest thing in the whole wide world is to see your baby with another girl.'

This song is too sad. And too slow paced. I need something at a faster clip. Don't you understand? Salvation is beckoning. My son – my sweet, sweet son – is up ahead. I need the energy and speed to catch his eye. One look and he will stop his skateboarding and run to embrace me, his father. We will cling to each other and I will smell his baby body scent once more – that wondrous milky odour.

'Sally go round the roses.'

Child of mine, listen out for me. Turn your head, acknowledge me and make this rapture complete. Hear my call. I am so, so sorry. I always tried to protect you. But you'd reached that restless age and I couldn't reach you any more. I even feel guilty when I am blameless.

'Roses, they can't hurt you.'

Dead rose petals on a tear-stained letter. His brain was flashing on a phrase that had come out of nowhere. It would make for a good line in a song yet to be composed. A song of regret and intense longing. A melancholy air. But in the here and now the words were just more clutter. He needed speed. He needed closure. He needed . . .

At that moment a jolting pain struck him in his upper torso. His legs began to buckle and his head tilted back. He was still moving at full pelt and to onlookers it must have appeared at first like he'd been the victim of a sniper's deadly whim. He tumbled to the ground in an ungainly heap.

'Saddest thing in the whole wide world . . .'

The record was stuck. The same line over and over again. Heartbeat on the frisk. Out of time – out of time – out of time – over and over. Goodbye, sweet youth. Goodbye, summer dream. This is the way the world ends. No blinding epiphanies; just more clutter in the brain. Done with it all. Over and out.

The woman working at a nearby florist's phoned in the accident. She'd seen the crazy old guy running like a loon ablaze.

Then – boom – he'd collapsed right there on the pavement in front of her place of work. Just tumbled over. Mashed up an arm and leg. Gaping bruises everywhere. She'd moved in close and checked his racing pulse. The guy was unconscious and that was disquieting enough but more alarming was the stream of blood running from his mouth and the vacant stare from his open eyes. She wouldn't place odds on him pulling through. After the ambulance left, she went to the bar three doors down to drink away her brush with death.

'Gentlemen, I fear there's been a misunderstanding.' The Russians had jockeyed the Boy into a waiting car and the four of them were now in transit. The atmosphere inside the vehicle was glacial and all their hostage could come up with as an opening salvo was some tired old line that he'd swiped from a film he'd once seen. Like he was Edward G. Robinson or Sidney Greenstreet – some highfalutin mobster.

The Ivans looked hard to impress. Frankly he was at a loss here. Normally his instinct for survival would assert itself and he'd be inspired to talk his way out of whatever predicament he'd tumbled into. But these were Russians. His gift of the gab would be lost on them. Still, no harm trying. Needs must and all that.

So he told them about his good fortune. A comeback on prime-time telly. He'd be back rocking the stadiums in no time. Everyone would be quids in. Old debts would get sorted while new revenue streams would open up like healthy veins. The Ruskies seemed to be listening but it was hard to gauge their response. Until one of them – Igor the other two called him – chose to address him.

'Your current career prospects are of little concern to us. You seem to forget that our organisation owns the rights to all your recordings. We already have you – how do you say? – over a barrel. Our boss Dimitri thinks it unlikely that you can make us more money by being alive. And he's very displeased with you also. You had sex with his girl-friend and gave her a very nasty infection. Dimitri caught it too. Ever since then, he's had difficulty urinating with comfort. The burning sensation in his penis reminds him of you. You can understand why a man of his standing would feel great anger towards one who had injured him so indelicately.

'So let's not talk about your career. Let's not talk at all. Just enjoy the view. Take in the scenery. Soak it up. You never know, it might be the last thing your eyes get to gaze on.'

The Boy felt very, very queasy indeed. He wasn't ready to die. One last desperate plea was all he had left to muster.

'Listen, Igor, you shouldn't be taking orders from Dimitri. Leave him and become my manager instead. I can guarantee you more money, more pussy, more clout . . .'

'Dimitri . . .'

'Is getting too long in the tooth, son . . .'

'Dimitri is my older brother. A person of your shabby standing could never comprehend the bond that unites us. Ridding the world of your kind is a privilege I've long savoured.'

'You're making a big mistake.'

'On the contrary, you're worth more to us dead than alive. Nothing makes a rock star more bankable than dying or going missing, permanently. And disappearing mysteriously only feeds the legend further. One day they might even build a shrine to you. But you won't be there to see it.'

Igor pulled out the shooter with the silencer attached, whispered, 'Say hello to Elvis for me, motherfucker,' and fired a round into the Boy's temple. The victim looked startled before crumpling over the car seat. One of the other two Russians checked his pulse. *Niet*. He nudged his compatriot and pointed at the prone corpse. 'No seatbelt,' he said. No one thought the remark merited a reaction. The body had to be disposed of before it started bleeding out and ruining the rental car's interior. They'd packed shovels in the boot. And some chemicals to dissolve bone tissue. It would be a long, messy night.

CHAPTER 15

Trevor was working the media graveyard shift when the call came through. Another rock icon had passed away. They were dropping like flies these days. This week it was one of Steely Dan. Like all self-respecting rock critics, he'd been a fan of their 1970s work. 'Bacharach and David with fangs', he'd just typed into his computer. Then the beeper had sounded.

It was Brian Hartnell again. 'Thought you'd like to hear the news. The Boy was supposed to meet with Roger Thornton. Roger said he sounded keen. But he never turned up to the appointment. It's bewildering to me. And very unfortunate. Roger's put the kibosh on any award for the Unstable Boys. He's lined up Simple Minds for the lifetime achievement statuette. At least he can count on them to be there on the night.

'One of Roger's assistants tried to contact the Boy. Phoned Michael Martindale's landline. A voice answered claiming he no longer resided at that address and that the tenant Mr Martindale has been hospitalised. Know anything about that?'

'No, I don't.'

'To top it all, there's a report circling on the internet that Ral Coombes is in hospital in critical condition over in Amsterdam and not long for this world.'

'Good Lord . . .'

'The good Lord's got nothing to do with this. That group was always cursed. I feel bad for Ral – he had skills. A nice fellow when his head wasn't too far up in the clouds. The other one? They should have called him "the liability", not "the Boy". Narcissistic personality disorder the size of Southeast Asia. Ungrateful. Sneaky. Divisive. Shiftless. The English language doesn't have enough bad words to list his flaws.'

'What do you think has happened to him?'

'Who gives a monkey's? He wore out his welcome many, many moons ago. Living on borrowed time. Maybe someone decided to terminate the loan. Or maybe he's split the country. I certainly hope so. I sleep easier at night when I know people like him aren't lurking around these shores.

'Still, what a story, eh! You should be thanking me. A bit of snooping around and you'll have something tasty to sell to your paymasters. The publicity would help shift those reissues and fatten my bank account, of course. But don't quote me by name. Sayonara.'

Two weeks after this conversation and two days before the event itself, the *Guardian* ran a story in its Thursday issue. 'Brits' Unstable Dilemma' was the headline. Trevor's byline was featured in bold type alongside a passport-sized snap of his face on the upper-right-hand corner of the page.

His story rehashed the information provided by Brian Hartnell, or 'an anonymous source' as he was referred to in the piece. Trevor had tried to contact other players in the saga but had come up empty-handed. Roger Thornton wouldn't return his phone calls. He tried to contact Michael Martindale to get news of the Boy only to discover Martindale's mobile phone number no longer functioned. He'd tried to speak to Martindale's agent and received an earful of lofty reprimands and a stern warning not to bother him or his client with 'such trivia'. The setup was all a bit fishy. But the raw ingredients were strong enough to make for a compelling piece of text. Aged sixties has-beens get the promise of a golden handshake only to be blown mysteriously out of the water by the fickle finger of fate. That was the theme.

It was something to read on the tube the day it appeared. Office workers probably mentioned it in passing when grouped around the coffee machine. But then just as quickly, they forgot. There was a mystery to solve – disappearances, the smell of death – but no one felt like picking up the gauntlet and seeing the case through to a satisfactory conclusion.

The Boy had cried wolf too often. His disappearance passed without further comment. No investigation as to his whereabouts was mounted. This was the curse he'd placed on himself with his profligate ways and vanishing acts: neither dead nor alive, unable to be mourned, pieces of him floating in cold waters, a tiny bullet hole in his forehead to go with the dissolute dimples in his cupid cheeks.

Where were all the wailing women and grief-stricken disciples? Why wasn't the sky crying too? A legend was gone. Where were the grieving observers, the candlelit vigils? His voice could still sometimes be heard when they played his group's early stuff on the radio. Otherwise his beautiful reward had turned out to be the endless sleep of nothingness. Fate had played its dirtiest trick on him.

But it was appropriate. Former acquaintances generally preferred to keep their memories of him locked away in a dingy closet deep within the storage space of their brains. Only a hardcore collective of fans remained to keep his legacy alive. There were a couple of websites dedicated to the Boy that came and went. Those who logged on and left messages seemed an odd bunch. One or two floated murder theories. A woman claimed to be the mother of a 'love child' sired by the singer. A man wrote in to remind the Boy that he still owed him fifty quid and could expect a 'good thumping' if they were to cross paths again.

But there were also tributes. Words of praise and encouragement from individuals dotted around the globe. One of the most touching was posted from Switzerland. 'The Boy is the greatest rocker of all. And he is my friend. We had many happy hours together. They were the greatest of my life. He is a wonderful guy.' The sender was Jean-Claude Messman.

Another of the slain singer's acolytes, Johnny Two Livers, hung up his spurs and breathed his last halting spasm of air five months after his hero's forced defection from the planet. A heart attack took him out after his immune system pretty much packed in. His son Darren was now the man of the house and was standing tall in an elegant tailored suit at the funeral service in a Crouch End church comforting his weeping mum and conferring with the priest to make sure all the arrangements were being adhered to.

As he watched the coffin being lowered into its grave, he'd mulled over the recent series of events to which he'd been party. His father's death hadn't hit him yet. He'd shed no tears. He had to stay strong for the others blubbering away at his side. He'd thought that if he'd got rid of that fucking leech known as 'the Boy', then his dad might have been granted a few more years of life. But it hadn't worked out that way. Sad. But there you go.

Originally he'd just wanted to scare the singing scumbag. Lead him up the garden path and then – whack! Hit him with a rake. Some broken bones and a scar or two. He'd have been in a wheelchair for a while. But he'd still have been breathing. Not brown bread. That wasn't on the cards until the Ruskies entered the scheme.

How they'd actually found Darren – that was still a mystery. But they had. In fact, they were waiting for him when he got back from Martindale's gaff – and they were very persuasive. He handed them the number of the phone he'd given the Boy earlier that evening and they just took it from there. They also handed over ten grand in cash to Darren as payment for his treachery. Even if no money had passed hands, he'd have done it anyway. You don't trifle with the Ivans. But he hadn't refused the bounty either. And here comes the irony of it all: the money was now paying for this very funeral. It was a funny old world.

For Michael Martindale, the months following his 'escape' from the Boy's suffocating clutches were ones spent in a state of earnest self-examination. After his agent had found him incoherent and spread-eagled on his sofa, an ambulance had

been called. Michael couldn't recall any details of the journey,
just of waking up in a strange room lying in a strange bed.
Unbeknownst to him, his stomach had been pumped. He
felt weak as though wracked with fever. His brain was still
too pickled to cogently evaluate his recent circumstances.

The days dragged by. The place he'd landed up in was a
kind of rehab facility situated somewhere in Surrey. The
mornings were taken up with psychological counselling, the
afternoons with him and other patients making stuff with
their hands. Apparently it was all interconnected: rebuild
your life while constructing a coffee table at the same time.

At first, he told them what he thought they wanted to
hear, the psychiatrists: 'Fame and tabloid notoriety threw
me for a loop and robbed me of my family. In my sorrow, I
fell into bad company who then introduced me to
substances that foolhardily I took. I am indeed lucky that
my episode with drugs terminated before I fell under the
vice-like grip of chronic dependency. I feel I have escaped
my very own season in hell. From now on I'll be walking
sobriety's path.'

In other words, he was crooning that old twelve-step
redemption song. The powers-that-be in the facility seemed
pleased with his progress and noted as much in their reports.
In truth, Michael was on the mend but still only half-cured.
He'd stopped thinking obsessively about the Boy. The penny
had finally dropped there. All the debris of his recent time
with that shameless, duplicitous charlatan still befuddled his
mind. But the conclusion was unavoidable: he'd been had.

So he didn't miss the Boy. But he did miss the pills. That
rapturous burst of energy in his brain. The cushion of sweet

oblivion descending. He'd feel their absence eating away at him at night time in particular.

But then Jane had visited him one day and he had something to live for again. Tenderness had been in short supply once she'd ascertained that he was out of the woods, health-wise. 'You've been a bloody fool,' she'd prefaced her remarks by snapping before running through a lengthy litany of her husband's shortcomings, both recent and not-so-recent.

He'd sat there shamefaced. He lost count of the number of times he'd said 'I'm sorry' in reaction to each and every accu-sation. But it was said sincerely. Finally, she started to soften. They'd commenced communicating without rancour, in civi-lised tones. He sensed a chink opening up in her armour, a ray of light peeping through.

The next time she came, their two sons accompanied her. The conversation between them was somewhat stilted but his family was once more united and his joy was hard to contain. Three visits later, a provisional scheme was hatched. When Michael left the clinic – any day now – he'd be housed in new, rented accommodation. The previous location contained way too many bad memories.

A period of courtship between he and Jane would then ensue. They'd go out on dates, learn to like each other fully again. 'Love' had become an elusive concept to both of them. They'd felt it once but then it had dissipated slowly. 'Like' was more attainable as a starting point. Liking someone implied a consistency of positive emotional interplay and that consistency could act as the right cement for reconstructing a failed relationship.

The yearning for pills meanwhile abated. Michael went all health conscious instead. He started lifting weights and jogging in the park. His body started shedding flab and his brain began fizzing from all the endorphins popping off. For the first time in ages he had true clarity of thought.

He'd been the perfect fool. First, set up by the treacherous tabloids. Then stalked and brainwashed by a former idol from his teens with a dastardly devilish streak. But he'd chosen to be corrupted. This was the breakthrough. No more playing that tired old victim card. He'd wanted to be corrupted because he'd wanted to know what it was like to throw caution to the four winds. He'd never felt that sense of reckless self-empowerment. He'd never sown his wild oats when the time had been most opportune. And now it was far too late to catch up.

The 82,357 words logged into his computer that now represented the Boy's last taped utterances were not returned to by the man who only a few months earlier had typed them in so enthusiastically. He didn't want to re-read them and the very idea of making them available to the public now disgusted him. He even considered deleting the text altogether but opted instead to box it away in some dim corner of his laptop's boundless memory vault, never to be reopened.

He toyed with the prospect of turning his recent misadventures into a piece of thinly veiled fiction but soon relented. No one would believe it anyway. A grown man brought low by befriending a childhood hero? Where were all the dead bodies?

The truth was – he still couldn't quite get his head around what he'd set himself up to have to endure. And he never would be able to fully fathom what had transpired within him to cause such a grievous lapse of judgement. But ultimately it didn't matter. He'd been put through a testing time but had managed – with difficulty – to clamber out the other end with all his vital organs still intact and functioning.

And now he and Jane were slowly on the mend. It wasn't the same as it had been back in the past. There was her stiffness and hesitancy to contend with now. But the ice was slowly melting. He was doing his level best to show everyone he'd turned over a new leaf and was no longer the shamed spouse but a new improved model, the steadfast man.

What made it work was that it was meant with absolute sincerity. When Jane finally let him move back into the family manor, his heart leapt with joy. Home at last, his inner core had yelped in ecstasy. And when one of his sons told him how much he still loved him, the healing process was almost complete.

A new phase of his life was quickly set in motion. With Jane to guide him on key issues such as plot trajectory and character development, he began writing again in earnest. More crime fiction novels got published. They generally managed to still sell well and were gently reviewed but didn't spawn spinoff TV series or potential Hollywood blockbusters like before. His years as a fixture in the mainstream were behind him now. Still, he took the demotion philosophically. The talk shows and panel programmes didn't call him any more but that was a blessing really; he'd hardly flourished when he let himself get caught in their headlights.

What he wanted to do most of all was grow old gracefully. He'd had his spell of growing old disgracefully and it had not suited him in the slightest, no matter what his brain had told him at the time. So he put his old Unstable Boys records and all his other rock vinyl into cardboard boxes and stacked them away in the loft. From now on, when he craved the sound of music he'd been reaching for the classics. Debussy and Ravel were particular favourites. Or some Bill Evans jazz. Soothing music – something stately and contemplative to enhance your twilight journey. Something quiet to take you into that dark night.

Dylan Thomas famously felt otherwise of course. But Dylan Thomas died in his late thirties, still in the grip of his roaring years. If he'd made it to his sixties, he'd have probably yearned for a quiet painless passing into the ether too.

He and Jane now slept in separate rooms. It was just as well: his snoring had always interrupted her sleep patterns. There was little in the way of physical intimacy between them. But they still found a connection through work. Together they would brainstorm fictional scenarios, drag characters hiding in their imaginations kicking and screaming into paragraphs on a computer screen. When a particularly good idea got voiced, a charge of joyous complicity would pass between them. This is what most nourished their reunion. It may not have been love in its purest most passionate sense but it was still something to cherish and nurture.

When Ral Coombes finally regained what he felt was some form of consciousness and had picked himself up from what had been the sidewalk of a winding Amsterdam high street, he became aware that everything around him had changed. Gone were the street, the shops and the billboards that lined it. Gone was the canal that ran parallel. Gone were the cars and the pedestrians. All signs of city life had been stripped from his new surroundings.

He found himself instead inhabiting some kind of pastoral retreat. The dramatic change of locale should have alarmed him but it didn't. Immediately he felt at home there. He was standing in some sort of forest. Stout oak trees bore leaves that shone like gold when the sun illuminated their branches. A brook close by was plaintively babbling out its own watery welcome. 'Have no fear,' the water seemed to say. 'You are among friends.'

He could hear music. It was coming from the building behind the everglades that he'd also just noticed. So he went to investigate. The front door was wide open. Nobody stood in his way. On the contrary, the thirty or so folks in the place welcomed him into their midst like he was a long-absent blood relation. Smiles all around. A glass of some foaming liquid warmly pressed into his hand. He placed the beverage on a table and eased into his new surroundings. It all felt so effortless. Like slipping into a pair of comfortable slippers after a long mountain hike.

Meanwhile up on the makeshift stage five men from different age groups were playing acoustic guitars. The oldest looked to be in his seventies with a long beard he'd laboriously woven into a dagger-like point while the youngest was still in his teens and untroubled by facial hair growth. The music they were playing was almost exclusively instrumental and came from a time when rock 'n' roll had yet to be identified as a musical genre. It was rooted in the unique fretboard wizardry of Django Reinhardt and his seminal recordings from the 1930s and '40s. This quintet were performing a homage to the gypsy guitarist while gainfully expanding on the possibilities he'd first set in motion.

Ral was enraptured by their dazzling interplay, the musical conversations, the fretboard duels, the high-spirited camaraderie on display. These five guys were way out of his league as musicians – bona fide virtuosos.

But then one of them had pointed to him and handed him his guitar; it happened so fast. The next thing he knew he was up on stage. The old bearded cat had counted a song in, the music struck up and his fingers suddenly knew just where to group themselves on that fretboard. Chord shapes he'd never known existed – suddenly he was shaping them without the slightest hesitation.

The music was now moving at a giddy tempo, faster and faster. All eyes fell on him. It was time to take a solo. He closed his eyes, let his fingers take flight and felt himself become airborne. Finally he was where he'd always wanted to be: cradled among the salt of the earth while channelling the music of the spheres.

But then something had disturbed his blissful jam. A hand had started grabbing at his arm while he played. He tried to ignore the intrusion. But the grip grew tighter. And then – just like that – he'd been yanked from the stage out into the woods and then . . . where? An elevator? Some kind of rapid movement was taking place. Was he floating upwards, downwards or sideways? It was so dark he couldn't tell. A ray of light materialised out of nowhere.

At first it was as tiny as a pinprick. But it kept growing until it engulfed his blurry vision. He opened his eyes and attempted to take in his current location.

His first reaction was one of rank bewilderment. He lay horizontal on – what – a bed, most likely. Yes, that was it. He could feel the sheet that was covering his bones. Then he felt the restraints on his wrists and the tube attached at needle-point to one of his arms. He experienced a stabbing pain in his chest like a scalpel incision. His eyes grew wide with alarm.

And that's when he saw them grouped around him. His new friends staring down at him with sleep-deprived faces. Pieter – just back from Spain – looked immensely relieved. 'He's alive,' he kept repeating as though he was witnessing a miracle from biblical times. And Magda – back from the land of the lost – was holding a bowl of grapes in one hand and wiping her eyes with the other. 'Are those tears for me?' he asked weakly. 'Don't flatter yourself, Englishman,' she retorted.

They pieced it all together for him. He'd collapsed in the street from a full-blown heart attack. The paramedics had been summoned by a local shopkeeper and he'd been trans-ported unconscious to the nearest hospital. It had been touch and go for three days and nights. He had been in a coma and his heartbeat had been kept going by artificial means. The doctors had opened him up and inserted a pacemaker. The bottle attached to the tube that was currently penetrating a vein in his arm was full of morphine and when he experi-enced discomfort – as he was bound to do given the nature of the operation he'd just undergone – he just had to press the neck of that bottle and a pain-blurring serum would be injected into his bloodstream.

Another face was staring down at him in that hospital room, a face he couldn't recognise. It was oval-shaped and expressionless and the black hair that framed it was tangled. Magda identified her for him: 'This is my beautiful daughter, Olga. I went back and I rescued her. Now we're reunited and we are safe once more.'

Ral looked at the girl. Even in his enfeebled state he could sense the damage within her though she was still in her late teens. She seemed remote and inattentive. Was she a trauma victim or a simpleton? Perish the thought. At least she was still alive.

It was then that Ral Coombes recalled why he'd fallen in the first place. He'd been chasing a ghost. A ghost on a skateboard that had resembled his son. He'd pursued the phantom until his heart had literally exploded. He'd wilfully placed his life in jeopardy to reconnect with his dead son. He'd gone to the middle of the air.

But death hadn't been ready to take him over its threshold. He was earthbound once more though still greatly weakened from his ordeal. Magda meanwhile had succeeded where he'd failed. He ought to have felt at least a twinge of envy. Yet no negative sentiments lurked within his reanimated heart and mind. They'd been replaced by a sense of overwhelming gratitude. He was just glad to be alive. He had his friends. He had the future. This was all that mattered now.

A week later he was off the morphine and sufficiently fixed up to return to his apartment. Magda moved in for the first few days to monitor his convalescence. Pieter was also a constant visitor, enabler and spirit-lifter.

A month after the heart attack, Ral Coombes was healing up nicely. He was taking short walks each day, had banned red meat from his diet and was stepping up his physical exercise regime. It was then that Pieter mentioned the Spanish beach house he'd inherited from his brother. He recommended that Ral, Magda and Olga join him for a lengthy getaway there. The tempting cocktail of sea air, sand under one's feet and a big fat orange sun would act as a perfect pick-me-up to counter-balance their recent scrapes.

Nobody needed to be persuaded. The four of them bought rail tickets and packed for an extended stay.

Before he vacated his rented Amsterdam apartment, Ral Coombes made two phone calls to the land of his birth. One was to Brian Hartnell to alert him of his change of country and address. Hartnell had sounded incredulous when they'd first spoken. 'I thought you were dead!' he'd fairly screamed. 'It's even been on the internet. It's a rumour for now but you know how these things can go viral. You need to post a denial, son – nip this bugger in the bud.'

'Oh, I don't know,' Ral had replied in measured tones. 'Let's be business-like about this, Brian. You know better than I – death sells. I believe it was Jimi Hendrix who once said when you die you've really got it made. What a visionary that man was. Death gives something once perceived as mundane and precocious mystique and gravitas.'

'Lofty words, Ral. You were always a bit of a poet. But what exactly are you saying?'

'I'm saying nothing. Let us neither deny nor confirm these rumours. People love a good mystery, don't they? And it pays to give the people what they want. I meanwhile have my privacy. I'll be lounging on a beach while my posthumous legend does all the heavy lifting from now on. Like Elvis, I've left the building. It's a perfect situation, don't you think,

Brian? Particularly for you. It must be so much easier managing ghosts rather than living human beings.'

That was when Hartnell had told him about the Unstable
Boys' Brits no-show. And just from the scant details he'd
heard over the phone, Ral knew the Boy was dead. No way
would he have missed out on such an event had there been
breath in his body. Only a bullet to the head would have kept
him away.

Hartnell said he thought there was something fishy about
the Boy's sudden disappearance but added quickly that it
wasn't out of character for him to vanish under bewildering
circumstances. 'You know what he was like.' Was like?
Already they were talking about him in the past tense.

And yet no corpse had washed up or ever would. The Boy
who would be king was most likely sleeping with the fishes,
but it was too abstract a concept. He'd have to focus on it
later to ascertain how he really felt.

One thing was for certain. Those Unstable Boy reforma-
tion bids were right off the cards from now on. And that was
a reassuring state of affairs.

His second call was to the care home where his wife was
staying. He needed to know that the payments he'd author-
ised were regularly going through and that she was comfortable and well-cared for. He'd developed a relationship of
sorts with one of the nurses, Jill, a kindly middle-aged woman
with a distinct West Country accent who was in charge of
Catherine's daily requirements. She told him his wife was
'stable' at the moment. 'She went through a phase recently
when she'd become easily agitated. She stayed in her room
and became abusive if anyone intruded. But then the doctors

upped her meds and she started to come around. Soon enough she was socialising once again. Alfred was thrilled to see her, of course.'

'Alfred?'

'You remember Alfred, don't you? You saw them together – him and your wife – when you last visited here. They're quite the couple nowadays. Always whispering and giggling.

'I'm sorry,' Jill interrupted herself. 'It must be hard for you to hear that your wife is with another man. I'm only telling you to let you know that she isn't suffering.'

Ral couldn't help asking: 'Does she ever have moments of lucidity? Does she ever talk about her past?'

'Not really,' Jill replied, 'not to me anyway. I'm sorry, I really am. It must leave you feeling pretty empty.'

Ral said nothing in reply. He felt empty but also absolved. 'Please tell Catherine that I love and still dream of her,' he asked the nurse after an especially long pause. 'And that I understand what happened and simply want her to be as happy as she can be.' Then he'd rung off.

Now there was nothing in the way. He could sink into his new surroundings without a backward glance. Beach life agreed with him. It was a drama-free environment. Even Magda had mellowed out in the weeks since they'd arrived here. The move had been good for all of them.

Pieter had blossomed as a go-between betwixt the townsfolk and the oddball quartet of foreigners Ral and company had first represented to the community. He'd smoothed things out and paved the way for a welcoming committee. The folks in the region generally seemed to lead aimless lives. They rarely worked and spent their days and evenings either swimming in the sea or drinking in a bar. At first, Ral had marvelled at their indolent lifestyle. But he'd quickly come to see the sense in it. He felt his own body clock relaxing within him. Just sit back on that rickety deckchair, feel the sand in your sandals and the salty air tickling your nostril hairs, and the hours will melt away painlessly.

That's where he spent most of his time these days. He could feel he was getting better. He was exercising daily and playing the guitar. A local fisherman was a dab hand at flamenco strumming and they'd get together from time to time to jam. A small crowd would sometimes congregate to hear these impromptu sessions and a few would throw money at them – coins more than paper – to register their approval. It wasn't lost on him that these modest soirees represented Ral Coombes's first paying gigs in over thirty years.

He was writing songs again too. Complete songs. Not just first drafts. One he was particularly pleased with was called 'King of the Refugees'. It was partly drawn from the ongoing global refugee crisis but also informed by its composer's own man-without-a-country status. He liked it because it didn't yield to desperation. It was a declaration of defiance instead.

> Bluebirds singing all around my head
> For I've returned from the living dead
> Can I hear a drum roll please
> For the king of the refugees?
> My wits are keen and my back is strong
> And I am sitting right where I belong
> On a throne not on my knees
> I'm the king of the refugees

Sailed on stormy oceans
Baked by a pitiless sun
Frozen in an Arctic tundra
But I came through
That's what I do

Pieter kept pestering Ral to let him record his new songs on the computer. At first, he'd shot the idea down. But he was starting to come round. He'd already warmed to the idea of recording them *Pink Moon*-style: one take, unadorned, just him and the stolen guitar. What would happen to them afterwards, though? Would they show up on the internet and blast his beloved anonymity to smithereens?

Perhaps he'd be better served just confining his music-making to his immediate locale then. These were issues that would get resolved in time, he knew.

Squinting from his deckchair with the sun full in his face, he could make out two figures playing together in the white ocean surf that rose up onto the beach. It was Magda's daughter and a local youth. The sounds of their laughter reminded Ral that the girl had lately come out of her troubled shell.

The first times he'd beheld her, he thought she might need some kind of psychiatric evaluation, so withdrawn was her demeanour. But – like her mother – she was made of sterner stuff. The Spanish sun and beach life in general had a transformative effect on her fragile ways. She shed weight, got bronzed up, started socialising. The language barrier meant she didn't speak much but she endeavoured to learn enough words in both Spanish and English to make do. Then she and her mother found work in a shop selling T-shirts, swim-wear and locally made jewellery.

Now it looked as though she'd found herself a boyfriend. It warmed his rickety old heart to see them cavorting around without a care in the world.

He hadn't forgotten what Magda had said to him just the other night. 'You're her father now too . . . If you want to be.' Then she'd kissed him on the lips for the first time. The sun had softened up the hard contours of her face and she'd looked radiant.

He looked into her eyes and saw his future reflected in them. It felt like an acid flashback in reverse – a flash forward. But it also felt right. His mouth spoke the same words that, unbeknownst to him, a famous crime novelist had once uttered to his former singer in very different circumstances.

'I'd . . . I'd be honoured.'

ACKNOWLEDGEMENTS

This book was improved by the contributions of Laurence Romance, Kalina Villeroy, Bernadette Marron, Howard Watson, Andreas Campomar and the ghost of Vince Taylor. I thank them all.